WICKED CURSES

THE SHADOW REALMS
BOOK 7

BRENDA K DAVIES

BRENDA K. DAVIES

CHAPTER ONE

SAHIRA GLIDED through the crowd filling the elaborately appointed pub. Conversations swirled around her, but she was still too shell-shocked by her current situation to register anything they said.

Instead, she tried to take in all the details of the large, open space with three crystal chandeliers illuminating the room. The subdued glow of the chandeliers indicated there was some power source here, but it must not have been much, as bronze lanterns with flickering candles hung along the wooden walls.

The place smelled of alcohol, sex, and cooking meat. Beneath it were the fainter aromas of wood and the earthy scent of the outdoors.

With its mirror-lined back, the stately bar took up the entire wall across from her. Bottles of different-colored liquids lined the glass shelves, but no labels marked what each contained.

Multiple gaming tables and high-top and low-top tables filled the room. She'd never seen such an eclectic mix of immortals in one place or getting along so well as they gathered around the tables, drinking and gaming.

More of them filled the stools lining the bar as they chatted and downed their drinks. *Why aren't they as freaked out about this place as I am? How long have they been here?*

Sahira gulped as she studied them. They must have been here for a while if they were all this calm. Most immortals, especially lycans, would have lost their minds over being trapped anywhere, but the lycans in this crowd were contentedly playing cards or eating dinner.

Sahira wasn't sure she would have believed it possible, but being trapped in this realm had bound them together instead of pitting them against one another. Though, she imagined there were times when they turned on one another like rabid dogs.

She'd only been here for ten minutes and was already feeling claustrophobic. Rubbing her neck, she resisted pulling at her collar. *I'm trapped.*

The words ran through her brain on a continuous loop. It couldn't be true. It *had* to be some sick joke.

She waited for the punchline but felt like she'd been punched in the gut when it didn't come. There *had* to be a way out of this place.

Orin wasn't the most trustworthy guy in the world. She wouldn't trust him to cross the street without throwing someone in front of a car.

And he'd gladly push her into the way or run her over if it suited his needs.

But if he's lying, why can't you open a portal out of here?

Recalling her inability to do so made her throat tighten; this time, she couldn't resist tugging at the collar of her blue peasant shirt with its bell sleeves. The loose-fitting, flowing shirt suddenly felt as confining as a straitjacket.

Her fingers itched to tear it off so she could breathe easier. Sweat beaded on her forehead and trickled down her back to cleave the thin material of the shirt to her.

I'm stuck here. I'm stuck!

Oh, shit.

"Easy," a deep voice rumbled.

Sahira hadn't realized she was on the verge of hyperventilating until the words came from beside her. A large hand rested on her shoulder; its claw-tipped fingers brushed her flesh.

Her head craned back as she looked at the towering figure. She almost fell over when she had to *keep* looking up as, standing at least seven feet, the demon was over a foot and a half taller than her.

"You're new here," the demon said. "It gets easier, but this place is a shock to all of us at first."

"It can't be real," she muttered.

"It is." He pushed a small glass full of amber liquid toward her. "Drink."

Sahira blinked at the fluid swaying back and forth in the glass. It blurred, came back into focus, then blurred once more.

Get it together, Sahira.

With a trembling hand, she grasped the glass. The cool reality of it helped to steady her a little more as the stringent scent of the contents drifted to her.

The whole place smelled of liquor, food, and immortals, but her senses became hyper-focused on the glass as she used it to ground herself in reality. It was smooth beneath her hand with sharper edges at the corners. Sahira ran her finger up and down one of the edges in a gesture that calmed and centered her.

Lifting the glass, she downed the contents in one gulp. The liquor burned down her throat, and she coughed as she set the glass down with a thump on the polished golden top of the bar.

She didn't drink often but welcomed the burn as it warmed her chest and belly. Her hand didn't shake quite as much when she released the glass.

CHAPTER TWO

THE DEMON CHUCKLED as he pushed the glass across the bar to the inner edge. With her brown hair swaying around her shoulders, the over-six-foot-tall lycan woman behind the bar strode down to refill the drink and slid it toward Sahira.

The lycan's brown eyes were intense as she spoke. "These are on the house because it's rough when you first get here; we've all been there, but there's no freeloading in this realm."

"Give her a minute, Belda," the demon said.

"I am, but you know the rules. Make sure she knows them too."

The demon raised his hand to his forehead and gave a mock salute. "Yes, sir, captain, sir."

Sahira stifled a smile as, not at all amused, Belda scowled at him. "No one likes a dick," the lycan snapped.

"I must disagree," a pixie said as she stopped to hover in front of Sahira.

Belda waved at the tiny creature who held her hand over her mouth to contain her laughter before zipping away. A trail of pink pixie dust followed her through the crowd.

"Are you okay?" the demon asked.

Sahira downed her second glass of alcohol and winced as this one seared its way onto her tastebuds. "Fine."

She coughed into her hand and blinked away the tears burning her eyes. When she set the glass on the bar, the demon leaned his elbow on the red leather padding the edge, while reaching over to grab the bottle Belda set down.

The demon refilled her drink before setting the bottle beside it. "Keep drinking. It doesn't make it better, but it's a little calming. I'm Drozeth, but everyone calls me Zeth."

"A demon," she murmured.

"You're very observant."

Despite her distressed state, Sahira chuckled. "I meant it's not often you run into a demon. You tend to keep to yourselves."

"That's probably why I'm the only one here."

"Are there witches here?"

"Yes, and warlocks."

"What about vampires?"

"They're here too. Are you going to have a problem with that?"

She laughed humorlessly as she flashed her teeth at him. Her fangs weren't fully extended, but, like all vampires, they were noticeable. "Not me."

"Oh, sorry, I thought you were a witch."

"I am."

His eyebrows rose as his eyes ran up and down her. "Interesting."

"So I've been told by some. Others don't find it so intriguing." She poured more alcohol into her glass but only sipped it this time. "How long have you been here?"

"Thirty years."

Sahira almost spit out the liquid as she choked on it. Setting the glass on the bar, she pulled at the collar of her shirt as the world blurred.

Zeth rested his hand on her shoulder again. "Easy. Deep

breaths. It doesn't seem like it now, but you get used to being here."

When she could see clearly, she tipped her head back to take in the handsome man. He had deep black skin, a broad nose, strong cheekbones, and a jaw that could cut glass. Two red horns curled out from the sides of his bald head and hooked toward the middle.

His yellow eyes shone with concern as he studied her. He had a narrow waist, and his broad shoulders blocked the bar behind him. Two sharp, bony hooks rose from the tops of his shoulders and curved toward his neck. They would make wearing a shirt difficult, which was probably why he was bare to the waist.

"It does get easier," he assured her.

"Does it?"

"You eventually adjust."

"That doesn't sound encouraging."

"Not much is around here."

Sahira laughed bitterly as she downed her drink.

CHAPTER THREE

ORIN HAD a little extra spring in his step when he opened the door to his room and closed it on the three women within. He'd kick them out when he returned and finished with them, but they'd earned their rest for now.

He couldn't stop smiling as he strolled the balcony; he had to resist the urge to whistle. There hadn't been anything to look forward to since getting stuck here, but now...

Well, now he had a witch to play with. Rubbing his hands together, he grinned as he contemplated how he'd torment his little witch.

She couldn't hide from him here or run away. He almost felt bad for the hell he intended to unleash on her, but she deserved everything she got after refusing to take her tracking spell off him. Getting herself trapped here, too, should be punishment enough for that.

It wasn't.

He'd break her, bed her, and make her pay for her refusal to do as he'd asked. His smile widened as he glanced at the pub below. Then it vanished when he saw the demon standing with *his* witch and plying her with alcohol. No one would play with his witch but *him*.

Orin rubbed his hands together, his smile returning as he descended the steps. Yes, there was something finally fun about this realm.

Once at the bottom of the steps, he crossed the scarred wood floors to where Sahira stood at the bar. She was still paler than normal but beautiful in the dim glow filtering over her.

And she was going to be so much fun to break.

Stepping between them, Orin grinned at the demon before shifting his attention to Sahira's still-stunned expression.

"Hello, witch," he purred.

Her unfocused eyes lifted to his before her vision cleared. She glared at him while sipping her drink.

"Do you two know each other?" Zeth asked.

"Unfortunately," Sahira whispered.

"Oh now, dear, don't be so glum. At least, now that you're here, we can comfort each other," Orin told her.

She finished her drink before setting it on the bar and focusing on the demon. "Is there somewhere I can sleep and stay while I'm here?"

"All newcomers stay here until their houses are built."

"Built?"

Orin almost felt a little bad for her. She was confused and upset, but empathy wasn't an emotion he liked to entertain.

And, he reminded himself as he lifted the bottle and poured more into her glass, *she's the reason she's here. She decided to play games by keeping my tracking spell on, and she lost.*

He'd make sure she lost the next game they played too. He drank the whiskey in her glass and set it down.

"The immortals here all help to build homes for the new arrivals," Zeth said.

"That's nice of them," she muttered.

"We were all you once too—stuck, confused, and convinced

there was some way to escape. It takes time, but you eventually accept there might not be."

Orin would never accept that, and from the look on Sahira's face, she felt the same way.

"You can always stay in my room," Orin offered.

"I'd rather sleep outside," Sahira murmured.

"No need," Zeth assured her. "There are plenty of rooms upstairs, and you two are the only ones residing here now. Everyone else has moved out. I can ask Belda to get you the key to a room, and I'll take you up."

"I'll be the one to take care of my family," Orin said.

"Family?"

"His brother is engaged to my niece, but we are *not* family," Sahira stated.

Some of her shock was wearing off, making things a lot more fun. He much preferred a feisty witch to this numb one.

"Thankfully, we're not blood," Orin agreed.

Sahira turned up her nose before shifting so her back was mostly to him. Behind Orin, voices rose as chairs scraped back and something clattered.

With his elbow on the bar, he craned his head as a lycan and vampire stood over a table. Each of them had their hands on the green surface of the table while they swore at each other.

"Hey!" Belda shouted, thrusting her finger at the door. "There's no fighting in here. Take it to the pit, or you'll each be in a cell!"

"What's the pit?" Sahira asked.

"It's where immortals settle their disputes in this realm," Orin told her.

When the vampire jerked his head toward the doorway, the lycan nodded his agreement.

"You're in for some fun today." Orin looped his arm through hers. "What a great day for you to arrive!"

"Oh, fuck off."

Orin laughed as he led her toward the door.

CHAPTER FOUR

SAHIRA WAS STILL TOO stunned to resist as Orin escorted her through the pub and toward the door. She frowned when she spotted the metal shutters pinned open inside the windows. The metal was at least two inches thick.

She forgot about Orin's hold on her arm as they followed the rest of the immortals out the door and onto the porch. "What's with the shutters?" she asked.

"Protection," Zeth responded.

"From what?"

She wasn't sure if Zeth didn't hear her over the growing din of conversation and excitement surrounding them or if he became distracted by the chatter as more immortals from the town joined the crush of bodies propelling them onward.

How is this possible? How can we be trapped here?

She had no idea, but they were, and she had to figure out if she could escape this mess. Trying to control her rising panic, Sahira focused on getting out of here as they crossed a red dirt road.

Finally getting her wits about her, she started taking in details of the town. It was a strange combination of old wood buildings and stately, elaborate structures that must have taken immortals, with their superior strength and speed months to erect.

A reddish hue bathed everything. The sun in the sky was redder, and the clouds were also a deep red as the sun touched the horizon. The dirt beneath her feet and the rocks and mountains stretching beyond the town were also various shades of red.

Even the lake, with the sun reflecting across its serene surface, appeared red—something that was confirmed when a mermaid's red tail flicked out of the water. A mermaid's tail changed color based on its surroundings.

The sun had sunk low enough that the vampires moved freely through its fading rays. As a half vampire, the sun didn't affect her like pure-blooded vamps. Sometimes, if the sun was too bright and she was in it for too long, it bothered her, but it couldn't kill her like it did other vamps. It was one of the few blessings of her rare birth.

She could teleport like vampires, too, but not as well. Many of them could cover vast distances; she could only go fifty or so feet at a time. However, she did possess the enhanced strength, speed, and senses of vamps.

Besides the immortals and the different-colored clothing they wore, the buildings and black rocks jutting up from the mountains and countryside were the only colors that broke the drab monotone.

They moved through alleys running between the buildings and onto more streets. The streets all ran parallel and curved around to the other streets like a big, expanding city block.

At the end of each street, the dirt roads stopped at the edge of a red, sandy desert that stretched onward before rising into mountains. Jagged rocks poked up from the sand that blew when a small breeze stirred the air.

The mermaid's tail flicked out of the water before it dove again.

"Did the witches create the lake?" she asked.

"No," Orin said. "It was always here."

"How do you know that?"

"I've been here long enough to learn about this place."

"And there was natural water in an outer realm?"

Orin shrugged, but when his black eyes met hers, they didn't gleam with amusement. Instead, they held a calculating light. The tips of his pointed ears poked out from hair as black as the crows the dark fae used to communicate.

His clothes hid most of his black ciphers, but the tips of the flame-like markings darkened the bottom of his neck. He had the slender build of all the pure dark fae, but one would be an idiot to think that made him weaker. Power and strength flowed through the chiseled muscles of the arm holding hers.

His narrow face, high cheekbones, and the slight point of his chin all combined for a lethal-looking appearance that matched his personality. His hawkish nose only added to his intimidating aura and handsomeness.

"It does look like an outer realm, doesn't it?" he asked.

"Isn't it?"

"I'm not sure what it is. I was picturing outer realms and portal hopping when I ended up here, but it's not the same as the others."

"No shit," she muttered.

Zeth had been here for *thirty* years, and she had no idea how much time any of the others had spent here. It could be centuries.

She gulped at the possibility as sweat beaded on her nape. In Dragonia and the human realm, fall had settled in and turned toward winter, but the temperature was warmer here.

The sunbaked land and sand gave this realm the air of a desert, but it wasn't hot. Instead, she felt like Goldilocks, who had found her perfect bowl of porridge. *It's just right.*

The temperature might be the only right thing about this place. She was in deep trouble here, but she would keep it together and get out of this realm if it was the last thing she did.

Orin led her past a golden building that was more like a mini palace with its pointed turrets, domed archway, and drawbridge lowered over the pit dug around the structure. The makeshift moat was a sandy ditch with nothing at the bottom, but the place looked built for royalty.

No one exited the golden home, but apparently the walk to the pit was a big thing, as more and more immortals filtered out of their homes and businesses to join the crowd. They made their way through another small alley, boxed in by two simple wooden buildings.

The scent of cooking meat wafted from one while the aromas of lavender, sage, and countless other herbs drifted from the other. One must be someone's home; she'd bet the other was either a witch's shop or home.

Usually, witches preferred to live closer to the earth than in a building, but this realm was far from the norm. The building intrigued her, but she had no idea how the witches in this realm would react to her.

Her friendship with Kaylia, and the battle against the Lord, had changed some of the witches' opinions about her. But this realm was locked away and the residents isolated; the witches here probably still harbored the same extreme dislike of her as many others over the years.

Which meant the fun times were going to keep on coming.

"What is this pit?" she asked, distracting herself from her morose thoughts. There was no point in getting bogged down in misery when there was little she could do about it.

"It's where the immortals in this realm go to solve their disputes," Zeth replied.

She was so focused on taking in the town, she hadn't realized the demon was still walking with them until he spoke. It also finally sank in that Orin was still holding her arm, and she tried to tug it free.

He held on.

Gritting her teeth, she glowered at him but didn't try to extricate her arm again. Fighting with him on this would only make him happy.

He proved her point when he turned his head to smile at her. Her fingers twitched into a fist as she pictured punching those perfect white teeth down his throat.

His crow-black eyes sparkled with amusement before he focused ahead again. Sahira ignored him as she shifted her attention to Zeth.

"They fight in this pit?" she asked.

"Yes," the demon said.

"To the death?"

"That's the victor's decision to make. They can allow their opponent to live or die."

"Everyone who enters the pit is aware of this," Orin said.

Brutal, but then most immortals were. "Do all disputes end up in the pit?" Sahira asked.

"If both opponents agree to it, they do. If not, they agree for the argument to end, but there is no fighting or attacks outside the pit. It keeps things in this realm more civilized."

"I see."

"Not all disagreements start in a fight in the pub, like you witnessed. Some immortals arrive and realize they have enemies here. They seek to end old disputes and take them to the pit."

Sahira focused on Orin. "How often have you been in this pit since you arrived here?"

"Five, but I don't start fights—I finish them."

She wasn't surprised by the number; he hadn't been gone long, but Orin wasn't exactly known for making friends.

"And how many of your opponents still live?" she asked.

There was that irritatingly obnoxious yet annoyingly striking smile again. She'd like that smile if it didn't light up his handsome face and cause his onyx eyes to twinkle so enticingly.

Did he have to be so handsome? And *why* did his hand suddenly feel so warm on her arm?

The worst part was he *knew* he was gorgeous and used it to his advantage, which meant he was trying to use it against her and anyone else.

Everything was a weapon to Orin, including his looks. She scowled at him, which only made his smile grow.

"I don't let anyone who threatens me survive," he said.

She'd expected that answer. Orin had the morals of a shark, and plenty would prefer him dead… with good reason. If he let them live, they'd only try to kill him again.

And she didn't blame them for trying.

They wandered through another street with more houses and buildings in all different styles, but none were as elaborate as the golden one.

"Who lives in the golden home with the moat?" she inquired.

"No one… anymore," Zeth said.

"Anymore?"

"Prince Cogsworth of the trolls used to reside there but was killed during The Reaping."

"What's The Reaping?"

"Here we are!" Orin announced as he released Sahira's arm to clap. "Let the fun begin!"

CHAPTER FIVE

ORIN GAZED at the hole the immortals of this realm had dug into the earth. Some of the black rocks jutted through the sand and into the pit. They helped make for some very interesting ways to destroy an opponent. He'd used them well to his advantage.

He smiled as he recalled smashing the berserker into those rocks. The look of astonishment on the man's face and the way his jaw dropped when he saw the rock jutting through his chest had been great fun.

Orin rubbed his hands together as the lycan and vampire descended the black stone steps into the pit. Someone cleaned the pit after every battle, but bloodstains still marred the sandy floor fifteen feet below them.

Some stains could never be washed, shoveled, or raked away. Mostly, he found the Cursed Realm extremely boring, but the pit provided a distraction from the mundane days and nights of their lives here.

For the most part, the Cursed Realm was well-ordered, had an established set of rules, and the immortals here usually got along. Whatever fights happened here were resolved in the pit... if both parties agreed.

If one fighter agreed and the other didn't, the rest of the immortals knew who the winner was and who the coward was. If both parties disagreed, it was all forgotten, and everyone moved on. If both parties agreed to a fight, they settled their differences in brutal hand-to-hand combat that one of them might not survive.

In this realm, everyone worked. Each of them had a job they had to do, and if they didn't, they were banished. They were given everything necessary to survive here if they pulled their weight.

Even he tended bar at the pub. It wasn't a job he'd ever imagined himself doing, but those who didn't work were thrown out of town and told to make their way in a realm with little to offer outside of this area.

And there were some battles he picked and some he didn't. He wasn't stupid enough to pick a fight with a woman who had this realm running so smoothly when it could be a complete shit show.

Being in this town was as boring as watching paint dry, but he wouldn't live in the outer reaches of some forsaken realm with *no* entertainment and no way to survive. He'd far prefer to sling drinks.

Besides, tending bar could be amusing, and he did learn all the gossip. Although, in this realm, not much happened.

Bartending also came with the perk of a steady supply of women. But that part of his life would have to change for a bit.

He glanced at Sahira as she stared into the pit with a furrowed brow and her full mouth pursed. With her here, he had a new source of entertainment, and he was going to enjoy breaking the little witch.

Provoking her was great fun, and there was so little of that here. But, if he was going to get her in his bed—and he *would*— he had to back off that source of entertainment and some of his other ones.

The more he rattled and annoyed her, the more she would resist him. And to appease a grizzly bear, one had to offer some honey, or so he assumed.

And she *was* like a bear, all cute and disarming, until she gutted you with her claws… or, in Sahira's case, her words. The witch had a vicious tongue—one he *would* feel against his cock.

So, until he got her in his bed, he'd have to be less irritating to her and work things differently. She wouldn't like his normal approach to getting a woman—being arrogant, flirty, and goddamn good-looking. Plus, he was fantastic in bed, a reputation that preceded him everywhere.

But his little witch didn't care about those things. She wouldn't respond well to them because they didn't matter to her.

What does matter to her besides her niece and brother?

She had a lot of pride, strength, smarts, and enjoyed her freedom. She wasn't one to fall for flattery or flirting. She was strong, independent, and could keep a secret—she'd helped Del keep Lexi's heritage under cover for over two decades.

He'd bet she was wild in bed. He couldn't wait to find out, but to do so, he'd have to stop irritating her. He'd never get anywhere if she continued to hate him.

He surveyed the witch's striking amber eyes and mahogany hair, which she'd pulled into a neat bun that had come loose to hang against her nape. She was beautiful with her heart-shaped face and Cupid's bow mouth, but she didn't flaunt it.

"Fight!" someone shouted.

Orin turned his attention to the pit as the lycan and vampire went at it. Unlike him, few in this realm went through with the kill. Most of those who entered the pit walked out again.

Probably because, while over three hundred immortals clustered around the pit, this was a small town. If they kept killing every time they went into the pit, the number of residents would be much smaller, and things would be even *more* boring.

Plus, most disagreements, such as this, were over petty things like cheating at gambling or because someone was in a pissy mood. His fights hadn't been either of those things.

When he arrived, some didn't like him, and others thought taking down a dark fae prince would be great fun. Those idiots never left the pit again, and no one else in this realm shared any of their grand plans, as no one bothered him again after that first week.

Other immortals would have kept coming at him if he'd allowed any of his enemies to survive. He'd put a quick and effective end to that.

The crowd cheered as the lycan punched the vamp in the face, spilling blood. And if there was anything immortals loved, it was blood.

The vampire dodged the lycan's next few blows, ducked under his arm, and leapt onto his back. He wrapped his arms around the lycan's shoulders and chest as he sank his fangs into the immortal's throat.

"Why doesn't he teleport?" Sahira muttered.

"Not possible in this realm," Orin said.

Her head lifted, and she blinked at him before her mouth pursed. Orin suspected she was trying to teleport and failing.

"How is that possible?" she breathed after a minute.

"That is the constant question of this realm."

"It would take so much power...."

Her attention shifted back to the fight. He felt she wasn't watching the fighters but trying to piece this place together. He hoped she had better luck at it than him, as he didn't have a clue what was happening here.

The lycan shifted into his wolf form and threw the vampire free with a violent shake of his thick coat. When the vamp hit the ground, the lycan pounced, clamped down on his head, lifted him off the ground, and flung him into the wall.

The distinctive sound of the vamp's back cracking radiated outward; he howled and hit the ground. The wolf prowled over, planted his paw on the man's chest, and lowered his muzzle until it was only an inch from the vamp's face.

"Mercy!" the vamp yelped as he slapped a hand off the sandy ground.

"How disappointing," Orin murmured.

He ignored the disapproving look Sahira shot him. It was disappointing; he'd been looking forward to a bit of death, and it was already over.

The lycan didn't move as he debated granting this mercy or not. Then he slapped the vamp's chest with his paw before prowling away from the broken man.

Cheers and groans erupted around the crowd. Those who bet on the lycan received slaps on the back and the extra pieces of food or drink they'd won.

There was no money here; everyone had to work for what they had, and their payment was the things they required to survive. It was almost a utopian society, except they were all trapped here, their friends and families weren't here, it was boring, they battled in a pit, and—

"So, what is The Reaping?" Sahira asked.

CHAPTER SIX

"THAT, my friend, is a soon-to-unfold horror story," Zeth said.

Sahira stared into the pit as the lycan crept up the steps and out. The vamp remained on the ground with his arms spread at his sides. When no one went to help him, she assumed his broken back and inability to walk were part of his added humiliation for losing this fight.

As if he were reading her mind, Orin confirmed this. "He'll stay there until he can get himself out. It's what he deserves."

"And why is that?" she demanded.

"No one should ever reward a loser, Sahira. Not ever."

She rolled her eyes but didn't respond. Of course he would think that. He was one of the most brutal and unrelenting men she'd ever encountered.

And Orin didn't lose. It was something she was keenly aware of now that she was stuck here with him and the object of a new game he planned to play.

"And what if the sun comes up before his back heals?" she asked.

"Then he'll die."

Sahira blinked at his callous brutality. She didn't know why it astonished her; she knew what kind of man he was, but still, the coldness of his words was unsettling.

With a hand on her arm, Orin turned her away from the pit. "Come, it's time you learn the rules of this place."

Sahira tried to ignore the small thrill his touch sent through her. The thrum of it ran to the tips of her toes, which she *refused* to let curl in her brown, soft leather boots.

She prepared herself for him to take control of her arm again, but instead of insisting on touching her, his hand slid away. She hadn't expected that but was grateful for the reprieve.

And she kept telling herself that as her body continued to hum from their contact. Orin strolled beside her but didn't encroach annoyingly on her as he often liked to do.

It made her suspicious. He was up to something, and she suspected this was a way to get at her.

"And what are the rules?" she asked.

"Everyone here works," Zeth said. "Belda will find you something you'd like to do, but you have to do it. *No one* gets a free ride here. Also, we all help to build one another's homes; until then, you can stay at the pub. That's where we all stayed when we first arrived."

"I'm still staying there," Orin said. "I won't be here long enough to have a home built for me."

"That's what we all said," Zeth murmured.

Sahira gulped at his cryptic words but chose to ignore them. "Where do you get building materials? This is an outer realm. There's usually not any building materials in most outer realms."

"There are some woods to the left side of the lake. You can't see them until you're closer to the lake, but they're there. There used to be more trees big enough for lumber, but they were harvested, and nothing has sprouted forth to replace them.

"Soon, we won't be able to build homes for everyone who arrives; they'll have to use the ones that aren't occupied anymore. There's more trees by the river, but they're too small to be useful."

"Where did you get the gold for the palace?"

"Some of the witches and warlocks cast a spell to give it that appearance. It's just wood, but that asshole troll was fine with it and stopped demanding a place fit for a prince afterward. The immortals trapped here didn't build everything in this realm either. Some of the buildings were already here when the first immortal arrived."

"They were?" Sahira asked in disbelief.

"Yes. The pub, infirmary, stable, library, jail, mercantile, and granary were all here before," Zeth answered.

"How do you know that?"

"From a book in the library and Belda. The first immortal wrote their story in what was originally a blank book; it became the first of many stories. She was a vampire who reported that no one else was here when she arrived, but she discovered those buildings, food, and drink."

"Was there blood?"

"No. She was nearly starved when a second immortal, Belda, arrived. Belda agreed to supply the vamp with her blood, and they worked together to try to uncover the secrets of this town. Neither of them ever unlocked those secrets, and the vamp died during the first Reaping. Belda's been here for four hundred and fifty years; she established most of the rules we live by."

Sahira's heart sank. "That's so much time."

"It is," Zeth agreed.

She glanced at Orin, whose jaw had tightened, but he didn't say anything. Then another uncomfortable possibility occurred as she looked around the town. "How do the vampires here feed?"

"They have someone who agrees to provide them blood," Zeth said.

"I will provide for you," Orin stated.

She'd rather starve than drink from him. There had to be someone else in this realm she could feed from, and she would find them.

"How is there food here?" she asked instead of engaging Orin in the argument he was probably seeking.

"Originally, a fair amount of grains and salted meats were stored in the pub's back room, along with some seeds. The vamp and Belda learned those seeds grow here."

"They do?" Sahira squeaked.

"This place isn't like any outer realm you've ever been to," Orin said. "It's more than being trapped here. This whole place is different than anything we've ever experienced before. Whoever made it impossible to leave here also set it up so those who arrived could survive."

The hair on Sahira's nape rose as she glanced at the reddened sky and buildings surrounding them. Feeling like she was in a snow globe, she waited for someone to shake their glass home and send them all spiraling into a dust-covered wonderland.

"Are we being watched?" she whispered.

CHAPTER SEVEN

ORIN COULDN'T DENY that he'd often wondered the same thing. Was this all some sick, cosmic game someone had set up, and now they were sitting by, watching it play out?

If that was the case, it was a boring game to play, but he didn't put it past some immortals to devise this twisted trap. It would be great fun initially, but over four centuries later?

A giant snooze fest. If he'd done something like this, he would have killed all the members of his game over four hundred years ago. He didn't know any immortals with the patience to continue something like this.

Unless they'd gotten bored and walked away, but that didn't seem likely. Mostly because... "Who would have the power to do such a thing?"

"The arachs, maybe," Sahira said.

"We've heard that one of them still lives," Zeth said.

"I see Orin has been talking."

"We like to be kept up on things, so when new immortals arrive, we usually bombard them with questions. You'll get them too. There was a lycan who arrived about a month before Orin.

He filled us in on a lot, but I don't think Orin has been questioned as much. I haven't asked him many."

"It's been a busy couple of months for new immortals arriving here."

"It happens. Sometimes new arrivals come at steady intervals. Other times we'll get two or three in a week and then no one for a year or two."

"It depends on the unlucky draw," Sahira muttered.

"Yep. So, this arach, does she have the power to do something like this?"

"She wasn't alive when Belda and the vamp first arrived here. And all the other arachs were dead, except for her parents. They wouldn't have had the power for something like this. They were powerful, but not *this* powerful. We can't open portals, and vampires can't teleport. That level of magic would have required *all* the arachs, and I'm still not sure they could have pulled off such a feat."

"Maybe, before they all perished, the arachs set up this realm."

"Why would they do that?"

"Why did they all kill each other?" Orin asked. "They're not exactly easy to figure out and weren't entirely rational."

"I don't see them wasting their time or power on a realm they had nothing to do with before they all started fighting each other," Sahira said.

Orin agreed, but when it came to this place, he was willing to explore *every* option if it helped them escape.

When they arrived at the golden palace, Zeth stopped walking and turned to face them.

Orin hadn't talked much with the demon since arriving, but he was one of the few who had his shit together. He wasn't a hothead or a whiny pain in the ass.

"I don't really get that vibe from this place either, but maybe they did do it," Zeth said.

Orin rocked back on his heels as he studied the tall, powerful demon. "What vibe *do* you get?"

"I think it might be a realm that… died or was starting to die. It's almost as if the inhabitants were starting to make a home here and were building the places they needed before suddenly abandoning it."

"If there were enough of them to build a pub, library, and jail, then they would have built more than one home," Sahira said. "Those things are built when there are bigger populations."

Zeth rubbed his jaw while studying the town. "We sometimes find debris when we're building the new homes. There were other homes here, too, but none of them remained standing. The sand eventually claimed and covered them."

"I'm surprised the other buildings are still around."

"The other ones have a steel foundation and frames. They may look like they're made of wood, but an extremely solid frame is behind that wood. We haven't found any evidence that the buildings that toppled had anything like it. We haven't discovered any other steel, besides what's inside those seven buildings, anywhere around here."

"So, at one time, there were more than seven buildings," Sahira murmured. "But what does that mean?"

"It's another one of the many mysteries surrounding this place."

"The fact that others once resided here explains the stored food," Orin said.

"But if they abandoned it because it was dying, they left early; it's been going for centuries since then. It's not the most vibrant realm, but there's enough to keep immortals alive," Sahira said.

"There are animals to hunt for food and other creatures that only exist to kill us," Zeth said.

"If there was enough to survive, and far more than most outer realms, why would they abandon it?"

"Another one of those mysteries. Besides, they might not have abandoned it. They might have all been stuck here, too, and finally died off due to The Reaping."

"What exactly is The Reaping?" Sahira asked. "Because it doesn't sound good."

"It's not," Zeth said.

Orin had already heard about The Reaping and wasn't looking forward to it, but he wasn't overly concerned. The Reaping and this place would not be how and where he died. He'd survived worse than what was to come.

"Once a year, the scarog beetles arrive," Zeth said. "We call it The Reaping."

CHAPTER EIGHT

SAHIRA'S STOMACH plummeted into her feet. She'd heard of scarog beetles before but, thankfully, never encountered them. She doubted any immortals *hadn't* heard about the ravenous creatures.

The scarogs were monstrous beasts who devoured anything in their way when they invaded a place. They stripped the flesh from their victims and ate it before consuming the muscles and bones.

Her knees almost knocked together before she stopped them. "How many of them come once a year?"

"Dozens," Zeth answered.

"Dozens?" She somehow managed to stop herself from croaking the word.

"Yes. Most times, it's difficult to count them because they move so fast and there are so many of them. They don't leave until they've killed someone."

Sahira frowned at this revelation. Scarog beetles were usually voracious and didn't care about who they did or didn't kill. They normally didn't stop until there was nothing left to feed on.

"They stop after killing some*one*?" she inquired, certain she hadn't heard him right.

"Only if a full day has passed. The beetles come in and, if they kill someone immediately, stay for a full day and continue hunting. If three days pass without a kill, as soon as they succeed in finally getting someone, they leave right afterward. So, they hunt and kill as many as possible for one full day. After that, they only hunt until they kill one immortal and then they leave again."

Sahira didn't know how to respond. She'd never heard of such a thing; it was ridiculous, insane, and impossible. "From what I've always heard, that's not how scarogs work. They hunt until there's nothing left to hunt."

"Maybe that's true in every other realm, but it's not how they behave here," Zeth said. "It's how the first vampire to arrive died. And it's how Belda has remained all this time. When the scarogs arrive, we all cram into the seven main buildings… if we can. Not everyone always makes it inside, and our homes are useless against stopping them."

Sahira stared at the pub as she pondered his words. A woman danced on one of the wrought iron balconies, but the place was subdued.

The dark wood facade certainly didn't hint at the steel beneath, but Zeth had no reason to lie, and she now understood those thick shutters a lot better. They would require metal that thick to keep the scarogs out.

"So, if only one immortal remained here when the scarogs arrive…." Her voice trailed off as the woman retreated inside.

"The scarogs would hunt them to death."

Sahira couldn't stop herself from tugging at her collar as she glanced around the town. Being trapped here was bad, but this… well, what *was* this?

"So, the scarogs are another thing that makes it seem like someone has set something up here. As if they control things that shouldn't be controlled—"

"Kind of like an arach with the dragons," Orin interjected.

"Lexi can't control animals or insects," Sahira protested. "And the person who sits on the throne controls the dragons. It doesn't have to be an arach. The power doesn't drive an arach insane like it does anyone else who tries to take control of magic that doesn't belong to them."

"We don't know if she *could* control insects and animals."

She opened her mouth to protest before his words sank in. He was right; they still had no idea what Lexi could do.

Before Lexi stopped drinking the potion Sahira created for her, she'd never seen her niece bring dormant plants back to life or heal others. She'd also never ridden on dragons or ruled all the realms before.

They hadn't tapped into Lexi's full potential and may never do so. Sahira didn't want to believe this was some trap set by the arach, but it might be.

"They helped establish the dark fae trials," Sahira murmured.

"And they set a nasty little surprise in there for Cole."

"It wasn't specifically *meant* for Cole."

"Does that matter?"

"No," she admitted.

She looked around the town again, trying to figure out what was happening. "But why would they do it?"

"Why did they all slaughter each other?"

"For power. This place doesn't offer them any power. There's *nothing* for them to gain here."

"So they did it for fun. They were a coldhearted bunch of freaks, and this might have been their idea of a grand old fun time."

Sahira pondered this before shaking her head. "That wasn't the arach way. They didn't play with others like this."

A fire burned in Orin's eyes. "They played with the dark fae and especially Cole."

"When they cast the spell for the Shadow Reaver, they didn't know Cole would be the one to unleash it. They set that trap because they were trying to protect the last living arach, not because they were trying to mess with the dark fae. Their plan worked."

Orin glowered at her before shifting his attention to Zeth, who was watching them with amused fascination. When they both stared at him, he smiled before speaking.

"We've all learned about current events, or as current as they can be, from new arrivals, but you two have the inside information. It's interesting."

"I'm glad we're entertaining you," Orin retorted.

"So am I."

He scowled at Zeth, but the demon didn't notice. Instead, he turned to Sahira. "If you're ready, I can talk to Belda about assigning you a room until you decide what kind of house you'd like to have built."

"I won't be here long enough to require having a house built for me," Sahira said. "But a room would be nice."

Zeth smiled grimly. "Everyone says that, including me. We all change our minds."

Sahira refused to let the sinking sensation in her belly take a firmer grip while she watched him walk away, but she couldn't rid herself of the feeling of doom descending over her.

"You're right," Orin said. "We won't be here long enough for them to build houses for us."

Sahira watched him walk away before shifting her attention back to the mysterious town. It was peaceful, and from how Zeth described it, the different immortals here had found a way to survive and thrive together.

Everyone here worked and pulled their weight, or they left. Disputes were resolved in a way that worked for everyone involved, and they all helped build homes for one another. The immortals here should be mostly relaxed, but she sensed an underlying tension in those hurrying along the streets.

Maybe the approach of The Reaping was making everyone tense, or perhaps it was always like this. It was impossible to relax while living in a snow globe that could be shaken to release flesh-eating beetles.

Sahira refused to let her uncertainty get the best of her, so she straightened her shoulders and stalked across the street to the pub. One way or another, she would get answers. Until then, she required somewhere to sleep.

CHAPTER NINE

"YOUR HIGHNESS," King Firth of the merfolk greeted in the accented voice of his people that resembled the Greek inflection of humans.

His pale blond hair flowed around his shoulders as his sea-green eyes surveyed Lexi while she sat on her throne. He was missing part of his left foot, but Cole wouldn't have known until he saw it, as the merking's limp was nearly indiscernible.

The end of his golden trident clicked against the rocky floor when he stopped only twenty feet away from her. Broad-shoul-dered and tall, he was an imposing figure.

At his side stood his wife, Queen Mira. Her head only reached her husband's chest, and her black hair nearly brushed the ground. Her lively blue eyes were inquisitive as they went from him to Lexi and back again.

Cole rested his hand on the back of Lexi's throne as he stood beside her. He wouldn't be king of this realm until they married, so he couldn't sit at her side but wouldn't leave it.

At her other side stood her father, Del. Alina, the speaker of dragons, sat behind the throne with her tail curled around it and her head over the top of Lexi's. Her three wyrmlings, rolling around on the dais, snapped playfully at each other.

They'd started to breathe fire, and little balls of it puffed from their mouths as smoke spiraled from their nostrils. Astarot and Belindo were locked together when Firth spoke but stopped tumbling around the stage. Belindo lay on her back while Astarot remained on top of her.

They rocked back and forth in their embrace as they craned their heads to look at the merking. Nithe, crouched like a cat about to pounce, wiggled her ass before jumping on her siblings. The three of them yelped before taking off behind the throne.

The merking and the handful of followers he'd brought with him watched the baby dragons with various expressions of amusement. That amusement vanished when wings flapped and shadows fell across the room as more dragons landed to perch on the edge of the open roof above.

Every dragon made it clear they could descend upon this room, and the merfolk, in less than a second as they craned their heads to peer down from their golden eyes with their slitted pupils.

"King Firth," Lexi greeted. "It's a pleasure to finally meet you and your wife."

"You as well," King Firth said, "and it's good to see you doing so well after your recent brush with death."

Cole's fingers twitched on the throne. Without Firth, Lexi would still be trapped in a stone-like state, and he was here to collect on that debt, but he could have waited until after dinner before bringing up the topic.

"And we have you to thank for helping to ensure that death didn't come," Lexi said.

"You do."

From the corner of his eye, Cole caught Del's glance toward him, but Cole didn't dare shift his attention away from the merfolk. King Firth wasn't a fool, and he had to know if he tried anything against Lexi, he'd end up dead.

Cole wouldn't tolerate this man being rude or disrespectful in any way. Firth might not have declared his allegiance to Lexi, but she was still his queen, and if the merking didn't treat her as such, he'd be dragon shit by the end of this day.

Cole looked to Lexi as her fingers constricted and relaxed on the arms of the throne. This was her realm and situation to handle, but he'd gladly beat the merking down if she asked him to.

"I appreciate all you and your wife did for me by taking Cole to the crudue vine. He's told me how difficult it was to retrieve it, but *he* did."

Cole inwardly smiled as, with those words, Lexi shifted some of the credit for the crudue vine from the merfolk to him. She hadn't played the game of politics for long, but she was smart and already becoming adept at navigating the field.

"Very few survive the Malignant Waters." King Firth surveyed Lexi with a little more interest. Then he shifted his attention to Cole. "But your fiancé did so successfully."

"And we are both alive because of that," Lexi said.

"Which is amazing. The last time I saw him, I was sure he wouldn't survive his injuries."

Cole bared his teeth in the semblance of a smile. "It will take a lot more than that to kill me."

"So it seems."

And Cole could tell the king was pondering what it would take. King Firth may not want to kill him, but every man sought to know the weaknesses of a possible opponent, and Firth wasn't sure what Cole's were... other than Lexi.

"What has brought you here today, King Firth?" Lexi inquired with more of an edge to her voice.

She must have determined the same thing about King Firth's

thoughts. Cole settled a hand on her shoulder as he sought to soothe and reassure her that he was fine.

It had taken some time, but he'd regained his full strength. However, she didn't like being reminded of his injuries or having anyone contemplating what it might take to kill him. She wasn't a lycan, but she was just as protective of him as a lycan was their mate.

"We have come to ask for the repayment of our kindness promised to us by—" King Firth looked around, his brow furrowed, before focusing on Lexi again. "—a woman claiming to be your aunt who was with them when they came to Atlantia."

Beneath his hand, Lexi tensed, but it wasn't because of Sahira's promise to this man. It was because her aunt hadn't returned yet. It should have been a simple mission to locate Orin, but as much as his younger, more carefree brother irritated him, something was wrong if Orin hadn't checked back in with them yet.

And there was a reason why Sahira was still gone. They needed to figure it out but couldn't with the merfolk here.

"Was she lying?" King Firth asked.

"My aunt doesn't lie," Lexi said. "Of course we'll repay you for your help."

Cole could have pointed out that Sahira lied to Lexi for years by slipping her a potion to suppress her arach powers. Now wasn't the time, and she'd done it to protect Lexi, something Cole was grateful to her for.

King Firth smiled as he lifted his trident from the ground before tapping the end of it against the stone floor again. "Thank you, Your Highness."

Beneath his hand, Lexi remained tense and unmoving. "What have you come to ask us for?" Cole inquired when she didn't say anything more.

Firth's smile widened as he met Cole's gaze. "I don't think you can help us with this, King Colburn. This is something your fiancée must do."

A ripple of unease ran through Cole. He'd go to war with all these fish before he let Lexi do anything reckless for them.

Behind him, Alina shifted. As she did, she drew the merfolk's attention back to her, as Cole suspected she'd intended.

Her presence was a good reminder to the merfolk of what they were dealing with in Dragonia. A war with the merfolk wouldn't be good—they already had more enemies than allies—but he'd do whatever it took to keep Lexi safe.

"And what would you like *me* to do?" Lexi inquired.

"The arach were renowned for their strong magical abilities. They made it impossible for anyone who wasn't an arach to open a portal into Dragonia. We would like you to do the same for Atlantia."

Silence descended as King Firth asked Lexi for the one thing she couldn't do—use arach magic.

CHAPTER TEN

LEXI DIDN'T KNOW how to respond to the man who had begrudgingly helped Cole save her life. Yes, they owed him for that, he deserved repayment, and she couldn't have the merfolk as enemies, but she couldn't do what he'd asked.

Even if she could figure out how to use her arach magic, Lexi couldn't pull off such a feat on her own… or at least, she didn't think she could. It took a lot of power and many arachs to seal Dragonia off from the other immortals; she didn't have either of those things.

"We are tired of other immortals coming to Atlantia in search of riches and trying to take our people for sex," Queen Mira said. "We gladly kill those who dare, but sometimes they get away. We wish our realm to be more secure and to be left alone. Our children deserve to grow up in peace."

That they did, and Lexi's heart ached for all the merfolk. They deserved the peace they sought, but she couldn't help them with this, and admitting that was also admitting to a weakness she'd prefer to keep hidden.

They already had enough immortals plotting to take her down, even with the Shadow Reaver and dragons at her side.

That number could grow if they learned she couldn't tap into her arach abilities.

"I'd like to help," Lexi said. "I truly would, but I don't possess that power."

Cole's fingers tensed on her shoulder. She understood he was trying to caution her to tread carefully here, but she wouldn't reveal that she couldn't tap into her arach magic.

"It took a *lot* of arachs to pull off such magic with the portals," Lexi continued. "I can't do it without them."

"Which is something you knew before coming here to ask for this," Cole said.

His gravelly, low tone caused a few merfolk to shift uneasily as they glanced at their king. King Firth's jaw tightened, and the knuckles wrapped around his trident turned white.

"The arach were excellent at keeping their secrets. It's what they did best, and apparently"—his eyes raked Lexi—"what they still do best."

Cole's fingers lengthened into claws as the shadows around them shifted. "Watch yourself."

Alina's claws kicked against the rock as she approached the throne. Cole didn't know where the wyrmlings had gone, but he hadn't heard a peep since they disappeared behind the throne.

"Easy, Alina," Lexi cautioned. "They're not here to fight."

"No, we're not," Queen Mira said as she rested a hand on her husband's arm. He relaxed a little beneath her touch, but his eyes remained cold. "They take our children, or they did before we banned them from leaving the sea. So that means our children don't see the sun or land until they're grown. How is that fair to them?"

Those words were like a punch to Lexi's gut as she blew out a breath of air. "It's not fair to any of you, but I'm not keeping anything from you. I am the only arach left, and it took the combined powers of many to shut Dragonia off from other immortals. I can't do it alone, but...."

She glanced at the dragons above and the guards at the back of the hall. She didn't have many fighters to spare, but she was alive because of the merfolk, and their children deserved to grow up in peace. She owed them and would do what she could to repay that debt.

"I can send some guards back with you," she offered.

Lexi looked to Alina before glancing at the dragons above again. She couldn't volunteer them for anything they didn't want to do, but they might be helpful here.

Cole's hand fell away from her shoulder as she rose. "If you'll excuse me for a minute."

Queen Mira bowed her head, but King Firth remained rigid and annoyed. Lexi stepped around Cole to approach Alina.

Cole rested his hand on her arm, stopping her before she could get to Alina. He bent his head to hers and asked in a low murmur, "What are you doing?"

"I have to speak with Alina. I'll be right back."

He glanced at the dragon before releasing her arm. When he stepped back, shadows crept across his face and through his eyes. He was drawing them to him, which made her uneasy, but she could take them from him later if necessary.

Lexi swept past him and over to Alina, who twisted her head and lowered it so Lexi could talk to her. "I'd like to send some dragons back with them. Are there two or three who'd go with them?"

"For how long?"

"Long enough to make it clear to other immortals that no one can mess with the merfolk without dire consequences. Their presence will show Atlantia is protected by Dragonia. If the dragons decide not to stay, they can switch off with others."

"That would be preferable for them," Alina said. "And many will volunteer for it."

"Are you sure?"

"Yes. Tell them the dragons will help protect their children."

When Lexi rested her hand against Alina's cheek, the dragon leaned closer before Lexi reluctantly turned away. She resumed her throne and settled in as she focused on the merfolk.

"I can send some guards and dragons back with you. They'll switch off with others and will help protect Atlantia."

Mira glanced from her husband to Alina. "We don't want dragons in Atlantia."

"You have nothing to fear from us; we will not hurt you," Alina said as she reclaimed her place behind the throne.

King Firth almost dropped his trident, and Queen Mira stepped back as the other merfolk gasped. "It *talks*," one of them whispered.

"Yes, *she* does," Lexi said.

"My fellow dragons will understand they're not to harm any of the merfolk," Alina continued. "They will only protect you as they seek to destroy any who attack you."

"This is the best I can offer you," Lexi said. "You can take some guards and a couple of dragons back with you to Atlantia, or I can offer you carisle as a monetary reward for what you did. You could also wait until you can think of something else you'd like as repayment for your help."

Firth looked from her to Alina and back again before he bowed his head. "We will take the dragons. If they attack my people—"

"That *won't* happen," Alina vowed.

Firth started to say something again but changed his mind. "Then we look forward to this partnership."

"Good," Lexi said as she rose from the throne again. "Would you like to join us for dinner?"

"We would like that. Thank you."

Lexi turned and held out her hand to Cole, who clasped it in his. She kept a smile on her face while worry churned inside her.

"Sahira should be back by now," she whispered as they walked toward the stairs together.

"I'll send some guards to look for her and everyone who went with her. We'll find her."

She hoped he was right but couldn't shake the growing pit of dread in her belly. When she met her father's eyes, she saw her distress reflected in them.

CHAPTER ELEVEN

ORIN DRIED the glass and set it carefully behind the bar with the others. The crowd in the pub was abnormally subdued today, but according to the clock on the wall, it was only ten in the morning.

He studied the clock as he dried another glass. It was the only one in the Cursed Realm, and he had no way of knowing if it was right, but judging by the rise and fall of the sun, he assumed it was.

This wasn't his shift, but the bar was packed last night, and those working it fell behind on the cleanup. Belda asked him to help this morning, and with little else to do, he agreed.

Normally, that wasn't a thing he would do. He didn't *help* others; he was a dark fae. He found it more amusing to watch people sink than swim, but she'd promised him that he could have his afternoon shift off if he helped clean up the mess this morning.

His agreement also allowed him to keep an eye on Sahira and discover what she would do once the full reality of this realm sank in. He was curious how the little witch would handle it because he suspected that if anyone could get them out of this, it would be her or him.

The only problem was that he'd talked to everyone in this realm over the past month and still had no answers on how to leave it. And neither did any of those who had been here for decades and centuries.

Orin refused to think that would also be his fate. He was not a man meant to be tied down or trapped anywhere. He was a free spirit, a wanderer who briefly had his wings clipped, but he was determined to break free of this cage.

Preferably before The Reaping, but he wasn't sure that would be possible. Last night was the busiest he'd ever seen the pub. And it wasn't because there was a new witch in town for them to pump full of questions.

Sure, they came out to see Sahira, who politely answered their questions before excusing herself and going to bed, but the realm had been active lately with new arrivals, so they weren't as excited about her as they were for him. But some of those who rushed out to greet him also had plans to kill him.

They'd failed, and no one was eager to take up their cause. Some immortals still eyed him warily, but no one had the balls to fight him after he beat that berserker into a bloody mess before killing him.

Normally such violent, bloody deaths weren't his way—that was more how Cole took care of his enemies—but Orin had sought to make a point with the berserker, and it worked.

Unlike when he arrived, the witches and warlocks crowded the pub to see Sahira. A few of them turned up after his arrival, but they all came last night. Most hung back as they watched her.

The warlock Radagast was the only one who went up to introduce himself. He and Sahira shook hands before Radagast retreated.

Another witch hung farther back from the others; he believed she was the one who lived in the log cabin down the road but couldn't be sure. She rarely came to the pub, so he didn't know her, and she was often alone instead of with the pack of witches and warlocks who lived near the lake.

Orin set another glass down as he studied the pub's occupants. Most muttered to each other or tossed cards on the table.

Over the past month, the tension in town had steadily increased as the imminent arrival of The Reaping drew closer with the end of the year approaching. He imagined during the years when The Reaping occurred in January or February, the rest of the year was much more relaxed, as they didn't have to worry about the scarogs arriving.

But the end of the year was approaching, and no scarogs had arrived yet. So that meant the beetles could arrive any day now.

Instead of remaining sober and keeping their heads, many immortals started packing the pub. They sought to distract from the impending certainty that one of them, if not more, would die.

He finished drying another glass and set it with the others. Carmella, the witch tending bar, scrambled to fill drinks as Orin washed and dried the glasses.

The small crowd was still demanding, and nothing had been clean when Orin first came downstairs. He was in no rush to finish washing the glasses, even if she kept telling him to hurry. The more she did, the slower he went.

Carmella snatched away his freshly dried glass and filled it with whiskey. The founders of this town had established a brewery in the pub's basement.

Belda said, when she first arrived, the storage room was full of barrels and bottles of alcohol. They now used their crops to make more of the liquid, something everyone in this realm was happy to have happen. This place would be much worse if they couldn't drown their sorrows in booze.

"Oh great, the abomination has arrived."

Orin had been so focused on his thoughts that he hadn't noticed the witch had returned to his side. Carmella's words pulled him from his musings, and he followed the direction of her glare to Sahira as she closed the door to her room.

Sahira's room was next to his, a soon-to-be convenient fact. He smiled as he set another glass down and tossed his towel on the bar.

And then Carmella's words sank in, and his eyebrows rose as he glanced from her to Sahira. Sahira wasn't exactly his favorite immortal in the realms, but she was technically almost family, and no one looked at or talked about his family like that.

CHAPTER TWELVE

"THE ABOMINATION?" he inquired.

"You do know what she *is*, don't you?" Carmella retorted as she poured some beer into a mug.

"I do."

"It's an absolute disgrace that her mother let a *vampire* rut between her legs."

"We've all done some rutting we've regretted." He gave her a pointed look as he slid another glass toward her. "And I've been disappointed a time or two."

Carmella shoved a loose strand of black hair behind her ear as she swung hate-filled brown eyes to him. Orin grinned at her before switching his attention back to Sahira.

He couldn't help admiring the way the brown fae pants hugged her enticing ass and firm thighs. Those thighs could probably cinch around a man and keep him locked inside her. He would find out.

Her black shirt was off the shoulder and had multicolored flowers running down the front and between her breasts. And the swell of those lovely breasts was emphasized by her low, scooped collar.

He shifted as his shaft stirred. It would be a long game with Sahira, and part of that game would be him playing the good guy role. He wasn't familiar with it, but he'd give anything a try at least once.

He couldn't take some other girl out back to fuck while he was working on getting Sahira into his bed. It was tempting, but it would give her a reason to stay away from him.

He had to play nice, and when he won the game, he could play with everyone again. Until then, he'd be the one thing he'd sworn never to be—a one-woman man.

Suppressing a sneer, he watched as Sahira reached the bottom of the stairs and stood with her hand on the banister as she surveyed the room. Her amber eyes were curious but also filled with unease.

"You might be interested to learn that witches and vampires worked together to bring down the Lord. And they continue working together to protect the new queen of the Shadow Realms. The queen"—he leaned closer to Carmella as he pitched his voice lower—"who happens to be the niece of the woman you just called an abomination."

Carmella glowered at him before shifting her attention to pouring another beer. "Not by blood."

"Blood isn't what always matters in life. Blood can be the death of you, while found family can be a savior. The last arach is alive because of Sahira and her brother, who is also a vampire. She loves them both, and they are under her protection. You and your little witch friends would do well to remember that."

Carmella slapped the beer tap closed as she spun to face him. "And you should remember that *none* of it means anything here. That world doesn't exist to us anymore. *This* is our existence now, and anyone who believes they're important because of who they were in their *old* life is wrong." She leaned closer to him. "Including dark fae princes."

Orin laughed as he lifted a strand of her hair and twirled it around his finger. She tried to slap it away, but he refused to relinquish her as their eyes locked.

"Even if we never return to our old lives and who we were, some of us possess more power than others. You're a little witch in a realm where it doesn't matter."

"Fuck you, Orin."

"Never again, Carmella. My hand has more moves than you."

Her face turned the color of a tomato. She tried to tug free of him, but he grasped her wrist, locking her in place as he released her hair.

"Now, get this through your pretty, empty head. If you or any of your other tree-hugging cohorts get any ideas about attacking her, I'll do whatever it takes to protect my family. And, *she* is family."

Besides, *no one* would mess with the witch… except him. He owed Sahira and would repay her for putting that tracking spell on him and refusing to take it off.

"You can't take us all on," Carmella hissed through her teeth.

"I can and I will. Not only do none of you spell casting twats scare me, but cursing another is forbidden in this realm. If you dare to try it, I will stop you, and you'll also bring down the wrath of Belda and her pack on your heads. Trying to curse someone as powerful as me will weaken all of you, and you'll either be destroyed in the pit or banished to the Barren Lands."

When she jerked at her wrist, he didn't release her. "Let me go."

"You're going to make sure all the witches and warlocks understand this too. You *will* tell them everything I just said."

He was sure he'd get more than a few dirty looks from the cauldron-loving, spell casting crew, but none were brave enough to come at him head-on. They'd die if they challenged him to the pit, which was their only recourse; he'd make sure they knew it too.

"Let me go!" she spat.

He did no such thing. "Are you going to tell them?"

"Yes!"

He smiled sweetly as he relinquished her. She rubbed her wrist and gave him a scathing glance before turning away. Despite her attitude, she couldn't hide the apprehension in her eyes before she did so.

He'd have to water her if her IQ were any lower, but he'd made his point. If she tried anything against Sahira, he'd kill her, and she knew it.

She'd also make sure the other witches and warlocks knew it too. If she tried to get all of them to attack him, it would be a battle, but he'd take them down.

Belda wouldn't sit back and let it happen either. She ran this realm with a fair, iron fist and didn't tolerate insubordination or a disregard for the laws.

Sahira entered the pub's main area and glided between the tables toward an empty one in the back. Zeth sat at a table with a couple of lycans and a vamp. The demon didn't notice her arrival, but Belda did.

Orin finished drying the last glass as Belda intercepted Sahira and led her to an empty table in the corner. They sat, and Belda pulled out the scroll Orin signed on his second day here.

The scroll contained the agreement to obey the rules of the realm. Broken laws were met with punishments, the worst of which was banishment.

With their heads bent close together, Sahira and Belda discussed the rules before Sahira signed the parchment. Belda promptly rolled it up, tucked it away, and pulled out the list of job openings.

He didn't know which one Sahira chose, but she put her initials next to something on the parchment. She could change her mind if she hated it.

Belda tucked away the list, shook Sahira's hand, and started to rise, but something Sahira said stopped the lycan. She remained half standing while they spoke and then gestured toward the bar.

Sahira's eyes darted to him as a muscle ticked in her clenched jaw. Orin couldn't contain his grin when he realized what they were discussing.

Sahira had just learned he'd already volunteered to be the one to feed her when she required blood. No one else would do it, and everyone knew vampires got a little excited while drinking.

His smile widened as he recalled that ass and those thighs. They were going to feel amazing beneath his hands.

CHAPTER THIRTEEN

SAHIRA STRUGGLED to keep her jaw from coming unhinged as Belda dropped a bomb on her. With red blurring her vision and teeth grinding together, she looked at Orin behind the bar, grinning at her.

That smug asshole knew what they were talking about. She wanted to smile back at him, to act like it didn't bother her, but she was too irate to smile. If she smiled, she might scream, making it so much worse.

"There must be someone else," Sahira said, tearing her attention away from the prick behind the bar. "Zeth said immortals volunteer for vampires to feed from them."

"They do. But some immortals refuse to let it happen, such as the witches. And others feel it's too intimate or that a vampire might take advantage of the situation and go too far."

"I would never do that."

"I'm not saying you would." Belda glanced over her shoulder at Orin as he tossed a rag on the bar. "But many here aren't willing to be a donor. Those who are have already been assigned to a vamp. Orin volunteered...." Sahira's growing panic must have registered with Belda as the lycan sat again. "I know Orin can be difficult."

"Difficult is an understatement. He's doing this to manipulate me."

"Probably, but he's agreed to keep you alive. I can ask for other volunteers, but I doubt I'll get any. This is something other immortals sign up for when they get their jobs. Orin is the only option, and he only agreed to feed *you*."

"Of course he did."

Sahira fisted her hands on the table as she glared at the scarred, dark wood surface. If Belda started asking around, word would get back to Orin, and he'd find it hilarious to know she was trying not to feed from him.

But, of course, he already knew that and was enjoying watching her squirm. She could feel those black eyes boring into her now.

He believed her feeding from him would lead to something else, as it could be an erotic experience for vamps, but that would *not* happen. It had been years since she fed from a pumping vein instead of a blood bag; it had been longer since she had sex, but she wouldn't let bloodlust take her over.

She also wouldn't give him the satisfaction of knowing she'd asked Belda to find *anyone* else to feed her. Plus, how humiliating would it be for the lycan to ask around this town and come up with no one?

"No," Sahira said. "Don't ask anyone else. I'll make do with him until we get out of here."

Belda inhaled a big breath and held it before exhaling. She patted Sahira's hand before rising. "Perhaps one day."

But the lycan didn't sound confident as she sauntered from the table. *No one* in this realm was confident of escape, but she refused to let that deter her.

If some powerful being was pulling the strings, there had to be a way to cut them, and Sahira would find it. If there wasn't, there had to be a way out, and she *would* find that too.

Until then, she'd have to feed from the asshole dark fae prince from Hell, but she would make him pay for putting her in this position. Thankfully, she was only half vampire and didn't have to feed as often as other vamps.

He'd given her more reason to get out of this realm, and she would do so before ever having to feed from him.

CHAPTER FOURTEEN

KNOWING she had to pull her weight in this realm or suffer the consequences, Sahira placed her hands on the table as she rose. She didn't look at Orin as she strode past the tables toward the door.

She was almost there when a small pixie with red hair and blue eyes zipped forward to bob in front of her. A trickle of red dust drifted from him as his wings fluttered, but something was off about his movements.

"Yer new 'ere," the pixie said in a slurred voice.

"I am."

"Wha's yer name?"

He let out an inelegant burp that caused him to float down before bobbing back up. She stifled a laugh when she realized the pixie was drunk. And not just a little tipsy but plastered.

"Sahira. And yours?"

"Fred."

"Fred!" she blurted.

The pixie's eyes narrowed as he floated closer. "You got a problem with Fred?"

"Not at all."

She'd never heard of a pixie with such a simple, non-nature-based name. They were always named after a tree, flower, or plant.

He grinned at her before flitting away to perch on the edge of Zeth's beer mug. The demon tried to shoo the tiny creature away, but Fred leaned over the edge and fell into the beer.

His hands and legs kicked, but his soaked wings didn't flutter as he tried to free himself. His dust turned the beer a maroon color.

"Idiot's going to drown himself," Zeth muttered as he plucked the soaked pixie from his drink.

He set Fred on the table. The pixie smiled as he curled into the fetal position, tucked his hands under his head, and fell asleep.

"Does he do that often?" Sahira asked.

"The Reaping has him all riled up," Zeth answered. "It's coming any day now, and some don't handle the pressure well."

Zeth draped a napkin over Fred before shifting his attention to her. "Did you sleep well?"

As well as she could in an unfamiliar realm and with a lot of noise coming from down here. Thankfully, she had a silencing spell, but he didn't need to know those details. "Yes."

"Good. Did you get a job?"

"I did. I'm off to start it now."

Zeth glanced at the clock. "I'll be returning to mine soon."

"Have a good one."

"You too."

Sahira made her way out the door and descended the steps. Once there, she realized she had no idea where to go and stood looking up and down the street.

It was much quieter today, and the only one around to ask was a witch glaring at her from the porch across the way. Preferring to be lost, Sahira turned to the right. They'd mostly gone toward the left yesterday, and she didn't recall seeing a library.

Unlike her brother and niece, she wasn't a big bookworm. She read occasionally but didn't spend every spare minute buried in books like they did.

She preferred working in the garden, where she tended her herbs and flowers. She was never happier than when she was turning the land over, planting seeds, and checking her plants. The feel of dirt running through her fingers always brought comfort and peace.

If she could live with her fingers in the earth, she would. She loved everything about it, from the smell to the touch to the worms crawling beneath the surface and making her plants healthier.

As a child, she'd spend hours in the gardens with her father. He wasn't a big gardener, but to make her happy, he'd sit there watching and helping her while Del read under the shade of the willow tree.

As she got older, he didn't have to supervise her, but he'd still sit there, trying to help in his awkward way. His fingers were always too big for seeds, and he lost more than he successfully planted.

He never gave up, and he never stopped coming to sit with her. It was their bonding time as they either talked about the plants and what was on their minds or sat in comfortable silence.

They were some of her best memories, and she smiled as she recalled them. He'd been gone over four hundred years, but his loss still caused a pang in her heart.

She would have much preferred the gardens to the library. She was part witch and, as such, felt a stronger connection to the earth and all living things. Even now, the life force of this realm vibrated through her boots and into her body.

This place was like an outer realm in many ways, but it had far more life flowing through it than any of the others she'd visited. That life was one more mystery about this place.

With a sigh, she studied the town as she walked. Life

thrummed through the ground, but no birds took to the air, and no animals scurried through the town. Despite the low hum of conversations, the realm was eerily subdued.

In the distance, the large gardens next to the lake shimmered in the red sun. The planted fields were opposite where the witches and warlocks resided in their tepees and homes.

Behind those residences were the remnants of a dwindling forest. The trees had no leaves but still stretched toward the sky.

Sahira suspected the witches did most of the work in the gardens, but she hadn't decided against working in them because of the witches. They'd been anything but welcoming since she arrived; in this realm, things were the same as they'd been for centuries.

She was fine with that and used to dealing with a bunch of assholes. She hadn't chosen the library over the gardens to avoid those snotty shrews; she'd chosen it because she hoped to find answers in the books there.

Or at least she hoped there would be answers. For all she knew, there were fifty books in the whole place, all on the joys of cooking.

She was sure that, with all the immortals here, at least a few had read through all the books. She wouldn't be satisfied thinking there was nothing to be found in them until she read them all herself.

She could always switch to working in the gardens if there weren't any answers in the library. She could ignore a bunch of witches if it allowed her to dig in the earth, and Belda said she could do some extra work and earn more things if she helped tend the gardens after the library.

For now, she hoped the library possessed some answers or something to help her flee this place. She'd find out when she got there.

CHAPTER FIFTEEN

SHE STROLLED PAST MORE HOUSES, stores, and immortals as she searched the eclectic buildings for the library. At the end of the road, a wooden tower with a ladder on the side and a pole descending from the center of it stretched fifty feet into the air.

A single immortal stood beneath the tower's bell; a rope dangled beside him. It was one of the bell towers she'd seen on the list of jobs Belda set before her. Unlike most other jobs, there weren't any openings for work in the bell towers.

Sahira stopped and shaded her eyes against the red sun as she turned to search the skyline. Another tower was located at the far edge of town to her right. Another rose from the earth back toward the pit, and a fourth was a couple thousand yards away, at the other corner of town.

Immortals manned all the towers; they remained resolutely focused on the Barren Lands beyond the town. Those in the towers would be the first to notice the scarog beetles coming for them.

Despite the warm day, a shiver ran down her spine at the reminder of those flesh-eating monstrosities. She wasn't looking forward to seeing those things and hoped to be gone before they arrived.

Sahira continued down what she considered the main street, but when she reached the end, she didn't see a library. She glanced at the different roads beyond this one; it wasn't a big town, but she wasn't in the mood to wander until she stumbled across her new place of work.

Hurrying toward the building at the end of the road, she climbed its sagging, wooden steps and stopped to read the sign in the window: Barber Shop. For a second, she couldn't move as she stood and blinked at the sign.

Everything here was such a surreal mix of the familiar and unfamiliar. This realm was broken yet whole in such a strange way. It met all their needs, yet this place lacked the life they were used to.

The squeak of the screen door opening drew her attention as a berserker strolled out. The well-muscled woman grunted at her before descending the stairs in a clatter of boots.

Behind the berserker, a light fae woman emerged onto the porch. She stopped when she spotted Sahira, and a smile lit her pretty face. "Have you come for a cut?"

"No, I was hoping for directions to the library. I'm supposed to work there today, but I forgot to ask where it was," Sahira replied.

The woman chuckled as she brushed her pale blonde braid over her shoulder. "So, you're new."

"Yes."

"This place throws you off when you first arrive. It's unlike anything you've ever known, yet it's similar to everything we've always known."

"That's exactly what I was thinking!"

"We all think it when we first arrive. And then we adjust to it, and eventually, it becomes"—the woman's eyes drifted to the road—"home."

The possibility of *that* happening scared Sahira more than the looming arrival of the scarog beetles. She had a home and loved ones she desperately wanted to see again.

She missed her friends, brother, niece, and her familiar, Shade. She would give anything to hug them again and scratch Shade behind his cute little black ears. He'd purr while tilting his head into her touch and watching from his golden eyes.

He was her fourth familiar; the first, an owl, found her when she was seventy-five. It was a bit late in life but not unheard of for a witch. They never knew when their familiars would find them, but once they did, they remained loyally by their witch's side until they died.

Familiars lived longer than other animals, but they weren't immortal. When they died, they reincarnated into another animal and found their witch again soon after. Some witches had to wait years before their familiar originally found them, but their spirits always returned within a day of their body's death.

She'd had the pleasure of loving an owl, mouse, and fox before Shade arrived at her door—a tiny black ball of fur with golden eyes and a tail already twitching with a cat's irritation. Sahira smiled as she scooped him up, rubbed her nose against his, and carried him into the manor.

Lexi was barely a month old when Shade arrived, and he'd been with them ever since. He'd chosen his name when he was an owl and conveyed it to her. They couldn't speak to each other but had their way of communicating.

For a black cat, Shade made sense, but her owl had been a beautiful snow-white color. She believed it amused him to choose such a name, and Sahira wouldn't argue with him.

Resisting the impulse to rub her chest as it constricted with emotion, she tried not to think about how unhappy Shade would be without her or how she might miss seeing Lexi walk down the aisle to get married.

Before she left, Lexi and Cole were putting off getting

married until they learned what had become of Orin, Brokk, and Kaylia. Now, she was on that list, but how long would they wait?

Sahira hoped it wasn't long. She was determined to get out of this realm, but so many had been here for so long; it could take her weeks or years to figure out how to escape. Lexi deserved happiness, and the realms would be more secure with Cole and Lexi united for all to see.

And there had to be a way. No matter what anyone said or believed, if there was a way in, there *must* be a way out.

But she didn't want Lexi to keep her life on hold until then.

Sahira swallowed the lump suddenly lodged in her throat as she glanced over the town while trying to ignore the tears pricking her eyes.

"How many immortals are here?" she asked when she felt better able to speak.

It was a question she should have asked Belda, but it hadn't occurred to her then. The only one better to ask about a town's residents was the barber. She was sure this fae probably knew everyone and all the gossip.

"The last new arrival, before you, was *that dark fae*. He brought the count to three hundred and fifty-two." The light fae's aqua-blue eyes came back to her. "You make it three hundred and fifty-three."

The way the woman said "dark fae" made it clear what she thought of them, and Sahira didn't blame her. They were assholes. She wouldn't tell the woman she'd been stupid enough to follow *that dark fae* into this realm.

"So many," Sahira murmured.

"And soon to be less."

"So I've heard."

"Good, someone has told you about The Reaping. Be prepared; it gets ugly."

She rested her hand against the dagger she'd strapped to her hip before leaving the pub. Thankfully, she'd brought the fae-forged metal with her when she went in search of Orin.

The light fae's eyes went to the dagger. "That won't do much against a scarog."

"Maybe not, but I'll be ready for them."

And that was only if she didn't figure out how to escape before then.

A dwarf arrived at the steps and stomped her way up. Her battle-ax thudded off each step as she climbed.

"I'm ready when you are, Alette," the dwarf said in her accented voice that resembled the humans' English accent.

"I'll be right in, Holgi."

The dwarf grunted before going inside. Alette turned back to her. "The library is two streets over that way." The barber pointed across the road. "It's almost directly across from us. There's a big sign; you can't miss it."

"Thank you."

"Anytime. My name is Alette; come see me whenever you need a cut."

"Thank you, Alette. I will." Sahira held out her hand. "I'm Sahira."

Alette clasped her hand in both of hers. "It's nice to meet you. I wish it was under better circumstances, but you'll learn it's not so bad here."

"It could be worse."

Alette gave her a wan smile before releasing her hand and turning away. "Excuse me; I can't keep Holgi waiting."

When the door closed behind Alette, Sahira jogged down the steps and across the road. She strode through an alley and found another street where she discovered more homes.

She traversed another alley and emerged to find Orin standing on the bottom step of a building marked Library. Everything in her tensed, and she braced herself as she crossed the road to him.

CHAPTER SIXTEEN

"WHAT TOOK YOU SO LONG?" Orin inquired.

He tried to hide his amusement over the fury radiating from her, but it was impossible when her amber eyes sparkled in that way and red stained her cheeks. Stalking toward him with fisted hands, she looked ready to punch him.

Who couldn't smile at that?

"Did you get lost?" he asked.

Her scowl was his answer.

"You should have waited for me," he said. "I would have walked you here."

"I decided to explore the town and meet some of its residents," she retorted.

Orin didn't believe that for a second, but he didn't argue with her. He leaned against the railing and propped his head on his hand as she stopped before him. He couldn't help admiring the way her clothes fit again.

Like him, she'd probably found a closet and dresser with assorted clothes inside. They were all different sizes and once belonged to those killed during The Reaping or in the pit.

Orin had no problem wearing a dead man's clothes, but he

suspected Sahira had squirmed as she put them on. She'd probably squirm more if she realized how good she looked and how he imagined peeling those clothes from her.

He was going to enjoy winning this game. And no matter how stubborn and prideful his witch was, he would win.

Before this realm, he'd noticed how pretty she was and her alluring hourglass figure, but she was always far too prickly for his liking. He preferred his women eager and compliant; they were much more fun that way.

She was still too prickly for his liking, but she was entertaining, and he suspected this little witch might help him figure a way out of here. If anyone could do it, it was this obstinate, intelligent woman who would do whatever it took to protect and get back to the ones she loved.

He wouldn't let himself think about the nearly four hundred other immortals here who, at one time, were also determined to leave. A rare few of them were probably smart, too, and they were still stuck here.

"Why are you here?" she demanded.

"Belda told me you signed up for library duty. I wasn't surprised."

Sahira planted her hands on her hips. "And why is that?"

"You seem like a bookish little witch."

"I don't know what a 'bookish little witch' is supposed to *seem* like, but it's not me. I would have preferred the gardens."

Orin tilted his head as he studied her. "Then why sign up for the library?"

He'd be extremely disappointed if she did it to avoid the witches. She'd never backed down from a challenge before, and he disliked weak immortals far more than prickly ones. He'd still have sex with her but wouldn't enjoy it as much.

"Why do you care?" she demanded.

"I'm curious."

"You do know what happened to the cat, right?"

His amusement returned. No, this woman couldn't have avoided the gardens because of the witches. She was too feisty for that.

"Are you going to kill me, witch?"

"I'm sure I'd have to fight through a pretty long line to get the chance."

"I chopped off that line in this realm. No one would dare to get into it now."

"I would."

He laughed as he leaned closer; the little witch didn't move away. She hadn't signed up for the library to avoid the witches. She didn't avoid anyone.

"So why the library?" he asked.

Sahira's attention shifted to the three-story wood structure behind him. Like the rest of the original buildings, the wood facade hid a steel frame that made it more secure against an attack.

"Because I figured that if there were any answers in this realm, the library might be the best place to start looking for them. Working here would give me more time to hunt for them."

Not only wasn't she backing down, but his witch was using her brain. He approved... even if she was going down a road he'd guarantee almost every immortal in this realm had already traveled. He'd started along it too.

"Don't you think most of the immortals here have already gone through most of these books?" he asked.

"I'm sure many of them have gone through *all* of them. But we could have ten thousand or a *million* immortals and humans all searching for an answer and never finding it. Then we could have *one* who looks at things differently, or sees something different, and discovers the answer."

He rubbed his chin as he returned to admiring the swell of her breasts. An enticing body to go with all that determination and brains. He liked it.

Of course, he was sure some of the other women he'd been with were smart and beautiful; he'd just never talked to them long enough to find out. Because of their relatives and now this place, he'd spoken with Sahira more. He was glad she was proving not to be a wilting flower.

"It only takes one to change everything," he murmured as he shifted his attention back to the library.

Maybe Sahira would see something in one of the books he'd read that he hadn't. He doubted it, but it was worth a try.

CHAPTER SEVENTEEN

SAHIRA ROLLED her eyes before brushing past him. Orin was sure she would have preferred not to touch him, but she couldn't get past him without doing so.

The honey scent of her filled his nostrils as her hand brushed his. Unexpected warmth spread from his fingers as she stomped up the wooden steps to the massive arched door with the small pane of barred glass in the center of it.

Orin followed her up the stairs and toward the library as a pixie fluttered in front of the window. She flitted away, and a second later, an orc replaced her.

Orin was prepared for the emergence of the tall orc who opened the thick wooden door, but Sahira wasn't. Her step faltered, and she almost stopped walking, but Orin nudged her forward.

Yes, it was rare to see an orc outside their realm and rarer to find one of the brutes running a library. Orin would bet his dick that such a thing had never happened before, and he truly enjoyed his dick.

Orcs were known for their destructive tendencies. They were

as violent as they were ugly, and Gromuck was no exception to this rule.

At nearly seven feet tall, the female orc towered over most of those she met. She had a broad forehead and clawed hands and feet. Her sandals emphasized the bent and twisted angles of her toes.

Orcs are probably so pissy because their feet hurt all the time. He hated it when he got a pebble in his shoe, never mind one toe caught under another.

Gromuck, like all orcs, wore a simple scrap of cloth around her waist, and another piece crisscrossed her breasts. Every inch of her consisted of chiseled muscle, from her broad shoulders to her hideous toes. She had pointed ears, but the left one stood straight up while the right flopped over.

Her canary-yellow eyes narrowed on Sahira as Orin nudged her into the building. Like many orcs, Gromuck's skin was green, but the flesh tone of orcs often varied between green and gray.

"Your new help has arrived," Orin announced as they entered the library.

Gromuck grunted as she closed the door behind them. Her large feet thudded against the wooden floor and quaked the walls when she walked by them and toward the library's main area. Like all female orcs, a single black braid dangled against her waist.

Orin didn't follow her as Sahira remained planted in the entranceway. Unlike the rest of the library, this section was only a single story and didn't reveal the enormity of the building beyond, but it did have a door to his left and one thing decorating its wooden walls.

"What is that?" Sahira asked as she pointed to the three-foot-tall symbol above the arched entrance to the library.

"No one knows," Orin said.

"What do you mean, *no one knows?*"

"I'm not sure how else to say that so you can understand. Nobody in this realm understands what that symbol is or why it's here. It's also in *all* the original buildings in town."

"They've been there since the first vampire arrived, and then Belda arrived," someone else said.

The witch from the log cabin strode out of the library and stopped beneath the arch. Her chestnut-brown eyes were questioning as she surveyed them, and her chocolate-brown hair had been braided and wrapped like a crown around her head. It emphasized her pretty features.

"I'm Elsa." She glided forward and extended her hand to Sahira.

For a second, Sahira stared at the hand before clasping it. "Sahira."

"It's nice to meet you."

Orin believed she might mean that, which made him suspicious of the woman. None of the witches and few of the warlocks were happy to have Sahira here.

"You too," Sahira said.

"I'm Orin."

The witch studied him briefly before shifting her attention back to Sahira. "I work here, too, and Gromuck asked me to show you around."

"Okay," Sahira murmured as she focused on the symbol again. "I didn't see this at the pub."

"That's because it's not as big or noticeable." Orin stepped closer until his chest brushed her shoulder. "I'll show it to you when we return."

CHAPTER EIGHTEEN

A SHIVER RAN down Sahira's spine, but she didn't know if it was because of that symbol and the knowledge that it was on every original building or if Orin's close presence caused it. His breath had tickled her nape when he spoke, and as much as she *loathed* the man, that breath had warmed her insides in a way they should *never* warm around him.

Focused on the symbol and Elsa, she hadn't realized he'd moved so close. *Damn the dark fae and their affinity with the shadows.*

That affinity allowed them to move as swiftly and noiselessly as the darkness they could envelop. And why did he have to smell so good?

His scent was of cinnamon and cloves, two things she loved and that had always brought her a measure of calm. No one should be calm around Orin; that was like being relaxed around a lion that hadn't eaten in a month. Sooner or later, she'd forget to watch everything and get devoured.

Sahira almost edged away from him, but he'd know he'd unnerved her if she did. Gritting her teeth, she kept her feet planted while studying the symbol.

A figure eight, or maybe it was an infinity symbol, was carved into the wooden wall. The eight stood straight up and down; piercing diagonally through the top circle was an arrow pointing downward. At the other end of the arrow was a set of feathers.

Another arrow went through the center of the eight; this one had an arrowhead at each end instead of feathers on one side. Those arrows pointed up and down.

Another arrow cut through the middle of the bottom of the eight. This time the arrowhead pointed up, and its feathers were at the bottom end.

Sahira had seen a lot of symbols over her lifetime but never anything like this, and she had no idea what it meant. Something wasn't right about it.

Shouldn't the arrow at the top of the symbol point up? It's the upper part of the eight. And shouldn't the one at the bottom face down?

Maybe I'm looking into this too much.

But the symbols had to mean something; why else would someone carve them into the original buildings? Or maybe they meant nothing, and this was just a way for whoever did it to throw them off and play with them.

She hadn't believed it possible, but she was beginning to hate this place more. It was such a complete mindfuck.

"What do you think?"

Orin's breath whispered across her nape and tickled her ear. Did he somehow manage to make himself smell even better?

It sure seemed like it as his scent intensified in the air, and the heat of his body eased the chill the symbol had created. She was pretty sure this man was created to torment her.

"It's not a witch symbol, but I'm guessing you already knew that," she said.

A tiny pixie with yellow dust fluttered down to hover before her. "That's what the other witches have said."

"I don't recognize it… from *anything*," Sahira said.

"Neither do I," Elsa said. "And I've been poring through all the books, hoping for an answer, but nothing."

"No one recognizes it," Orin added. "I've done a lot of traveling, met almost every immortal there is, and I've never seen anything like it."

"Just one more mystery about this place," Sahira muttered.

"You hate it as much as I do."

Sahira was aware of the pixie and Elsa studying her, but she couldn't deny the simple truth. There was no way they loved this place.

"I do," she said.

Before Orin could say anything more, and needing to get away from him, Sahira strolled toward the ten-foot-high arch and beneath it. She came to such an abrupt stop that Orin almost walked into her but sidestepped in time to avoid it.

That didn't stop his chest from brushing her shoulder as he did so, and she suspected it was on purpose. At least he didn't stand too close again; instead, he gave her space as she gawked at the building.

She tipped her head farther and farther back to take in the numerous rows of books surrounding her. She had no idea what she'd expected from the library, but it certainly wasn't this vast display of knowledge, mystery, and adventure trapped within countless tomes.

The only wall space not covered with shelves and books in the wide-open, three-story room were the two windows at the back of the building, the two on the side, and the two at the front. Each of those windows had thick metal shutters beside them.

Three chandeliers with thick, crystal clear beads reflected the light as they dangled from the ceiling. They provided the only illumination in this place. Judging by the steady dim glow, magic instead of fire kept them lit.

"Who keeps the lights on?" she asked.

"We don't know," Elsa answered. "They were on when the first vamp arrived and have remained that way."

"But there's not light everywhere." She had to use a lantern and candles in her room last night.

"No, but the lights in the main area of the pub are the same," Orin said. "It doesn't extend to our rooms."

Sahira bit her lip as she pondered this while taking in more of the library. Books covered every available shelf space, and more lay on the tables spread throughout the room.

Some immortals sat at those tables, flipping through pages. Three comfy armchairs rested near the side windows; immortals occupied two of them, and books were piled on the tables beside them.

Two winding staircases twisted up to the balconies lining the second floor before continuing to more balconies on the third. More immortals strolled those balconies as they searched for books, and rolling ladders were set up on each floor.

On the third floor, a dwarf was using one of the ladders to remove a book from the top shelf. An imp on the second floor spun around a ladder while rolling it toward the end of the bookcase.

Everyone looked up when it stopped with a clatter, and Gromuck slammed her hand on the table. Barely two feet tall, the imp's big round green ears bowed over a little as it gave a sheepish grin before darting up the ladder to retrieve a book.

On the first floor, more rolling ladders leaned against the shelves. A lycan stood on one, examining the spines before pulling a book free.

Whatever hope Sahira held about quickly finding answers here deflated as she took in thousands of books. Even if she managed to read one book a day, it would take her decades to get through them all.

She'd expected a small, one-story library with maybe a hundred books. She'd been completely wrong.

"Daunting, is it?" Orin inquired.

For the first time, she didn't detect any arrogance in his voice. He was simply stating the sad, deflating truth.

"Shit," she breathed.

"But it also makes you think there's an answer here, right?"

"Or it's another freaking game set up by whoever created this place."

"I've considered that too."

"I think we all have," Elsa said. "But every new arrival comes here and starts reading."

"Are you still reading?" Sahira asked her.

Elsa smiled sadly as she surveyed the shelves. "I've been here for ten years, and I'm about halfway through the second floor."

Sahira's heart sank into her stomach. *Ten years!*

"I'm not giving up. Besides, what else is there to do here?" Elsa didn't wait for an answer as she pointed to a large wooden desk sitting kitty-corner between two windows. Books were stacked two and three feet high on top of it. "When you're ready, I'll be behind the desk cataloging returns. We can start on your training then."

Elsa walked to the ornate desk they must have built with the place, as it was attached to the wall and floor. A couple of baskets sat beside the desk; more books filled them.

Despite her every intention not to engage with Orin unless necessary, she couldn't stop herself from asking. "Have you started reading?"

The corner of his mouth twitched toward a smile. "I'm on book fifteen."

Sahira looked over the books again. "Has anyone read them all?"

"A couple dozen immortals have," the pixie said in her tiny voice. "Most give up hope; what's the point in going through them all when other immortals have discovered nothing?"

Sahira hated to admit she was wondering the same depressing thing. She could be in the gardens, with her hands in the dirt and the power of the earth beneath her fingers.

It was a much happier place than this dimly lit, vast place with desperate immortals clinging to hope as they flipped through these ancient works. Still, she couldn't give up. She *wouldn't* give up.

"What are all these books about?" she asked.

"A little bit of everything," Orin responded. "There's romance, sci-fi, fantasy, nonfiction, tomes on the warlocks, lycan, dark fae, witches, and so on and so on."

"No one has ever found anything of use." The pixie fluttered her tiny wings while hovering before Sahira. "But there must be something, don't you think?"

Sahira wanted to agree with her, but she was becoming less and less certain about *anything* here. This place was like a maze, and they were the rats hunting for the cheese. Except there was no guarantee of a prize at the end of this labyrinth.

Standing here won't help you.

That was the truth, but this room was more daunting than the dragons when they were under the Lord's control.

Still, it was time to dive in and find a way out of here. Clasping her hands together, Sahira took a deep breath and walked to where Elsa waited behind the desk.

CHAPTER NINETEEN

ORIN WAS PLAYING cards with a berserker, lycan, and vamp when Sahira returned to the pub later that day with an armful of books. It wasn't often a group of such varied immortals were together, but he'd experienced it many times in his life.

As one who, in many ways, preferred to live on the fringes of society, he'd spent more than his fair share of time with the rejects from the various immortal groups. He'd gathered a bunch of them to help fight against the Lord.

Orin threw his cards on the table and rose when Sahira slunk into the crowd. "Excuse me."

The lycan grumbled about his abrupt departure, but no one complained too much since they only played for pride and to kill time. The berserker gathered Orin's cards, shuffled them, and dealt them out again.

"Did you discover anything?" Orin asked when he arrived at Sahira's side.

She glanced tiredly up from beneath the thick fringe of her long lashes and hugged her books to her chest. "Yes, I solved the mystery that countless others haven't been able to solve in eight hours. It's a *fucking* miracle."

Orin lifted an eyebrow while he studied her. Normally, that was his kind of sarcasm; he didn't appreciate having it turned on him. "Did somebody wake up riding the cranky train today?"

"What does that mean?"

"It means you're a little testier than normal. Is it that time of the month?"

"I hate you."

"I don't think so. Deep down"—he rested his finger against her chest—"you want me."

Sahira smacked his hand aside, but not before her eyes darted away. He sensed he'd struck a nerve. *Is it true?*

It wasn't surprising, of course. He was pretty irresistible, but he thought he'd have to work harder to get her in his bed. Maybe it wouldn't be so difficult after all.

"I'd have sex with a wendigo before you," she said.

He didn't believe it, mainly because *no one* desired a wendigo. But now wasn't the time for flirting with his little witch; he had far bigger fish to fry... like getting out of this realm.

"I have faith that if anyone can pull off a miracle and get us out of this, it's you," he said.

"Thanks, but maybe you should pull off your own miracles."

"I'm trying, but when I do, I'll take you with me."

Her tired gaze returned to his. "Thanks."

"I expect the same from you."

"Sure."

She said it, but he wasn't confident she would. Even if she did want him, the witch would prefer to leave him behind.

However, she'd come here because Cole and Lexi wanted him back. She wouldn't return to tell them she'd found and abandoned him.

"Where is the symbol in this building?" Sahira asked.

She stiffened when he clasped her elbow but didn't try to pull it free.

"This way," Orin said.

~

SAHIRA RESOLUTELY IGNORED the tendril of warmth spreading from where he'd touched her to the rest of her arm. Did he have to be so warm? And *why* did he make her tingle in all the wrong places while her heart beat faster?

But then, the dark fae were built for two things: sex and deception. Orin was the perfect example of that, so of *course* he affected her when she didn't want it. That was the *only* reason why. She was sure of it.

Mostly.

Orin led her to the back of the pub and into the shadowed alcove where two bathrooms were located. When she returned to the pub yesterday, she got the key to her room from Belda and went upstairs to settle in. Since there were also two bathrooms upstairs, she hadn't explored this area last night.

Brass lanterns hung on the walls. The candles inside them jumped and danced to illuminate the shadowy space, but she immediately spotted the infinity symbol with the three arrows sticking through it. Other than being a lot smaller—this one was only three inches tall—it was identical to the one in the library.

"What does it mean?" she muttered. "Something or nothing?"

The door to the men's room opened, and Zeth ducked down so he could exit. He rose and froze when he spotted them, but then he followed the direction of their gazes to the symbol.

"Ah, so you've discovered another one of the many puzzles from this realm," he said.

"Have you ever seen anything like it?" Sahira asked.

"I've seen countless symbols over the years; demons have a way with them. But no, I'd never encountered this one before coming here. I have no idea what it means or why it's on the original buildings. No one does."

So she'd been told, but it never hurt to ask. "Have you looked through the books in the library?"

"I'm not much of a reader, but I made it to the third floor last week. I've been going through them since I arrived."

And it had taken him thirty years to get there. He was a slower reader than Elsa, or the second-floor selection wasn't as interesting to him as the first.

"And you haven't found anything in them?" she asked him.

"Not one little thing."

"Great."

"If you'll excuse me, I have some lycans who will take over my job in the stables tomorrow if they lose one more hand of cabul." He rubbed his hands together as he grinned over the possibility of winning another round of the card game immortals often played. "I sure wouldn't mind an extra day off."

After he walked away, Orin spoke. "That's about all we have to play for here, extra time off, but most won't wager it as they don't want to do more work. I'm amazed he got those lycans to agree to bet it."

"Hmm." Sahira wasn't really paying attention to him as she stepped closer to study the symbol. "Does it seem off to you?"

"What seems *off* about it?"

"Shouldn't the arrow at the top be facing up and the one at the bottom down?"

"Maybe, but it's a symbol. They're all strange and can be drawn however their creator decides."

"I'll be back."

Before Orin could respond, Sahira turned and walked out of the small alcove. No one paid attention to her as she set her books on a table, grabbed a chair, and carried it to the symbol.

"What are you doing?" Orin asked.

Sahira set the chair down and climbed onto it. Once there,

she was high enough to reach the symbol. Tipping her head back, she examined it before lifting her index finger to hover it over the figure eight.

There was power in symbols, and messing with one could unleash someone else's magic, but she couldn't be the first to touch one of these things. She was sure countless other immortals had traipsed along this same path.

Before she could think about the possibility that she might unleash something malignant, she pressed her finger against the top of the eight and traced its curving contours.

CHAPTER TWENTY

"What are you doing?" Orin demanded.

Since she had no idea what she was doing, she didn't answer him. Instead, she followed the grooves carved into the wood and the feathers and sharp points of the arrows.

As she worked, she felt no magic from the symbol, and nothing happened, but these things *must* mean something. Why else would they be here?

Tomorrow, before she went to the library, she'd find the other symbols too. She had to know where they all were.

When she finished tracing over the symbol, she stopped and stared at it as she waited for something to happen. Nothing did. She had no idea what she'd expected, but it all felt so anti-climactic.

She rested her palm against the symbol. Beneath her hand, she felt the thrum of the earth as it vibrated up through the wood. The power here came from the ground and not the symbol.

Removing her hand, she climbed down, lifted the chair, and returned it to the main room. When she set it down, she lifted her head to discover a couple of witches had entered the pub.

They stared at her with looks of such utter contempt they

would have made her shrivel inside when she was younger. Now, she smiled and waved at them.

Their scowl deepened at her wave, and Sahira returned to the alcove. Though she almost ran over to hug the witches when she spotted Orin in the doorway with his hand against the wall while watching her.

She'd prefer the fallout from that to getting past this far too enticing and soul-destroying dark fae. It was too late now, and she was on a collision course with the man blocking the doorway and looking at her with an amusement that shouldn't be sexy but was.

He lowered his arm before she reached him and stepped back a little. "Making friends, I see."

She was relieved he'd moved out of the way but also a little skeptical. Orin liked to push boundaries and get into her personal space. She didn't trust this new, more respectful man.

It had to be part of his game, but she was thankful he wasn't trying to touch her all the time. As much as she hated it, she also loathed how her body reacted to his.

"Everywhere I go," she replied flippantly.

She felt his dark eyes following her as she walked over to stand before the symbol again, but she didn't look at him. "Can you take me to see the others tomorrow?"

He was the last one she wanted to ask for help, but she didn't have any friends in this realm, and while Zeth might help her, she couldn't impose on the demon. She'd prefer not to intrude on Orin either, but she'd never have enough time to locate the symbols before work tomorrow.

"Of course."

Sahira rolled her eyes at his smug tone. "I'll have to leave early to see them all before work."

"I'll be ready to go."

She'd made a mistake. Having Orin help her with anything was a bad idea; he'd find some way to use it to his advantage.

She should have asked for directions and found the symbols on her own, even if it took her a couple of days. But she'd already asked him for help and couldn't back out now.

"I'll see you in the morning, then," she said.

Brushing past him, Sahira ignored the increased beat of her heart as his scent engulfed her. His steps followed her from the alcove as she reclaimed the books she'd set on the table, but she refused to look back at him while focusing on the stairs.

The pub was starting to fill with assorted immortals looking to forget their troubles while ignoring the guillotine of scarogs hanging over their necks. Sahira hadn't thought much about the beetles today; she'd been too busy learning her new job and getting to know her coworkers. Gromuck was an orc of few words, but Elsa was surprisingly friendly, considering the witches in this realm didn't like her.

Sahira was so focused on her day, and her coworkers from the library, that she didn't notice a witch stepping into her path until she almost crashed into her. Coming to an abrupt halt, Sahira tipped her head back, and her eyes widened on the tall woman with blonde hair and hazel eyes.

She almost apologized for almost walking into her but stopped when she realized the woman purposely stepped in front of her. She had no idea who the woman was, but the witch studied Sahira like she was lower than dog crap. Just what she needed to cap off her oh-so-enjoyable time in this realm.

Unwilling to engage with the witch, Sahira went to step around her, but the woman moved to block her path. Sahira glowered at her. "What's your problem?"

"Is your mother Lydia?"

"She gave birth to me, but I wouldn't call her a mother."

"Who would want to mother an atrocity such as you?"

Sahira rolled her eyes. Maybe she'd be shocked and upset if this was her first time hearing something like this, but it wasn't.

She'd developed a thick skin over the years, and this witch was far from unique.

"I knew her," the witch continued.

"Good for you. I'm sure you knew her more than I did." Sahira waited for her to move, but when she didn't, Sahira sighed. "Would you like a cookie or something?"

The woman's stony face remained unreadable as her icy eyes ran over Sahira. She contemplated lowering her shoulder and shoving past this ignorant bitch, but she wasn't looking for a fight or to end up in the pit.

"What's going on, Blair?" a nearby voice inquired.

She turned to see the warlock Radagast standing to her right. He was a tall man with a regal bearing, golden blond hair, and eyes the color of raisins.

Blair's lips quirked in a cruel smile. "Just learning more about our newest addition."

More like just being a bitch, but Sahira kept that to herself.

"Good. We all rely on each other to survive in this realm," Radagast said.

The witches would throw her out to the scarogs if they got the chance, and they all knew it. The hair on Sahira's nape rose as a stark reality set in—she had more than the beetles to fear when The Reaping arrived.

CHAPTER TWENTY-ONE

"Is there a problem here?"

Sahira hadn't realized Orin had come up behind her until his scent filled her nose, his body warmed her shoulder, and his low, menacing tone sent a shiver of unease down her back. Blair's eyes darted to Radagast before shifting to Orin.

They didn't care about messing with her—they saw her as weaker because she was half vampire—but none wanted to piss off Orin. He was much more ruthless and powerful than any of them individually.

They could team up against him, but that would only piss off Belda and the lycans. Things wouldn't end well after that.

"I was introducing myself," Blair said.

"I'm sure Sahira's thrilled," Orin replied in the droll, mocking way he had that irritated her, but seeing it turned on another was amusing.

Sahira couldn't stop the smile twitching at her lips when Blair's lips pursed and her eyes narrowed. Orin stepped around her, so his chest was against her shoulder. When he did, Blair hesitated before edging out of her way.

She glanced at Orin and nodded but didn't thank him. If he believed she owed him, he'd use it against her.

His face remained stony as he stared at her before returning his attention to Blair. If looks could kill, the witch would be dead and buried a hundred times over.

Tired of all the tension and just plain exhausted, Sahira strolled past Blair and upstairs to her room. She closed the door behind her and leaned against it as she tried to sort through the emotions pummeling her.

From below, laughter rang out, shouts of revelry filled the air, and glasses clinked together. She was in a building filled with nearly a hundred other immortals, and she'd never felt more alone.

When she lived in the large manor with Lexi and Del, the place was too big for them, but it was *never* lonely. Their estate overflowed with love, the smells of home, and the comfort of family.

Even after they were told Del died fighting the Lord's war, the manor never stopped feeling like home. It had been emptier without his presence, but she and Lexi still filled it with love.

Now, she was completely alone and had no one to turn to. Orin didn't count; he'd sacrifice her to save his ass. He was only interested in her because he hoped she might figure a way out of here or she would screw him.

If they were anywhere else, and if she slept with him, he'd give less than a rat's ass about her. No, she had no allies here, but she had plenty of enemies because of her bloodline and a bunch of ignorant assholes.

She couldn't end up in the pit. She was a strong, capable witch, but without being able to teleport, she would be at a disadvantage against someone who had stronger magic than her.

Besides, though she'd killed in the battle against the Lord, the idea of such intimate hand-to-hand combat made her stomach twist. Witches were about celebrating life, not destroying it.

At least Radagast didn't have a problem with her, which meant the other warlocks probably didn't either. The witches' hatred for vamps was sometimes mirrored by warlocks but not always.

The vamps probably weren't thrilled about her birth, but they wouldn't bother her either. It was just the witches and maybe some warlocks, so only a dozen or so immortals would prefer to see her dead.

How fun.

Pushing away from the door, Sahira crossed the room and opened the curtains covering her window and the thick metal shutters. Belda had told her to close the shutters whenever she wasn't in the room.

She'd also suggested sleeping with them closed, but Sahira craved fresh air and had left them open last night. The bells would wake her if the scarogs were coming.

Opening the shutters, she locked them into place before resting her elbows on the windowsill and gazing at the street below. The dwindling sun illuminated the dozens of homes she could see from her angle and the passersby below.

Purples, reds, and oranges so bright she'd never seen the likes of them before streaked the sky. It was strange that this cursed land held so much beauty, but even if it was rather monotone, it was spectacular.

She watched the sunset until it vanished and the colors bled from the sky. The music and voices from below grew louder with the onset of night.

Stepping away from the window, Sahira walked over and plopped onto the full-size mattress. It was a small room that lacked the opulence of Orin's, but it was cozy.

She suspected Orin had done some decorating in his, and it had looked identical to hers before he turned it into a sex den. Belda had told her to make herself at home and that there were other furnishings in the barn behind the pub, but she wouldn't bother to change anything.

Even if she never left this realm, she'd never fully accept her fate by turning this room or a house into her own. Besides, the room was perfectly fine.

The mattress was firm but not too hard, and a quilt of numerous colors covered the bed. She traced the stitches between the soft fabric as she ran her fingers over the quilt.

She hadn't slept much last night, but burrowed beneath the blanket, she'd been warm and cozy. The aromas of the room's wooden walls and grass-scented candles made it more inviting.

The linens were all clean, and the scent of the outdoors lingered on them from when someone hung them to dry. There was no electricity in this realm, and whatever powered the library and pub didn't stretch to the rooms up here, but she'd discovered plenty of candles in the nightstand drawer.

The closet across the way was full of different clothes in various styles and sizes. She didn't like wearing a dead immortal's clothes, but beggars couldn't be choosers, and she had no other options. She'd arrived here with only the clothes on her back; they wouldn't last long if she wore and washed them daily.

The room didn't have a bathroom, but if she went out to the hallway, it was located directly to the right of her room, so she didn't have to go far. To the left of her room was Orin's.

He was a little too close for her liking, but at least a wall separated them, and her silencing spell had worked well to block out the noise last night, so hopefully, she wouldn't have to hear him and numerous partners. She cringed at the possibility.

No pictures decorated the walls, but a few pretty black stones sat atop her bureau. One was heart shaped, the other resembled a horse, and the third looked like a rose in full bloom.

She suspected Belda, or whoever decorated this room, had left them there. If they belonged to the previous resident, they would have taken the stones with them when they moved into their home.

Or maybe they were killed during The Reaping and never allowed to move out. That possibility made them a little less pretty, but she wouldn't remove them.

CHAPTER TWENTY-TWO

SAHIRA ROSE FROM THE BED, stripped off her clothes, and opened the bureau. Tucked inside was the same white nightgown she'd worn the night before.

Belda had told her there was a river at the edge of town where the others washed their clothes. The rocks in the water made it a better washing place than the lake.

A laundry basket was tucked neatly into the back of her closet, but since she wasn't rushing to scrub things on rocks, she'd wear the nightgown for at least a few more nights. She'd go through all the clothes that fit her before trudging her ass to the river.

Belda had also informed her that once the clothes became too tattered to wear, the seamstress and tailor took them and remade them into something new. They'd also patch any holes for her.

Sahira tugged on the nightgown that settled around her toes and brushed the ground when she walked. Lifting the wooden brush, with its hairy bristles, from the top of her bureau, she ran it through her hair as she tried not to think about who had used it before her.

There was also a toothbrush, some eucalyptus powder, and a

bar of soap in the top drawer of her bureau. She should have brushed her teeth before retreating to her room, but it hadn't occurred to her, and now she couldn't bring herself to go back out there.

Unlike the hairbrush, the toothbrush and powder were never used before, as one of Belda's pack members gave them to her last night. The man had informed her some workers made the toothbrushes kept in the mercantile down the street.

Since no one used currency here, the only way to earn a new brush was to work, and those who did work received a new one every three months. The lycan had explained this was monitored, as was the powder, so she shouldn't waste it.

He'd also informed her there were potions for birth control there and suggested she get some. Sahira might have taken offense to this if it wasn't for the fact that she was sure there was birth control for the men, too, and they were all on it. No one wanted a baby in this realm.

Sahira had thanked the lycan before retreating to her room. One of these days, she'd have to make it to the mercantile, but since she had no intention of having sex any time soon, that could wait.

Standing there, staring at the brush and powder, she brushed her teeth and rinsed with the glass of water on her nightstand. She'd brought the water up last night and left it there this morning, but she wasn't returning to the pub to get more.

Plopping onto her bed again, she stared out the window before rising and retrieving the books she'd taken from the library. Lifting the first one, she studied every detail of its cover and binding before setting it on her nightstand and shifting her attention back to her room.

She'd been too exhausted to explore it last night, but she went over every inch of the small space with meticulous care. When she finished examining the closet and walls, she crawled under her bed to look at its wooden slats. Afterward, she scooted out, lifted her mattress, and inspected it as well as the top of the slats.

Discovering nothing, she flipped over her nightstand and moved the bureau before getting down on her hands and knees to examine underneath it the best she could. No matter where she looked, she found no sign of the symbol, or any other symbol, in her room.

When she finished, she returned everything to where she found it, closed the curtains, and settled on the bed with the book categorized as 01 from the library. She figured there was no better place to start than the beginning, but many others had probably felt the same way.

Book 01 detailed the story of every immortal who had arrived in this realm. It was a history of what they knew about this land, the immortals who'd come and gone, and the deaths or banishments many had faced.

When she reached the end, there were blank pages for her to add her story. Orin hadn't added his yet. She understood why, as everything in her recoiled against becoming such an ingrained part of this place.

She'd do it, eventually, but she hoped she was gone by the time anyone new arrived to read it.

CHAPTER TWENTY-THREE

ORIN TOOK Sahira to all the locations of the original buildings and the symbols carved into their walls. Their last stop was the stable, where they encountered Zeth arriving to feed the animals.

The demon stopped and smiled when he spotted Sahira. "What brings you here?"

"I wanted to see all the symbols and the original buildings," she answered.

"Ah." The demon rubbed his chin as his attention shifted to Orin. "You got to this stage a lot faster than most."

Orin didn't respond. Unlike Sahira, he'd assumed the other immortals here were idiots, and he'd find a way out of here. But first, he'd spent time with some women, looked for crudue vine, wandered the library, and stalwartly continued trying to open a portal.

When none of those things proved useful, and Belda started threatening to banish him if he didn't get to work, he realized this place and his circumstances were more dire than he believed.

He could have told Belda to fuck off, though it would have resulted in a fight with her, her pack, and probably half the town.

He could take down a good chunk of them, but he had to admit, he couldn't destroy them all.

Orin finally came around to Belda's way of thinking and started working, but he wouldn't stay in this place or work for any longer than he had to. He'd been here for a week before he set off down the same road Sahira now traveled.

"Does everyone ask to see them?" she whispered.

Orin didn't like the defeated tone of her voice. She'd hoped to be on a new path. He knew she wasn't, but he decided not to take that hope from her; they all needed it in this place.

She acted like it didn't bother her, but she had enough to deal with when it came to the witches and their shitty attitudes. He admired that she refused to back down or hide from them.

He'd nearly laughed out loud when she asked Blair if she wanted a cookie, but he was too annoyed by Blair to laugh. If those bitches tried anything with her, he'd make them pay, something he'd made clear to Carmella, and he hoped she'd passed it along to her fellow twats.

If she didn't, *he* would.

Zeth rested a hand comfortingly on Sahira's shoulder. "Yes, eventually."

Orin bristled, and his eyes narrowed on that hand before they shifted to the demon. He couldn't tell if Zeth was competition for her, but if the demon decided to pursue her, he'd have to wait until Orin finished with her.

The demon could have her after that. Until then, it was hands-off.

When Orin stepped closer, he forced the demon to move aside and lower his hand from Sahira. Zeth shot him a look that Orin chose to ignore.

"Let's go see the symbol," Orin said as he rested his hand on the small of Sahira's back and guided her toward the closed stable doors.

Zeth slid open one of the doors, and Orin guided her inside.

The lamps on the wall held a steady light like those in the chandeliers in the library and pub. Every one of the original buildings possessed that magical glow.

"There are horses here," Sahira breathed.

"Some of the new arrivals came on steeds," Zeth said. "But there were horses here when the first vampire arrived."

"This realm is so strange," Sahira muttered.

"It really doesn't make sense," Zeth agreed.

"I used to hate the smell of the stables," Sahira whispered. "That was Lexi's favorite place, but I preferred to stay away. Why do I like it now?"

"Because it's familiar," Orin said. "It's a reminder of home in a place with little of them."

She looked at him like she didn't know him, and her forehead crinkled like she was trying to figure him out.

He bent closer to whisper in her ear. "I'm a man of many mysteries."

That earned him the scowl he'd been expecting. Throwing her off was one of his favorite things to do.

Zeth removed one of the lanterns from its hook and carried it to the end of the barn. He stopped a few feet from the far wall and lifted the lantern to reveal the symbol.

Like the one in the library, this symbol was larger. It stood nearly five feet tall and took up almost half the wall. And like *all* the other ones, it stood straight up and down. As with all the others, Sahira claimed a nearby chair and dragged it over so she could climb onto it and examine the symbol more closely.

She traced her finger over the entire symbol before leaning back to examine it. Planting her hands on her hips, she studied it like she was about to punch it. When she finished, she climbed off the chair.

After a few minutes, she finally spoke. "There's only seven symbols."

"But it's the number eight," Zeth said.

"Or the infinity symbol," Orin said.

Sahira bit her bottom lip before climbing back on the chair. Resting her palm against the symbol, she turned her hand over to look at it before shifting her attention back to the mark.

"What are you trying to do?" Orin asked.

"I don't know." She stepped down from the chair again. "Something. *Anything.* There has to be an answer, but does there?"

"What do you mean?"

"I keep thinking these symbols have to mean something, but they don't have to mean anything. They could be symbols that whoever originally lived here carved into the walls for protection or because they were bored. They don't have to mean anything."

"They don't," Zeth agreed.

"Do you believe that?" Sahira asked.

"No."

"Do you think any of the other immortals here believe that?"

"Some have probably convinced themselves they mean nothing simply to take a break from constantly throwing themselves against a wall they can't break."

"I'm going to break that wall," Orin said.

Zeth's eyes were assessing as they ran over him. "I hope someone does."

Sahira traced the feathers on the bottom arrow before moving to the arrowhead. "I don't understand this place at all."

"None of us do," Orin said.

"Is there a map of the whole town?"

"And now you've moved on to the next stage," Zeth said.

Sahira's shoulders sagged in defeat, but when Zeth walked away, she straightened them again and lifted her chin.

Good. She won't be like the others who have let this place defeat them.

Zeth stopped beside a trunk outside one of the horse's doors. One nickered, the other kicked the wall, and a third banged against the door. The sheep and goats baaed as they shifted impatiently in their stalls. Two of those sheep and goats were pregnant.

"Sorry, guys. I'll get your food in a minute," Zeth assured them as he opened the trunk.

Zeth removed a large piece of parchment from the trunk, closed the lid, and set the roll on top. "It's a map of the whole town and every building. There are plenty of them floating around, but I made this one myself. I placed an X on the buildings with the symbols. I have to feed the animals, but feel free to take a look."

Orin strolled over to the trunk lid and unrolled the parchment. After staring at the symbol for a few seconds, Sahira walked over to join him. They each held a side down to keep the map from rolling up again while they examined it.

CHAPTER TWENTY-FOUR

HE STUDIED Zeth's extremely detailed map with admiration. He'd spent hours poring over the one Belda created, but she didn't have the demon's artistic talent with a pencil.

Sahira put her finger on the stable where they stood, then drew a line toward the mercantile and pub. She moved her finger around the map as if searching for a pattern.

"I don't think witches had anything to do with this," she said.

But if they did, the pentagram was one of the witches' favorite symbols. "There's too many symbols to create a pentagram."

"Or too few," she murmured. "Don't forget the inner points on a pentagram. There would have to be ten symbols and buildings for that."

"They don't form into what could become an octagon either... not without another symbol."

She bit her lip while studying the map. "No, they don't."

He wondered if she was beginning to see what he'd seen after studying Belda's map. He could point it out to her but preferred to find out if she could do this alone. If she couldn't, she was much less useful at helping to find a way out than he'd hoped.

He considered her smart; it would be disappointing if she proved him wrong.

Her finger landed on a spot at the end of a road. When it did, he knew she'd caught on to what he had.

Good girl.

"What's here?" she asked.

As he passed them, Zeth looked over her shoulder to where her finger sat. "The pit. It exists because immortals dug it in the hope of uncovering the eighth symbol. When that didn't work, they turned it into its current function."

"Son of a bitch," Sahira muttered.

Orin understood her frustration; he'd experienced it too. "If there was a symbol there, they would all form a compass rose."

"With the pit being the south part of the compass," Zeth said.

"Or north," Sahira said.

Zeth pointed to the top of the map and the library. "This is north."

"That's what *we* know north to be, but this realm isn't like anything we've ever known. The pit could be east or west, and we're standing at north. If it is an infinity sign, it's been turned upright instead of on its side, which could mean this whole place is shifted onto a different axis."

"Anything is possible here."

Orin turned his attention back to the symbol on the wall. He released his piece of the map before walking over to examine it.

He'd come to the same conclusions as her a few weeks ago. This place could be completely backward from everything they knew. It was unlike anything they'd ever encountered, and he wouldn't rule out any possibilities.

When he first got his hands on a map, he tried to match the points of the arrow to other places on the map. He'd also twisted the symbol around so the arrow pointed in all different directions. Afterward, he'd gone to all the buildings the arrows could have pointed to, but he soon realized that was futile.

"The arrows can point anywhere on the map. We don't know how long their points are supposed to be, how much distance they indicate, or if they're supposed to indicate *anything*," Sahira said.

And with those words, she'd come to the same conclusion as him.

"Everything is useless here," she muttered.

Having finished feeding the animals, Zeth returned to stand beside her. The demon rested his hand on her shoulder again, and Sahira smiled tremulously up at him.

I'm going to have to break his hand, Orin decided as he returned to them.

"Not everything. I still have hope, and I've been here for thirty years," Zeth said.

"I'm not discovering anything new, am I?" Sahira inquired.

"No, but a fresh set of eyes is always welcome. Maybe, one day, it will be what helps us escape this realm."

"It's time to get you to work," Orin said as he rested his hand on the small of Sahira's back again and drew her away from the demon.

Zeth gave him an amused smile as he released Sahira's shoulder. Orin didn't know what to make of that smile; was the demon trying to screw with him or her?

He suspected it was him, as Zeth did seem to be trying to help her through this, but he was getting in Orin's way. And he wouldn't let that happen.

"Can I come back and look at this again later?" Sahira inquired.

"Sure," Zeth said. "I'll be here for a while; even once I finish feeding, doing the stalls, and exercising the animals, I stick around for a bit. It's peaceful here."

"Thanks," Sahira said.

Great, now he had to return to this shit-smelling place to run interference with the demon. Except he'd come back early to find out exactly what kind of game Zeth was playing.

CHAPTER TWENTY-FIVE

ORIN ARRIVED at the stable five minutes before Sahira finished at the library. Zeth was talking to the animals as he tossed what looked like baled grass into their stalls.

He didn't ask where the grass came from; he'd seen it growing by the river. It was one more thing about this place that gave him a headache.

Orin tilted his head to the side as he studied the demon. Most of the demons he'd known were loud, brash, and ruthless. None of them spoke softly or gave any consideration to those they could steamroll over.

Demons loved to fight, and they enjoyed a good kill more. Who was this freak of nature, and what did he want with Sahira?

"You're a lot different than any of the other demons I've known," Orin commented.

Zeth didn't look at him as he tossed more grass to the goats. "And you're no different than any other dark fae I've known."

"Oh, I'm very different," Orin assured him. He was far more lethal than most, which was saying something, as the dark fae weren't known to hold back when it came to killing. "What's your story?"

When Zeth glanced at him, the nearby lantern only illuminated half his face. Orin didn't trust the demon; he acted calm, caring, and like he was trying to figure out this mystery, but *everyone* had ulterior motives.

Okay, maybe not everyone, but almost everyone. And this demon most certainly did; he was sure of it.

"I don't have a story," Zeth replied.

"We all have a story."

"Then what's yours?"

"I'm sure you already know it."

"Second oldest son of King Tove, king of the dark fae."

"Not anymore."

Zeth turned so his face was more illuminated. "I heard. The lycan who arrived before you said the Lord ordered the death of King Tove."

"He did."

Zeth shifted his attention back to the wheelbarrow full of food he was pushing down the shedrow. The demon didn't say he was sorry to hear about Orin's father; it would have been the polite thing to do, but also a lie. It said something about the demon that he chose the truth over politeness.

Most weren't sorry his father was dead. King Tove was a good man to the dark fae and his sons, but few in the Shadow Realms liked him.

And why should they? He was a ruthless ruler who sought only the best for his followers. He wasn't the Lord, who slaughtered far too many innocents and sought to take control of all the realms, but his father didn't take shit from anyone.

And neither did his sons.

"My older brother, Cole, is now the king of the dark fae, and when he marries Lexi, he'll also be the king of the Shadow Realms."

"But she's the one with all the power."

Orin smiled as he leaned against the wall and crossed his

arms. "Those who truly think so don't last long. She has the dragons, but he has the shadows."

"All dark fae have the shadows."

"Not like Cole. None of us have them like Cole."

Zeth grabbed some grass from the wheelbarrow and tossed it over another door. "I see."

He didn't. Without seeing him in action, no one could understand the Shadow Reaver, but Orin wasn't here to discuss his brother.

"And you are Drozeth Carmosa of the Carmosa family. Your family rules the demon realm, and your uncle is king."

"If you already know my story, then why ask it?"

"That's not your story."

"It's not?"

"No. That's your history, and all I care to know of it. Your story is unfolding now and consists of what do you want? What are you after? What do you hope to gain out of all of this? *That's* your story."

"Gain out of what?"

"Sahira. What do you want from her?"

"I think you're talking about yourself, dark fae. And when it comes to you, I think we all know the answer to that question, including Sahira."

"I should hope so; I've made it obvious that I'm going to fuck her. But you're playing some game, and I want to know what it is."

Zeth tossed the last of the grass into the final stall, stood the wheelbarrow against the wall, and wiped his hands on a towel. He neatly rehung the towel before walking back to Orin.

When Zeth stopped a few feet away, his yellow eyes met and held Orin's. "I stopped playing games when I realized they were for children. Maybe one day, you'll finally learn the same."

Orin gave him a tightlipped smile as he kept his face expressionless. Inwardly, he seethed while contemplating taking this demon to the pit and bashing his brains in against the rocks.

He didn't think Zeth would accept his invitation, even if the other immortals in this realm saw him as a coward for refusing. Zeth didn't care what anyone here thought of him. It was a trait Orin would have admired if it wasn't so infuriating.

"I don't want anything from Sahira. I'm simply seeking a way to return home, and each fresh set of eyes who comes into this place offers an opportunity to see this puzzle differently. I'll do whatever I can to help them solve it since so many others here, including me, have failed to do so."

He surveyed Orin from head to toe. "Some new arrivals offer more of an opportunity to escape than others."

And just like that, Orin went from contemplating Zeth's demise to being amused by him. "I didn't offer you the opportunity?"

"Not like Sahira. To you, this is still a bit of a game. You have immortals to fuck with here, and that takes some of your attention away from the grander picture of getting out. Sahira's far more serious about getting out of here than you, but she has to be."

"And why is that?"

"Because, in case you haven't noticed, more than a few here would prefer to see her dead."

CHAPTER TWENTY-SIX

OH, he'd noticed, but… "I've seen her going into battle against the Lord's army, wendigos, berserkers, and countless other immortals; she's far stronger and more capable of protecting herself than many others. If anyone fucks with her, they'll regret it. I'll help make sure of that."

"And why would you do such a thing? What's your game?"

"When it comes to keeping her alive, there is no game. We're not family yet, but we will be, and I protect mine."

"Didn't you fight against your father and brothers in the war?"

"It was a very talkative lycan who arrived here."

"What else do we have to do but learn everything we can from every new arrival?"

What else indeed? "You haven't asked me any questions."

"I know everything I need to know about you. I have some questions for Sahira, but I'll wait until she's ready."

"You're a very brave demon," Orin muttered.

"Why is that?"

"Because you have no fear of me killing you."

"I'm not going to fight you or anyone else, fae. I had my one battle in the pit; I'm still standing but won't return."

"I thought demons loved to fight."

"We do, but I have more important things to focus on."

"Such as?"

"Not dying in this place."

Orin studied him as he pondered these words and the demon. The asshole irritated him more than itching powder on his dick, and he should know, as his younger brother Drax once dumped a bunch on him while he slept. It had been created by a witch and a living nightmare to get off.

He'd almost killed the little shit for it and had scratched himself raw for a week, but he couldn't stop smiling at the memory. Drax had been the brother directly beneath him and another full dark fae.

He'd been mischievous and always smiling. They'd shared many drinks, laughs, and nights out together as they relished the freedom that came with power, wealth, and devastating good looks.

Drax was full of laughter in a way none of their other brothers were, not even himself, and he considered himself a fairly easygoing guy as long as everyone did what he wanted them to. That wasn't too much to ask.

And when the Lord decided to unleash war on the human realm, Drax broke off from their father and followed him to his death during the Lord's war.

Orin's happiness over the memory of Drax vanished as he recalled his brother was dead because he'd chosen to follow *him.*

But then, some of his other brothers stayed with their father and died too. There once nine of them; now, only four remained. And he would do anything to get back to his brothers and ensure their safety.

He'd fought against his family, but they'd always been the

most important things to him. They always would be, even if they annoyed the shit out of him sometimes.

He wasn't the reason Drax was dead, the Lord was, but he'd always bear the guilt of his father's death. The Lord killed King Tove because of *him*; there was no denying that and no fixing it, yet Cole, Brokk, and Varo still loved and trusted him just as he would always love and trust them.

They were all so completely different, but they were a unit. They worked together, fought together, and protected each other, even when on opposite sides of a war.

The guilt of his father's death was a constant weight around his neck. One that would haunt him until the day he died.

He'd done what he believed was right when he sided against King Tove. His father's plan to bring down the Lord was more subverted, but Orin thought they needed to do more. They'd both failed in their missions, but his father lost his life because of *him*.

He could never change that or make it better; he had to live with it. Never one for self-flagellation, it wasn't something he beat himself up about every day, but it was something he regretted.

And now Brokk was also missing, or at least he was before Sahira arrived here. He could have returned since she left Dragonia, but he had no way of knowing.

If his younger brother hadn't returned yet, then Orin had to get out of here to help Cole and the others find him. He couldn't lose another brother. He didn't think his heart could take another loss like that.

"They're going to try to kill her," Zeth said.

Orin frowned as the demon's words pulled him from memories of his family. "Who?"

"The witches."

"I've made it clear she's off-limits to Carmella."

"And witches trip over themselves to obey others."

Orin ignored Zeth's sardonic tone as he pondered the

demon's words. Sahira was one of the toughest immortals he'd ever met. She'd spent decades protecting her niece and working with her brother to cover up the *biggest* secret in all the realms.

He'd also seen her with her mother, an uncaring bitch who obviously had nothing to do with raising her daughter. The two of them couldn't have been any more opposite in personalities. Sahira was kind, loyal, loving, and would do anything for her family. Lydia would die before acknowledging her daughter.

Lydia's callous attitude toward her child didn't affect Sahira when they ran into her. He suspected her thick skin had taken many years to grow... or maybe she was good at hiding any pain her mother inflicted on her.

"I don't see the witches or warlocks challenging her to a pit fight. Even if they did, Sahira could say no, and that would be the end of it," he said.

She was a prideful woman, but she wasn't stupid enough to fight someone more powerful than her. Everyone here would respect her decision; she wouldn't be shunned or banished to where so many others had most likely died.

"Would it?" Zeth asked.

"If they tried to do something outside of the pit, they'd break the law, and Belda would make them pay. There's no way they would risk banishment from this town."

"I don't think they care. They want her dead."

"Then they'll have to go through me to get her."

He planned on bending the little witch to his will and having her in his bed, but no one else would mess with her.

"Do you think you could stop *all* of them?" Zeth asked.

Orin laughed as he rested his hand against the wall and leaned against it. "I have no doubt."

Zeth looked doubtful, but even before the demon's eyes went past him, Orin knew Sahira had arrived. Although her step was silent, her honey scent preceded her.

Lowering his hand, he turned as she stopped in the doorway a few feet away. "How was work, dear?"

She rolled her eyes at him before shifting her focus to Zeth. "What if it *is* an infinity symbol, and all the symbols are also supposed to be a compass rose?"

Zeth's brow furrowed, and Orin tilted his head, as her question intrigued him. Where was she going with this?

"What if they are?" he inquired.

"I'm not sure," Sahira muttered. "I haven't figured out what it might mean, but if we're missing south—and I'm going to say it's south instead of wondering if the compass is flipped around, upside down, and crazy here—what if an infinity symbol means south is supposed to go on?"

"Go on to where?" Orin asked.

Sahira looked helplessly at him before turning to the symbol on the wall. "Beyond this town."

Orin studied the witch before focusing on the road and the buildings beyond. He couldn't see the pit from here, but it was out there.

"What about the arrows?" he inquired. "What do they mean?"

"I have no idea," Sahira admitted. "I'd like to go back to the pit."

The sun was setting, and he was scheduled to be at the pub soon, but he wouldn't miss this. She might be onto something.

What that something was, he didn't know, but he could handle Belda's wrath. Besides, no one got banished after their first offense.

Belda would understand they were chasing possibilities. He smirked, as even he didn't believe the lie, but he would see where the witch took this.

CHAPTER TWENTY-SEVEN

Sahira stopped at the edge of the pit. Dirt kicked out from under her feet and clicked against the sides as it tumbled to the bottom of the large hole.

She wouldn't consider it a canyon, but it was a good two hundred feet in every direction. It was wider than deeper, but that was probably because they were searching for the mark to be etched into stone.

"What if they hacked the mark away while digging?" she asked.

"Belda said they were extremely careful not to do that," Zeth said. "It took them years of excavation to form this pit. Before then, they settled disputes in a ring."

"What if they have to go deeper to find it?"

"They can't. They couldn't dig any deeper with the tools they had. There's about a foot-deep layer of dirt over it now because of the wind and drifting sand, but it's solid rock underneath. Not even the witches had a spell to break through it."

Blowing out a breath, Sahira lifted her head to examine the rocky mountains in the distance. Despite their inability to open a portal out, the town was safe and remote, except once a year when the scarogs came to play.

"Has anyone explored beyond those mountains?" she asked.

"Many of the banished have headed for the mountains; no one's seen them again," Zeth answered.

"They never left this realm," Orin said.

"How do you know?" Sahira demanded.

"Even if only one of them escaped this realm, they would have told their story to anyone who would listen. And that story would have gotten around."

"That doesn't mean we would have heard it. We've been preoccupied with other things recently."

"*I* would have heard it. I have immortals who report to me from all over the realms. Such a story would have made its way back to me. I'm sure of it."

Sahira planted her hands on her hips, but she didn't argue. He *did* have immortals all over.

"I went out there for a couple of days a few months after I first arrived. It was the same old scenery to me, except there's no food, no drink, and no shelter," Zeth said.

"But what if we're meant to go farther than the mountains?"

"And then onward for an eternity?" Orin asked.

She had to admit that sounded a little ridiculous and impossible, but... "I'm just trying to figure it out. If the symbols and original buildings are meant to form a compass rose, then there should be one here, but there's not. The symbol is an eight, so there should also be eight of them, but there's not. And since it's not here, maybe it's meant to be an infinity sign showing us this should go on forever or at least farther than we think."

"So, instead of being trapped here for eternity, we're meant to wander out there for one," Orin said.

He didn't sound sarcastic but more resigned and curious about this. When he turned to look at her, a calculating gleam shimmered in his eyes, and she could practically hear the wheels spinning in his brain.

"Is going out there worth the risk of death?" Orin asked.

"Is that any worse than being trapped here for eternity?"

"I don't know."

"And maybe *that's* what the symbols mean. Maybe they're meant to tell us we're stuck in this crazy upside-down, right-side-up, no-idea-about-anything realm for infinity."

"I don't believe that," Orin stated.

Neither did she, but she had no idea what to do about this. Was it worse to go out there and roam until they died? Or was it worse to stay here and rot?

She wasn't sure how to answer those questions, but she suspected the answer could change in a few days, weeks, or months. And it might change every day with the way things were going.

"Do you know of anyone else who's gone out there?" Sahira asked.

"Many have. I don't know if they've all gone south. I did, but I'm sure not all of them did. Some may have traveled in different directions," Zeth said. "I've also traversed the other direction with no luck, but I only stayed there for a week. I didn't see the point in staying out there longer if I didn't find any answers."

"So, you've already considered this too."

Zeth's wan smile was response enough. She wasn't coming up with any groundbreaking information here. When she looked at Orin, his face confirmed he'd already traveled along this line of possibility.

Lowering her head, she rubbed her temples as she tried to puzzle it all out. All that did was make her head throb.

"Even if the symbol does mean we're supposed to wander forever, what about the arrows?" Orin asked.

"I don't know," Sahira admitted. "They could be another piece of the puzzle or some red herring that means nothing."

"Well, this has been fun," Orin said. "But I have to get to work before Belda demotes me to busboy. If anyone has the answers to your questions, it will be her."

CHAPTER TWENTY-EIGHT

ZETH RETRIEVED his map from the stable before meeting Sahira at the pub. She already sat at a table with Belda, who was still glaring at Orin. He either didn't notice her or didn't care as he handed out drinks to the patrons already filling the seats. Sahira suspected it was the latter.

When Zeth joined them, a few other immortals looked over as he set his map down, and Fred fluttered over. The pixie held a bottlecap full of beer as he hovered above the table, shedding red dust everywhere.

Belda wiped the dust from the table and waved her hand at Fred. "Stop that."

He covered a burp before muttering, "Sorry," and landing on the table with a small thud. With the grace of a buffalo, he crossed his legs and plopped onto the table.

"How's it going, toots?" he asked Sahira as he lifted his cap toward her.

Sahira rolled her eyes at the grinning pixie. He was feeling pretty good, but at least he wasn't as drunk as the last time she saw him.

"Great," Sahira told him.

He grinned as he swayed back on the table before falling over. He laughed as he gazed up at the ceiling and lifted his cap in salute to it. Belda looked tempted to brush him off the table with the remainder of his dust, but she left Fred alone.

As Zeth unrolled the map, Sahira filled Belda in on what they'd discussed today. As the alpha lycan nodded, Sahira realized she'd heard this theory many times before; she was placating her by sitting here and listening to it.

"I've heard it before," Belda confirmed as soon as Sahira stopped speaking. "I've spent a combined total of two months out past the mountains of this valley in search of... something."

Before Sahira could reply, a shadow fell across the table, and she looked up at Radagast. "Can I join you?" the regal warlock inquired.

Sahira hesitated; he'd been respectful to her, but the witches and warlocks still made her uneasy. They were unusually close in this realm.

Most of the time, they tended to run in their own circles and do their own things. Despite having a similar brand of magic, they lived completely different lives. But here, the warlocks built their stately homes amid the witches' tepees on the shore of the lake.

She wouldn't turn him away and possibly make an enemy of someone who'd done nothing to deserve it. "Yes," Sahira finally said.

Radagast didn't take any insult at her hesitation as he pulled out a chair and settled onto it. "May I?" he asked Zeth and waved at the map. Zeth pushed it over to him, and the warlock studied it for a minute. "Impressive."

Sahira shifted her attention back to Belda. "You didn't find anything out there when you went looking?"

"Nothing but sand, rocks, hideous creatures, and more despair."

Sahira's heart sank at her words. "You don't think there's a way out."

"Leaving this place is still the dream, but every day, I wake up to the reality that I've been here for centuries, and I'm no closer to getting out than I was before."

Sahira tamped down the sorrow trying to rise. She would *not* give up hope, no matter how discouraging it seemed.

She looked to Zeth, but his attention remained on the map as his fingers drummed on the table. Radagast was focused on the map again. Fred suddenly sat upright; he blinked at them before taking another sip of his drink.

"What did I miss?" he asked.

She felt like Sisyphus rolling the boulder up the hill, but Sahira chuckled as the pixie looked around at them and grinned at her. "Hiya, toots!"

Apparently, that was going to be her new nickname from him. At some other time, it might have annoyed her, but she didn't have it in her to get snippy when she was contemplating burying herself in a bottle too.

A brush against her shoulder alerted her that Orin had arrived a second before he rested his hand on the table beside her. With a casualness that made it seem like they were comfortable with each other, he leaned over her to look at the map again.

His cinnamon-and-clove scent engulfed her as his warmth sent a shiver down her spine. She pushed aside her impulse to lean closer and touch him.

He was standing too close on purpose, but did he have to smell and look so good? Edging away, she resisted shoving him when a smile tugged at his lips. The bastard knew *exactly* what he was doing.

"What does everyone think?" Orin inquired.

"I think you should be behind the bar where you belong," Belda growled.

Orin gave her that dazzling smile Sahira was sure had caused countless women to get naked and jump him. It caused her heart to flutter, which made her dislike him even more.

Belda, a much better woman than her, was not impressed. She folded her arms over her chest and stared stonily back at him. Orin didn't turn off the charm or walk away as his gaze returned to the map.

"You know this place better than anyone; is there any chance of escaping it?" Orin asked.

Sahira already knew what Belda thought about this but didn't say anything.

"The longest I've spent exploring beyond this town was two weeks. I went south with the hope the symbol would be out there... somewhere," Belda said. "I went in as straight a path as possible and did everything I could not to veer off it.

"I was determined to get somewhere and to discover something other than black rock and misery; I found nothing but death and destruction. There's more than the scarogs out there. There's also a land of bones so white they could rival any cloud, a place of monsters you can't see, but you hear them hunting at night, and there are no resources to survive on.

"At the end of my weeklong journey into the Barren Lands, I had to choose between returning here or forging ahead to find food and drink. I risked losing everything if I continued, so I came back.

"When I left, I took as much as I could pack with me; when I decided to come back, all I had left was enough water for one more day. I crawled back into this town, a sunburned, starving mess. My pack took me in and bandaged my wounds. Many wanted to go with me, but I told them to stay here to watch over the town and promised I'd be back for them if I discovered anything.

"All I learned from my journeys was nothing good is out there, no eighth mark exists, there's no escape... only death. And the *infinite* finality of death."

Sahira didn't miss her emphasis on the word *infinite* and understood Belda believed that was what the symbols represented.

"Who brought the depressing gal to the party?" Fred muttered as he drank more from his cap.

Belda's gaze flicked to him before she rested her hands on the table and looked at each of them. "I understand none of you have been here as long as me. You still hold out hope, as you should, but I can guarantee there's nothing you haven't considered that someone else hasn't already."

Sahira couldn't breathe as Belda's words sank in. Beside her, Orin's fingers constricted on the table until his knuckles whitened.

When she glanced at him again, his jaw was clenched, and his eyes burned. For a second, she swore a flicker of black crossed the back of his hand, but it vanished so fast she couldn't be certain.

Was it a hidden cipher? She'd probably never know the answer, but she suspected it was.

"I don't believe that," Orin said through his teeth.

"You don't have to believe it, but one day, you will." Belda rose and tapped her hand on the table. "I think you could all use a drink."

"Hear! Hear!" Fred shouted as he lifted his cap.

"Orin, bring them some glasses of whiskey; it will do them good on a day like today."

Before Sahira could refuse the alcohol, Belda turned away and blended into the crowd. Her gaze fell back to the map, and she stared blankly at it until Zeth rolled it up and set it on the table beside him.

"I don't believe it either," the demon said.

"Neither do I," Radagast said.

"Believe what?" Fred asked.

"That there's *no* way out of this place," Sahira said.

"Oh." Fred closed one eye and peered into his cap. "I don't believe that, but I do believe I'll have another drink." Despite his inebriation, the pixie leapt to his feet with amazing grace. "I'll be back, toots!"

Sahira refused to believe they were stuck here, but doubt niggled like a rancid worm at the back of her mind.

Orin didn't move or say anything as he stood staring at the table. His body vibrated with barely leashed fury beside her.

She had the inexplicable urge to rest her hand over his to calm him, but she doubted she'd have any effect on him, and that *definitely* was not their relationship. Instead, she dug her nails into her palms and rested her hands in her lap.

When Belda called out Orin's name, he turned and stalked into the crowd.

A minute later, he returned with a bottle of whiskey and three glasses. He set it between them before leaving again.

CHAPTER TWENTY-NINE

AT THE START of this night, Sahira had every intention of retreating to her room early and starting another book. She hadn't returned the first book yet, mainly because she hadn't written her story, but she finished reading through it last night.

Orin hadn't left his story in the book yet, and she felt weird adding hers to it first, but she would. He probably believed he wouldn't be here long enough to write his story, but that time had come and gone for him.

She admired his tenacity, so she wouldn't say anything. As far as she was concerned, after learning everything she had today, she'd been here for too long not to have written something in it.

Instead of traipsing her ass upstairs like she should have done hours ago, she sat and drank with Zeth and Radagast without speaking for the first hour. Eventually, as time passed and the whiskey kicked in, they started talking.

She learned Zeth's uncle was the king of demons, and his father was dead. As far as he knew, his mother was still alive, and her brother was king.

"She's still alive," Sahira said, "or at least she was recently.

Not much is known about the demons—you guys like to keep yourselves hidden—but the king fought against the Lord in the Lord's war. His sister was at his side throughout it."

"The demons got involved in the war?"

"I don't think they had any loyalty to anyone; they were there for the fight."

Zeth chuckled as he finished off his glass of whiskey, set it down, and refilled it. "That sounds like them."

"Some of the demons fought on the Lord's side. I'm sure that didn't go over well with your uncle."

"He likely didn't care. They probably all just showed up to a battle and started fighting. I doubt they knew which side they were fighting for as long as they got to kill."

Radagast's lip curled in distaste as he elegantly sipped his whiskey before setting it down. Many warlocks sided with the Lord but didn't enjoy the brutality of the demons, berserkers, and many others.

"It didn't sound like the demons had any real loyalty to either side," Sahira said. "Or at least that's what I heard. I was in the human realm with my niece. That realm was devastated, but we mostly stayed out of the fight. My brother, Del, was in the war, but after the Lord's men told us he died during a battle, it was up to me to keep Lexi safe, so I kept her as far from the fighting as possible."

"I'm sorry for your loss," Radagast said.

"Don't be; it turns out he was alive but living in a jail cell *Orin* stuck him in."

She turned to glare at the dark fae pouring drinks behind the bar, but he didn't notice her.

"Interesting little history you two have," Zeth remarked.

"If he wasn't Cole's brother and about to be family, I'd have gladly killed him… more than a few times." She didn't delude herself into thinking she'd succeed but would sure like to try. "I like his brothers, Cole, Brokk, and Varo; it would upset them to lose him."

"Are you sure about that?"

Sahira squinted one eye shut and poured herself more whiskey. "Yeah, for some reason, they love the jerk. And though he's many things, most of them obnoxious, Orin is loyal to those he loves."

"Didn't he fight against his father in the Lord's war?" Radagast asked. "That's what some lycan told us."

"Yeah, but they've forgiven him, and he had his reasons."

Zeth grunted and resumed drinking as Radagast stared at the bar. "What about you?" Zeth asked. "What's your story, warlock?"

Radagast frowned at him, apparently unimpressed by Zeth's blunt manner. "I don't have a story. My family is mostly dead. I had a cousin who was still alive before I came here, but I'm not sure if he still is. I was searching for a good time when I ended up here."

"How long have you been here?" Sahira asked.

"Seventy-two years."

Sahira's eyes watered when she downed the rest of her drink. She shook her head and suppressed a yuck sound as Zeth poured her more.

The clock behind them ticked away the minutes until Zeth spoke again; his voice was a little less steady as he did so. "What do you think about what Belda said?"

"I'm trying not to," Sahira answered.

Radagast sipped some more of his drink. "The whiskey is helping with that."

"Have you given up hope of leaving?"

"I'm not sure," Radagast admitted.

Sahira wondered if the alcohol had something to do with this admission or if he would have said it without the whiskey. He stared at the back wall as if it wasn't there before drinking some more and setting his glass down.

"I've also searched the Barren Lands with no luck. I haven't spent as much time out there as Belda and some others, but I think we've all traveled those inhospitable lands by now, even the pixies. It's tough to retain hope for anything after being out there."

Squinting one eye closed again, Sahira raised the bottle and poured the last few drops into her glass. The bottle clinked against the table when she set it down.

Zeth lifted it. "Would you like more?"

She and Radagast nodded, and Zeth rose to go to the bar. Belda handed him another bottle, and he returned with it. He set it in the middle of the table as Fred returned to perch on her shoulder.

"Sing a song with me, toots!" the pixie shouted.

She was drunk enough to do exactly that, but... "What song?"

"Fields of Many Flowers!"

Sahira was familiar with the pixies' drinking ballad but didn't know all the words. That didn't stop her from singing along as Fred belted the song from her shoulder while she swayed back and forth.

At some point in their drunken torture of others, Zeth chimed in, and Radagast mumbled a couple of lines from "Butterflies Dancing in the Rain." Fred mainly stuck to pixie ballads, but Sahira didn't mind. She'd always loved listening to the pixies sing.

Fred gave a loud cheer when they finished their fifth song before passing out on her shoulder. Sahira giggled as his tiny snores filled her ear.

"Beautiful silence!" Radagast said as he lifted his drink, and they all clinked together in the middle.

The whiskey had relaxed him enough that his neatly ordered

hair was now disheveled from running his hand through it. Red color stained his pale cheeks, and his eyes twinkled.

"You're only saying that because he's not snoring in *your* ear," Sahira said with another giggle.

Time blurred as they continued drinking and talking until the pub's occupants started clearing out. She didn't notice this until Orin lifted the empty chair beside her, turned it around, and straddled it as he joined them.

Orin picked up the nearly empty bottle in the middle of the table. "Five bottles, little witch. I didn't think you had it in you."

Sahira squinted at the three blurry images of him as he grinned at her. Normally, immortals could hold their liquor, but she hadn't eaten when she returned to the pub, and it had been at least five days since she last had blood.

The alcohol had hit her harder than it normally would. Zeth still looked mostly functioning, as did Radagast, but as her head swam, she suddenly wasn't so sure she could stand.

"Shit," she muttered.

Orin plucked Fred from her shoulder and set him on the table. "You look like you're seeing double."

"I think I'm seeing triple."

Zeth placed a napkin over Fred as he released an inelegant snore and flopped onto his back. "I'll take her to her room," Zeth offered.

CHAPTER THIRTY

THOUGH ORIN WAS HIGHLY AMUSED by Sahira's antics over the night, especially her atrocious singing with a big old smile on her reddened face, some of his amusement vanished at the demon's offer. They were getting a little too close for his comfort. She was his conquest and game to play.

Zeth could have her when he was done. Until then, the demon wasn't getting into her room.

"I'll take her," Orin said.

"You still have work to do," Zeth said.

"Work can wait, but *I'll* make sure she gets safely to her room."

Sahira held up a hand as her head bobbed forward. When her chin hit her chest, she lifted it to glare at him. Orin tried not to laugh at the disgruntled expression on her face.

"I can take myself up," she stated.

He was pretty sure she knew that was a lie, but his witch was stubborn. To prove her point, Sahira rose from her chair and stood with her hands on the table as she swayed a little.

A few remaining patrons glanced their way, but most didn't pay her much attention. They had their own shit to worry about.

Orin rested his hand on her shoulder and steadied her while leaning closer. "Let me help you to your room."

She opened her mouth to say something but promptly closed it again. Orin pulled the chair out and guided her away from the table with a hand on her back.

"Don't be a prick, dark fae," Zeth said. "You better not try anything; she's drunk."

"I've got plenty of willing women; I don't need to fuck intoxicated ones."

"What about intoxicated ones unwilling to fuck you when they're sober?"

Orin smiled as he contemplated tearing out the demon's tongue while guiding Sahira away from the table. He wouldn't be such an annoying prick then.

"Taking advantage of women isn't my style, demon. Perhaps it's yours if you're so concerned about it."

He didn't look back at Zeth as he draped Sahira's arm around his shoulders and guided her up the stairs to the rooms above. Six doors lined the hall; one was the bathroom, but the others were all bedrooms.

Thankfully, they were the only two immortals staying here now. He didn't like immortals enough to be sharing the pub with them.

He led Sahira to her room and waited as she fumbled to remove the key from her pants pocket. It trembled in her hand before tumbling free and hitting the floor with a clatter.

Orin leaned her against the wall before bending to retrieve it. He unlocked the door and pushed it open to reveal the room beyond. Much like his was before he did some redecorating, hers was simple yet welcoming and smelled of grass and wood.

He guided her inside and over to the bed. She plopped onto the edge of the mattress, and her head fell forward.

"I ha'en't been t'is drunk in centuries," she slurred.

Orin stared at her bent head before kneeling to untie her

boots. He tried not to think about the fact that he, a dark fae *prince*, was kneeling before a woman and removing her boots with no hope of spreading her legs, but here he was.

He set the boots on the floor beside the bed and looked at her bent head. Some of her hair had fallen from her bun and tumbled forward to shield her pretty features, but her eyes were still open and bloodshot.

The little witch had tried to bury her troubles in a bottle, ensuring she'd have a bad headache tomorrow. He brushed back a strand of her hair; for some reason, his thumb lingered on her silken cheek while he studied her.

"I'm na gonna have sex wit' you," she muttered.

Orin chuckled as he ran his thumb across her cheek. She was so supple and warm; the feel of her spiked his pulse and sent blood straight to his groin, but he willed his arousal away.

"Believe me, witch, when we have sex, and we *will* have it, you'll be perfectly coherent and begging for more. Besides, I'll make sure you remember every detail of it."

"We're *never* having sex."

"One day soon, I'm going to prove you wrong."

Before she could reply, he grasped her ankles and gently lifted her legs onto the bed. She plopped back and rolled over so her back was to him. Before he could say anything more, his pretty little witch started snoring.

Orin stared at her for a minute, intrigued by her combination of strength and vulnerability. She'd never show that vulnerability, but it was there beneath her beautiful surface.

Finally, he tore his attention away from her and retreated to her door. He locked it and glanced back before closing it and returning to work.

CHAPTER THIRTY-ONE

SAHIRA HAD no idea what time it was when she woke, but her room was dark, her mouth dry, and her head felt like someone had taken a hammer to it. When she attempted to swallow, it made her stomach lurch.

She started to moan and lifted a hand toward her head but stopped when something shifted in the darkness. Her breath caught, and she froze as the shadows in the room's corners crept closer to her.

At first, she didn't understand what was happening and how the shadows could move. She didn't know where she was, as nothing in the room was familiar, but then the smell of whiskey and grass hit her, and her memory of this place returned.

She was in the Cursed Realm, a place where she didn't belong but couldn't leave. She'd become ensconced in a maze with no exit.

She'd become encased in Hell.

Then the shadows moved again, and a surge of hope deflated her misery. *Is it Cole? Did he find us?*

But that didn't make sense; Cole wouldn't creep through the

shadows if he were here. He'd make himself known instead of spying on her.

Did he send the shadows ahead of him? Have the shadows found us and are now reporting to Cole?

But something wasn't *right* about these shadows. Not that the ones who were a part of Cole felt right either; they were ominous, lethal things that could tear the heart out of someone... and often did.

Cole's shadows moved freely as they crept around a room and went about their destructive way. These shadows, or whatever was moving through them, didn't coalesce or split up and divide to attack; they moved together in an insidious dance that sent a chill down her spine.

Because of the pounding in her head, she could barely do more than squint her eyes at the shadows... that might not be shadows. They were a single form coming toward her, stretching a hand out—

A scream caught in Sahira's throat as she lay, watching and waiting for the shadow thing to connect with her. Its warmth brushed against her neck, but that couldn't be right. Shadows weren't warm; they were...

Well, she had no idea, but they certainly weren't *warm!*

Their tendrils or fingers, or whatever they were, crept toward her throat. Fingers reached forward—

Sahira threw herself backward with a startled cry. She tumbled out of bed and crashed onto the floor with a thud that shook the nightstand beside her. When she hit the ground, she kicked something aside, and it skittered into the darkness.

For a second, she contemplated crawling under the bed and hiding, but stubborn pride and self-preservation propelled her to her feet. With her body tensed for battle or to throw up, her eyes shot around the room.

Nothing moved.

What is going on?

The question screamed through her mind as she listened and searched for any movement, but nothing stirred. With a trembling hand, she felt for the candle on her nightstand and found the matches beside it.

It took four tries, but she finally got the match to ignite; a small flame sputtered to life at the end. Any attempt at steadying her hand failed as she brought the fire to the wick. When the candle caught, the light in the room grew brighter but didn't chase away the shadows in the room's corners.

Gulping, Sahira lifted the candle and, with a confidence she didn't feel, carried it around the room while she inspected it. There was nothing there. *Nothing.*

She stopped and turned in a small circle in the center of the room.

Did I imagine it?

It was possible as, now that her adrenaline rush was wearing off, the effects of the alcohol came roaring back to the forefront. Her head pounded with renewed intensity, and her legs quaked as her parched throat begged for water.

She could have been having a nightmare and thought she was awake. It wouldn't be the first time she'd dreamed she was awake when she wasn't.

But it had been *so real*. She could still feel fingers of *something* brushing her flesh.

Resting a hand against her throat, she searched for any sign something was there, but nothing was. Lifting the candle, she carried it to the mirror to study her reflection. She was paler than normal with shadows under her eyes, but nothing unusual stared back at her.

"What the…?"

She turned to search the room again. Nothing moved, but as much as she wanted to believe she'd dreamed the whole thing or was still drunk and imagining things, she couldn't shake the feeling that it had been *real*.

Yet she remained alone.

Sahira carried the candle back to her bed and plopped onto it. She was exhausted, and more sleep would probably help her headache, but as she lay back, she knew it would be impossible to sleep again.

CHAPTER THIRTY-TWO

SAHIRA SPENT the next two days in more of a fog than when she first arrived. She focused on work, read two more books, and barely saw Zeth, Radagast, or Orin as she trudged through her days.

Whenever she walked into the pub, Fred would land on her shoulder and start singing, but though she sang a few lines with him, she didn't jump into the whole song again. He didn't mind as he kissed her on the cheek, called her "toots," and flitted away.

She tried not to think about the symbols, compass, or anything else about this place as she focused on the books. Last night, she'd finally added her story to the first book. Even if she planned to escape this place, her story should be there so others would know she'd made it to freedom and have hope.

Sahira had no idea how they would learn of her escape, but she'd somehow ensure they did. She kept her story short and sweet, less than one page. It was all that was required to say what she had to say.

Like all the others before her, she left a small space after her name. The ones who had something written in that space had it done in a different hand than the one telling their story.

The sentences in those spaces were only one or two lines conveying how that immortal died and where they were buried. She suspected they did this so, if the immortals somehow figured out how to escape, the loved ones of the dead could return to claim their remains.

Life here was beginning to fall into a rhythm of work and reading. She didn't know if that was a good or bad thing, but having a purpose helped to get her out of bed every morning.

She waited for something more to happen in her room, but the nights remained calm. The more time passed, the more she believed she'd dreamed the whole thing.

Another two nights went by before she was pulled from sleep by the certainty that something was in her room again. Sahira lay there with her eyes closed as she inhaled and exhaled.

She had no idea what woke her, but the hair on her nape rose as that certainty grew in the pit of her stomach. Every one of her instincts screamed something was wrong.

Something else was in the room with her, and it wasn't good. She felt it creeping closer as it came for her.

She had to react, but she didn't know how to get away from whatever this was. Then the floor creaked to her right and from behind her back.

There was something behind her. Something she couldn't see as it crept closer. And this time, there was no alcohol clouding her judgment and making her question her sanity.

Whatever was in her room was real, and it wasn't any good. *Nothing* good crept around someone's room at night.

After first encountering this thing, she'd stashed her dagger under her pillow. With slow, cautious movements, she slid her hand beneath it, wrapped her fingers around the hilt, and pulled it free.

Taking a deep breath, she kicked her quilt off and rolled to the left before leaping from the bed. Enough light filtered through her open windows to reveal the black mass on the other side.

She couldn't see much else about it as it hovered near her bed, but the blackness was thicker over there. When she first woke and sensed this thing in her room, she'd *known* it was there, but seeing this blob was like a kick in the teeth.

Part of her yearned to turn and flee, but the other part refused to be intimidated by this thing… *whatever* it was. With the dagger in hand, Sahira released a small cry as she leapt onto the bed and ran across to the other side.

She swung out with the dagger and sliced downward as she cleaved through the mass, but it was gone. Confused by what happened, Sahira turned to examine her room, but nothing was there.

"What the…?"

She was certain it had been there. *Certain!*

It wasn't a trick of the light; that darkness was real, and she'd heard the floor creak. It had been here, but where did it go? How did it get in? And *what* did it want?

Her shoulders heaved, and her heart raced, but though it was gone, she knew that thing had been there!

And it appeared to have been made of shadows. With a sinking sensation, a horrible realization settled over her.

No one controlled the shadows like the dark fae.

Sahira's attention shifted to the door as her fear and confusion turned to rage. Orin's room was next to hers. Orin, who hated the word *no*, who hadn't been as overt in his sexual advances as he once was but still schemed to get her into his bed because she was a challenge, he was bored, and what a fun game for him to play.

Why *wouldn't* he screw with her in this way? He might believe it would push her into his bed instead of trying to kill him.

He was wrong about that.

With the dagger in hand, Sahira stalked toward her door, unlocked it, and entered the hall. She didn't question why it remained locked when something had been in her room—locks didn't stop shadows.

She looked left and right, but no one stood there, waiting to pounce on her. The building was dark, quiet, and shrouded in shadows that swayed and parted as she stalked toward Orin's room.

Sahira didn't know when everyone had left the pub, but she'd guess it was at least a couple of hours ago, as the light coming through the windows was turning gray. She shifted the dagger to grasp Orin's doorknob.

She didn't plan to knock; he'd come into her room uninvited, and she would do the same. However, she was annoyed to discover the knob didn't turn beneath her hand. It didn't astonish her, but it did irritate her.

Taking a deep breath, she battered the door with her fist. "Open up!"

She didn't stop knocking to hear if he'd risen; she just kept pounding until the door flew open, and her hand fell forward. Her knuckles skimmed his arrogant, too-handsome face instead of giving it the full blow it deserved.

"What the *fuck* are you doing?" she demanded.

He blinked at her from eyes still swollen with sleep. His black hair was tussled around his head, but his pointed ears still poked through it.

If she didn't know better, Sahira might believe he'd been sleeping, but she didn't believe it because she *did* know better.

"What the fuck are *you* doing?" he retorted.

Sahira's eyes narrowed on him. "Why were you in my room?"

He yawned and rubbed his face. "Little witch, if I was in your room, I'd still be between your thighs."

She thrust the dagger into his face and held the tip beneath his chin.

His amusement and confusion vanished as malice glimmered in his crow-black eyes. "You better watch where you point your blade. I've been nice up until now, but I don't take threats lightly."

The low growl of his words and the menace emanating from him probably should have caused her to retreat, but she wouldn't back down from this asshole and whatever game he played. She didn't move the blade.

"You and your shadows stay *out* of my room. The next time I catch you in there, I'll gut you from your balls to your throat."

With that, she turned on her heel and stormed away. She pushed through the door of her room when she felt him pressing against her as he followed her inside.

CHAPTER THIRTY-THREE

SAHIRA TURNED with the blade as she swung it at him because, by Hecate, she wanted him to bleed. If anyone deserved it, it was this bastard, but he was as fast as the shadows he controlled as he ducked her swing and grabbed her wrist.

She bit back a cry when he squeezed down, but her fingers instinctively released the blade. Cursing, she kicked at him, but he swept her legs out from under her before she could make contact.

If it wasn't for his hand on her wrist and him seizing her other arm as she started to fall, she would have gone down. Instead, he kept her upright as her back crashed into the wall.

Before she could react, he drove his thigh between her legs, and his face hovered only inches from hers. It was only when his chest pressed against hers that she realized how bad her mistake was, because not only was Orin's thigh between her legs, but he was naked.

In her fury, she hadn't noticed his nudity before. The horrible reality of it was crashing over her as she tried to maintain her calm while inwardly screaming against her body's involuntary, physical reaction to his. She should *not* like how this felt, how warm he was, or how good he smelled, but every part of her liked it.

This disgusting man had been spying on and touching her, yet her body still tingled from his caress. Her traitorous nipples hardened against the thin material of her nightgown.

Gritting her teeth, she willed herself not to react to him, but it was impossible when his mouth was so close to hers. And those utterly alluring lips were twisted into a cruel smile that created a knot of unease in her belly.

"Hello, little witchy witch," he purred.

Sahira refused to react. He was one of the most lethal immortals in all the realms, and he'd turned his wrath on *her*. But no matter what he did, he wouldn't intimidate her.

And if he planned to try to kill her, she'd put up a fight so big they'd hear it throughout the town. Belda and the others would make him pay for not taking her to the pit like he was supposed to.

His breath tickled her neck as he inched closer. When the beat of his heart thudded in her ears, a sudden burst of clawing, insatiable hunger caused her fangs to prick.

She'd never gone so long without blood before; there was never a reason to. Now the reason for her thirst was staring her in the face with that malicious grin and calculating gleam in his eyes. He'd made it so she could only feed from him, and she was determined not to do so.

Orin had been different since she got here; he hadn't been pushy, overly touchy, careless of boundaries, or with other women. Sahira was sure he was still screwing plenty of other women—he was a dark fae, after all—she just hadn't seen him with any since having the misfortune of walking in on his orgy when she first arrived.

Her stomach curdled at the reminder. However, a man determined to escape this place had replaced *that* Orin. They'd acted like a team while working to figure out an escape.

That teammate was gone, and in his place was the dark fae she equal parts loathed, distrusted, feared, and desired. Unlike Cole, Varo, and Brokk, Orin was pure dark fae. He was everything that represented his race—cold, calculating, vicious, and with only the ability to care about his family.

Sure, Lexi and Cole's relationship had twined them into a larger family web, but they weren't blood, hadn't grown up together, and throughout most of the time they'd known each other, they could barely tolerate one another. Even if it devastated Lexi and pissed Cole off, he'd kill her if he believed it would benefit him.

And he'd also mess with her if he believed it would benefit him. He'd marked her as his prey, a game he would win, and he'd started tormenting her by entering her room at night. Had he done it so they would end up like this: him nude and against her while she wore only a thin nightgown?

She wouldn't put it past this manipulative prick to have done it for this moment. He knew she'd gone a while without blood. Maybe not the exact amount of time she'd gone, but at least the five days she'd been here. He'd have to know that if they got too close, she might find the lure of his blood too enticing to resist.

And, as a dark fae who survived on feeding off sex, he would also know that drinking from the vein of another could be an erotic experience for a vampire. That was the reason he'd volunteered to be the one who fed her.

Orin's head tilted to the side as it did when he was studying things. Unfortunately, she'd become the object of his attention.

His smile became crueler as he shifted his hold on her wrists until he locked them within his grip. There were chains more breakable than his hold as she jerked against him.

The annoying prick lifted his index finger and waved it at her as he chided, "Uh-uh."

Sahira stiffened at his condescending tone, but she didn't move as he used the tip of his finger to trace her bottom lip.

When she jerked her head away, he grasped her cheeks with one hand and turned her back so she had to look at him.

She glowered at him as the continued beat of his pulse pounded in rhythm with the throbbing of her fangs, and her traitorous body yearned for more of his touch. Determined to get her desire under control, she couldn't stop her eyes from falling to his mouth again.

Orin released her cheeks and returned his finger to her mouth. She tried to clamp her lips shut but couldn't keep them closed against his prodding.

When he lifted her upper lip, he grinned at her elongated fangs. "Hungry, witch?"

CHAPTER THIRTY-FOUR

IF LOOKS COULD KILL, he'd be dead a thousand times over from a million stab wounds while his balls dangled from a necklace around her neck. Thankfully for him, looks couldn't kill.

Also thankfully for him, his fiery little witch was quite beautiful when she was mad. She was a sight to behold in her simple white gown, her cheeks all red and eyes glistening.

He had no idea what she was so incensed about or why she accused him of being in her room, but it had gotten them here, which made him happy. He'd followed her into the room to punish her for waving a blade in his face right after he woke up, but now, as he sensed her growing hunger, a new plan started to develop.

Orin hadn't fucked anyone since she arrived; if he was going to play the game of getting her into his bed, then he couldn't traipse past her door with a different woman or six every night. But he was a dark fae who had needs, and she wasn't the only one famished.

She would break first; he was certain of it. They both required something the other had to survive, but he had to deny himself to win the long game with her. After he won, he could go back to screwing every woman in this realm.

He leaned a little closer so her breasts brushed his chest. The connection sent an electric thrill through him.

Her eyes widened when his cock lengthened against her belly, and her heartbeat accelerated. She could deny it all she wanted and fight him until the bitter end, but she craved having him inside her.

"My blood isn't the only thing you hunger for," he murmured, lowering his mouth so his lips skimmed her throat.

She jerked as she tried to pull her wrists from the wall, but he slammed them back into the wood. He hadn't finished punishing her for shoving a dagger in his face.

Resting his free hand against her hip, he stroked her flesh through the soft material before lowering his hand toward the junction between her thighs. When her fingers started twitching, he pulled his hand away and grasped hers to stop the motion.

Leaning back a little, he smiled. "No spell casting, little witch. That's not playing fair."

She bared her teeth at him. "And coming into my room while I'm sleeping is?"

He pressed closer to savor her honey scent and how her body yielded to his. Too much time had passed since he'd been with a woman; she was a delectable temptation he couldn't resist.

Lowering his mouth, he kissed her neck as he told her, "This is only the second time I've ever been in your room. Remember, I helped you upstairs when you had too much to drink."

"Liar! And stop that!"

Orin grinned as he nipped at her neck. When she shivered beneath him, and the hardened buds of her nipples rubbed her nightgown, he bit back a groan as his dick jumped in anticipation.

The woman was a study in contradictions, so unyielding in many ways yet so warm and enticing in others. She was also going to learn he didn't take commands from anyone… unless they were fun ones.

"I don't lie," he murmured as he released her fingers to graze his knuckles down her nightgown and around one of her breasts.

His mouth watered when her nipple became more visible, and her body swayed toward his. She may think she wanted him to stop, but her body told a different story.

"I saw you!" she accused.

The tone of her voice pierced through his increasing haze of lust. Reluctantly, he leaned back to study her. "I wouldn't creep around someone's bedroom at night. I don't have to; women welcome me into their rooms."

"I don't!"

Orin glanced at her breasts before sliding his hand between her thighs. "Don't you? You're the one who came to *my* room tonight, and you're so wet right now, I can feel it through your nightgown."

She squirmed and tried to clamp her thighs shut, but he refused to move his hand. "Don't touch me!"

He stroked her with his finger and watched her pupils dilate when he found her clit. She was so ready for release he could have her coming in less than a minute. "Why deny yourself something you're enjoying so much?"

Her breath came in small pants as she continued to give him that death stare. "I hate you."

"That would only make the sex so much better."

"Fuck you!"

He smiled as he caressed her again, and her legs trembled. "Gladly."

She bit her lip, sinking her fangs into her bottom lip and causing a tendril of blood to slide down her chin. Leaning into her, he continued stroking her while kissing the blood away. She also tasted of honey, he decided as he ran his lips across hers.

She kept her mouth locked against his kiss, but her body was relaxing and the death grip of her thighs easing. His body thrummed with excitement; he would hear her cries of pleasure and feel her body coming apart against his.

When her hips rose toward his, Orin reluctantly pulled his hand away. She was so close; a few more strokes and he'd learn what she sounded like when she came, but he planned to win this game and wasn't giving her a free ride.

He grasped her nightgown and started pulling it up when she shifted and thrust her hips into him, knocking him back a little. "No!"

Orin's hand fisted in the fabric as he met her frightened eyes. Her breaths came faster as her gaze ran over his face.

He'd never seen fear from her before, but it was there now. She'd enjoy this, but not even he was that much of a bastard to push it on her.

Reluctantly, he released the nightgown and let it fall around her feet. "I'm going to have you, Sahira. And when I do, you'll beg me for more."

"After what you did tonight—"

"I wasn't in your room," he interrupted. "I'm many things, and I freely admit to most of them, but I'm not someone who enters someone else's room without their permission."

"Then you sent your shadows to do it."

"I have great control over the shadows, but I'm not my brother. I can call them to me and use them to cloak me, but I can't send them out to do things for me. Cole is the only dark fae with such a power."

CHAPTER THIRTY-FIVE

SAHIRA TRIED to focus on his words, but she was acutely aware of each thump of his heart and his rigid erection nudging her belly. She also couldn't deny the almost painful ache between her legs.

She'd been so close to release and experiencing the pleasure he could give before he stopped. *Because he knew you were close and hoped you'd let him have sex with you.*

True, and it was a cruel thing to do, but he had her wound tighter than a spring and on the verge of pleading for release. However, she didn't beg, and she certainly didn't screw someone who'd scared the shit out of her earlier.

She told herself that, but her body continued to pulse with anticipation, and her skin had become far too hypersensitized. The slightest touch might make her whimper.

It had been too long since she'd fed and far more time since she last had sex. She hadn't thought her reckless actions through when she confronted Orin tonight, but she also couldn't let him keep coming into her room without saying *something*.

But was he the one here tonight?

Before leaving this room, she was *certain* it was him, but he had a point. Before Cole, the dark fae could only cloak themselves in shadows; they couldn't use them as weapons sent out to destroy their enemies.

Or at least, that's what the dark fae let everyone believe. They could be hiding a stronger, more nefarious ability.

She trusted the dark fae as much as a lion that hadn't eaten in a month. At some point, it was going to feast.

And that was what the dark fae did. They devoured anyone in their way and cared little for anything beyond themselves and their loved ones. They shadow kissed others and moved on without any regret over the mindless, sex-craved beings they left in their wake.

She'd always despised the heartless dark fae. Cole had changed her opinion on them some, as had Brokk and Varo, but Orin only solidified her dislike.

"And I'm supposed to just believe you?" she inquired. "The dark fae lie."

"Not me."

"You kept my brother locked away and let us believe he was dead. You manipulated and blackmailed Lexi into keeping you hidden in the tunnels beneath our manor."

Orin shrugged as he stroked her hip. "Those weren't lies; they were simple omissions for things I needed done."

If she had her hands free, she'd wipe that arrogant look off his face. It was unfair that someone so cold was this handsome.

How can I be turned on by a man I despise so much?

She had no answer, but it made her loathe him more.

"You twist things your way," she said.

"I get what I want."

"And you don't care who you hurt in the process!"

Orin leaned so close his breath warmed her skin again. She'd woken him from sleep, or at least that's how he portrayed it, but the hint of mint remained on his lips.

"Why should I care?" he asked.

"Because that's what decent immortals do!"

He grinned at her, but it wasn't a smile of happiness. It was the look of a hunter stalking its prey, and she was the deer trapped in his crosshairs.

"Come now, witch. We both know I'm *far* from decent, and you like me that way." When Sahira's fingers twitched, he clasped them again. "No spells."

"I *abhor* how deceptive and manipulative you are."

"I'm not deceptive. I've made it quite clear what I want and what I *will* have." His thigh nudged between her legs again as his shaft grew thicker and longer against her. "We both know it's only a matter of time before you part those pretty thighs and *beg* me to take you."

Sahira ignored his words; she wouldn't dignify them with an answer. Mainly because, after tonight, she feared he might be right. Instead, she focused on something else. "You're not deceptive?"

"Not at all."

"Then how many ciphers do you really have?"

Orin's eyes glittered with amusement as they both shifted their attention to the ciphers running across his chest and down his arms. The black marks all dark fae possessed looked like a cross between flames with their sharp edges and water as they flowed over their bodies.

Some dark fae had more ciphers than others. The more markings a dark fae possessed, the more powerful they were. Being able to sense the vitality in things was part of being a witch, and she'd always felt an extremely strong current emanating from Orin.

Many suspected some dark fae, if not *all* of them, hid some of their ciphers to conceal their true strength. Cole possessed the most Sahira had ever seen, but she doubted she'd seen them all.

The fact that Cole triggered the arach spell during the trials that made him the dark fae king backed up her theory. The arach designed their spell to turn the strongest dark fae into the Shadow Reaver, and Cole had claimed his place in history as such.

Because of that, she suspected Cole *and* Orin had *many* more ciphers. She'd seen that flicker of black on the back of his hand in the pub, and he had more than she'd ever seen on anyone except Cole. But then, she'd never seen any dark fae as bared to her as Orin was now.

His ciphers ran across his upper chest and shoulders. They encircled his arms before ending at his wrists. He displayed an impressive amount of his power, but it was far from all of it, and they both knew it.

"You think I have more ciphers than this?" he inquired.

"I know you do."

He smiled at her. "But you'll never know how many."

"More of your twisted deceptions. I'm tired of this. Get out of my room."

He lowered his thumb to run it across her bottom lip. "But we were just starting to have fun."

Warmth spread through her belly, making her legs almost useless, but Sahira refused to melt. "*Nothing* is fun with you."

He lowered his mouth until his lips brushed hers while he spoke. "We both know there's something *very* fun we could be doing together now."

"That's never going to happen."

He chuckled as he unexpectedly released her wrists and stepped away. "You have to feed sometime, vampire. And we both know what blood can do to a vampire's libido."

She'd told herself she wouldn't look, but her eyes involuntarily went to his vein. He pulled her lip up again and smirked at her fangs before sauntering toward her door.

I will not *look at his ass.*

She looked at his ass; it was as chiseled as the rest of him. His back muscles, flexing with each of his steps, caused her mouth to water. Tendrils of his ciphers ran along the tops of his shoulders and grazed his back.

He was magnificent, and he knew it.

Orin stopped in the doorway and, grasping the knob, looked at her over his shoulder. "And no matter what you think, I wasn't in your room earlier, witch. You must have been dreaming."

With that, he closed the door behind him.

CHAPTER THIRTY-SIX

SAHIRA SPENT the next couple of days focused on work and reading through the books she borrowed from the library. Elsa had told her one was a really good read while the other two were more boring than dirt, but Sahira was determined to get through them.

She also trusted Elsa's taste in books and looked forward to some entertainment. Over this past week, she'd come to learn the witch loved books and didn't care about Sahira's half-vamp status, or at least she didn't seem to, as she was the only witch who openly talked to her. Elsa always smiled, waved, and hurried over to greet her when Sahira arrived at work.

When new immortals came into the library, she talked with them as she sought to learn more about her new reality. None of them had any useful information. A few had theories about what was happening here; some even believed it could be a warped reality or alternate universe.

Some believed the symbols were for protection; some were sure they were a curse. Others thought they meant nothing and could be right, while others believed they meant *everything*.

None of their theories sounded more or less crazy than

anything she'd already considered. One thing was clear: nothing they said gave her answers; they only raised more questions and confusion.

Her lack of sleep and growing hunger didn't help with that. Every night, she stayed up and read until she passed out. And every night, she woke to the certainty that something was in her room watching and touching her.

Last night, cool fingers brushed her face and ran down her shoulders before she rolled over and leapt out of bed to confront it. Laughter trailed it as the creature disappeared from her room.

She still hadn't glimpsed anything more than shadows, but unless Cole controlled those shadows, they couldn't laugh. And this wasn't Cole's doing; she was certain of that.

She was too tired and starved for blood to handle anything properly, but she didn't know how to stop it. She'd cast a protective spell around her room that should have kept *every* unwanted thing out, but whatever this was, it had waltzed right through her magic.

Last night, she'd set traps around the room too. One would stab anyone who stepped on it, another would lower a net on her intruder, and finally, she'd spread glass around her bed.

The thing had come, but it hadn't set off any of her traps, and not one drop of blood littered the glass. She hadn't expected shadows to bleed, but something had to be controlling them.

This entity had intruded in her room every night, but she still hadn't gotten a good glimpse of it. Last night, her candles were blown out before she woke.

It had to be Orin. She had no idea how he was doing it, but he had to be controlling the shadows and unleashing them on her. It could be one of the other dark fae here, but most of them ignored her, and the few who didn't had no reason to torment her this way.

Orin did.

Rubbing her eyes, Sahira yawned as she hugged her books to

her chest and climbed the steps to the pub. She opened the thick door to raucous laughter and music.

Immortals had packed the pub for the past couple of nights. She hadn't been down there to drink again, but she'd seen Zeth and Radagast in the crowd. She waved to them and said a quick hi to Fred when he plopped on her shoulder.

Before returning here, she'd grabbed some bread and salted meat from the mercantile and ate it on her walk back. She usually ate the same thing every morning during her walk to work.

Once, there was cheese from goat's milk, but that was a few days ago. Her new staples weren't the best, but she didn't like eating in the pub with so many other immortals and *Orin*.

When she felt eyes on her, she glanced at the bar to discover Orin standing behind it. He had a glass and towel in his hand while he watched her. She didn't acknowledge him as she trudged up the stairs to her room.

Every piece of her was exhausted; she swore even her hair was ready to sleep as she slipped into her room, locked the door, and leaned against it. Before leaving this morning, she'd removed the traps from last night; they'd proven useless, so there was no point in keeping them out to clutter her room.

She placed her new books on the dresser and opened the shutters to look out the window. Since her nightly guest had started arriving, she'd taken to closing the shutters while she slept, too, but it did nothing to keep whatever it was out.

Resting her elbows on the sill, she inhaled the earthy aroma of the realm. Sand drifted through the streets as the wind kicked up. The immortals on the road ducked their heads against it.

Sahira's attention shifted to the immortal in the one tower she could see from here. They stood beneath the bell. Immortals had excellent vision, but if the scarogs came at night, they'd have less notice about their approach than if they attacked during the day.

She should probably be worried about the impending arrival of the beetles, but she didn't have it in her. There was far too much for her to worry about already.

All she could think about was how to keep that thing out of her room, and she was completely out of ideas. She should ask Belda for a new room, but the immortals here would see her as weak if she couldn't even protect *her room.*

She had enough issues with the witches, who continued their catty looks and snide remarks, without making herself a target for others too. And as much as she liked Zeth, Radagast, and Elsa, she didn't trust anyone enough to tell them about this.

Tonight, I'll stay awake. Tonight, I'll see it coming.

She'd vowed this to herself many times over the past week, and every night, she failed. It was impossible to stay awake when she was already functioning on so little sleep. No matter how much the thing frightened her or how hard her adrenaline pumped, eventually, exhaustion won.

And when it did, the thing would come.

~

ORIN FROWNED as he watched Sahira slog up the stairs to her room. Her shoulders hunched forward, and her hair, while still in a bun, had fallen to her nape; strands had straggled free to frame her face.

If he hadn't known better, he might have assumed she was rolling around on the library floor with someone, but that wasn't his little witch's style, and he didn't smell sex on her. Besides, the dark shadows under her eyes and the exhaustion she emanated were most likely the reasons for her disheveled appearance.

Was there really something in her room the other night?

The two of them hadn't spoken since her unexpected arrival in his room, something he would have to remedy soon as his hunger grew. He'd been trying to give her space, but couldn't let this drag on much longer.

At the other end of the bar, Carmella laughed at something the lycan leaning toward her said. Boris, Belda's beta, had his hand on the bar while he spoke. His blond hair fell to his shoulders, and when he lifted his head, the light from the windows shone off his brown eyes. Orin suspected the lycan's interest in Carmella was purely physical, as she wasn't interesting to talk to.

A dwarf huffed and puffed as it clambered onto one of the stools. "Whiskey, and keep them coming," the dwarf said.

Like all other dwarves, his accent resembled the humans' English accents. Orin grabbed the bottle and set it on the bar as Sahira closed the door to her room.

He didn't know what was happening with the witch, but he'd have to fix it soon. Because not only was he growing increasingly ravenous, but so was she, which wasn't good for either of them.

CHAPTER THIRTY-SEVEN

SAHIRA CAST A STRONGER protective spell around her room. It could keep out anything, and if something managed to slip past, a horrible shrieking noise would alert her to an intruder.

It didn't work.

Instead, what alerted her to the presence of an intruder was fingers clamping around her throat, digging down, and choking off her air supply. She woke in a frenzy of flailing arms and legs as she gasped for air.

When she swung her hand at her attacker, it came up against nothing. The dim radiance of the candle on her nightstand revealed the shadowy figure hovering over her, but there were no other details, and it was difficult to make out much about the figure as lack of air caused her vision to blur and darken.

Whatever this shadowy thing was, it shouldn't have such strength. The shadows Cole controlled could do this and far worse, but this creature wasn't like them. She'd already be dead if it was.

Sahira flopped on the bed as she sought to break free, and this time, when she swung out, she connected with something solid. Shadows didn't entirely make up this thing; they appeared to, but it was something *more*.

And she had to break free before she passed out and this thing slaughtered her. Throwing herself to the side, she yanked herself from its formidable hold. Her forehead and right arm crashed off the nightstand before she tumbled to the ground.

A groan escaped, her head pounded, and a knot formed on her forehead as the room spun. Her brutalized throat burned while she wheezed in air as she forgot about the unconsciousness trying to take her under.

She started to rise when something pounced on her back, propelling her into the floor as hands, or whatever they were, encircled her throat. Rearing back, she tried to buck it off, but the thing clung to her like a burr to clothing.

Struggling to remain conscious while seeking to break free again, she fumbled for her bed and the dagger tucked beneath her pillow. When her fingers enclosed on the cool metal, she yanked it free as a crash reverberated around the room and shook the floor beneath her.

~

At first, when the noises from the witch's room stirred him from sleep, Orin cursed her for being so loud. But then, as he lay there listening to the ensuing silence, he began questioning if something was wrong.

He waited for the scrape of furniture as she moved it back into place, but there was nothing. Lifting his head off the pillow, he listened while telling himself to go back to sleep.

He had no idea what time it was but was certain he hadn't fallen asleep long ago. It had been another busy night at the pub; it had taken a lot of prodding to get the immortals to leave, but they finally did.

And he'd just gotten to sleep only to be woken by the woman

who would like nothing more than to cut off his nuts. He started to turn over to go back to sleep but couldn't.

Tossing aside his blanket, he swung his legs out of bed and rose. He didn't care about his nudity; it never fazed him.

Besides, if she was going to be rude enough to wake him, then she would have to deal with seeing him naked again. It would serve as another reminder of what she was missing.

He left his room and walked to her door. Orin was about to knock, but the scratching, fumbling sounds from within stopped him.

Frowning, he stared at the door before leaning closer so his ear nearly touched it. He had no idea what was happening in there, but it wasn't good. He couldn't announce his presence to whatever lay within by knocking.

Orin strode back until he stood near the balcony railing. Lowering his shoulder, he ran at the door and smashed into it.

Wood splintered and flew inward as it gave way beneath his weight. What remained of the fractured door rebounded off the wall and swung toward him.

Orin threw out his hand to keep it from crashing into him as a low, piercing screech started to sound. At first, he had no idea what it was, but when he tried to enter the room, a shock hit him, and he realized the witch had set up a security system.

One that had failed to stop whatever was happening in this room.

Stepping back, he took in the dark room, but all he could see was the empty bed and a toppled candle only a few feet away.

Then he noticed the dark blob hovering before him and over the top of Sahira. When the thing turned toward him, the darkness grew. It expanded toward him before retracting and scrambling under the bed.

Orin waited for it to reemerge, but it was too dark for him to see that side of the room, and if it reemerged, he didn't see it.

When Sahira moaned, Orin forgot all about the creature as he shoved his way through the electric jolt.

His body jerked and twitched from the power hitting him, but once he was through, the screeching stopped. With his hands still twitching from the lingering effects, he scrambled over to Sahira.

He knelt beside her and gently grasped her shoulders to turn her over. Her pale face turned toward him, and even in the darkness, he could see the dark circles encasing her throat.

Her white nightgown was a tangled mess around her legs as she lay unmoving before him. He searched for the rise and fall of her chest but saw nothing.

Was she dead? Because that would suck. He was looking forward to seeing how this game between them played out, and now some asshole may have cut his fun short.

He didn't like admitting he might also miss her. She made this realm a little more bearable, and he admired her strength, but acknowledging such a thing was too close to admitting he liked this woman more than most others.

"Shit." He reached to check for a pulse when her eyes fluttered open.

"Why are you doing this?" she whispered before passing out.

Orin sat back on his heels and rested his hands on his knees as he surveyed the room, but nothing moved through the shadows. He'd have to get better light in here.

"Fuck," he whispered.

He removed the dagger from her hand and set it on the nightstand before carrying her from the room. There was no way he would leave her there after what he'd witnessed, and he had to examine this room more closely.

Orin carried her into his room and settled her on the bed before returning to her room. He gathered the candle and lit it again before restoring the nightstand.

Once he finished, he closed the broken door the best he could. He'd have to fix the door before anyone returned to the pub. There was no way he was letting anyone know something happened here tonight, especially when he had no idea what that something was.

He didn't trust anyone in this realm, and that trust had just gotten much smaller.

With relentless determination, he searched every inch of her room but saw no sign of whatever was there.

That must be why she looked so exhausted and accused him of being in her room, but he had no idea what it was or how it got there. With a sigh, he returned to his room and stood beside the bed, staring at Sahira.

The bruises on her throat were already darkening and becoming more visible. He recalled when she arrived to accuse him of being in her room but understood that night better now.

He hadn't lied to her; he didn't have that kind of control over the shadows and didn't think it was some shadow creature in there. The only dark fae who could exert so much control over them was Cole, and he would *never* do that to Sahira.

And there was no way Cole had been in there. If he had, his brother would have found a way to get them out of this realm, not attacked her.

Besides, if Sahira had done something so horrible to unleash Cole's wrath on her, he would have come here and killed her in person. No, whatever was in her room was entirely different than the Reaver.

He didn't know what it was, but he would find out.

His fingers skimmed her brow and the purple lump there. Her breath was slow and steady, but she required some medical attention, and the witches wouldn't help with this. Besides, he didn't trust them to be anywhere near her.

The light fae could also help, but most would shut the door in the face of a dark fae before he could tell them why he was there. Besides, that meant involving others, and he'd already decided against it.

Retreating from his room, he left the door open so he could hear her if something happened again. He descended the stairs and went to the bar to gather supplies to help her.

He couldn't find any bandages, but he grabbed some towels and cold water to take to his room. Hopefully, it would help with her swelling.

CHAPTER THIRTY-EIGHT

SAHIRA WOKE to what felt like an imp happily hammering away on her brain. She scrunched her eyes closed as she tried to bury the nausea churning in her belly.

Why does every part of me hurt so much?

"Easy," a voice murmured.

A cool hand resting against her forehead eased her discomfort, and the cold compress that followed helped more. She settled down as she forgot about trying to figure out what happened.

She didn't know how much time passed as she floated in and out of consciousness, but she stirred to voices before slipping under again. More time passed, and more voices drifted to her, along with laughter, music, and the clink of glasses and silverware.

When she rose from unconsciousness again, she blinked against the darkness suffocating the room. Her head felt better, but a dull throb still pulsed in her temples. She searched the shadows for answers but couldn't find any.

I'm not in my room.

It was similar to hers but smelled more masculine. Instead of grass and wood, the scents of cinnamon and clove permeated the air. Her bed was a perfectly fine full-size, but now she lay in the middle of a king.

Instead of her pretty quilt, a deep red blanket covered her. Sheer red gauze draped over the tops of the four tall posts and spanned over the top of the bed.

Orin's room, she realized with a sinking sensation.

She'd seen it before, and her skin started to crawl when she realized she was in *his* bed, where she'd walked in on him with *three* other women when she first arrived. She hoped he'd washed the sheets.

Turning her head, she rested it against the pillow and sniffed. The soap and fresh air aroma wafting from it was a welcome relief.

She craned her head to take in the lantern on the nightstand. Its small flame danced across the walls as the night's events crashed over her.

Her hand flew to her forehead. Her fingers tentatively felt over the lump there before falling to the swollen flesh of her throat. When she gulped, pain accompanied the movement.

She was in Orin's bed, probably exactly where he wanted her after he attacked her last night. Or at least, she thought it was last night. She had no idea how long she'd been out.

Indignation rising, she propped herself up to settle against the headboard. It took a few seconds, but she finally swung her legs out of bed.

Nausea rolled her stomach and nearly drove her to her knees. The pounding in her head increased as tears of frustration and anger burned her eyes.

She'd known Orin was ruthless and would do whatever it took to win, but she'd never expected him to unleash this cruelty on her. She didn't have high standards for any dark fae, but somehow, he managed to sink lower than she'd ever believed possible.

She was about to rise when the knob turned and the door crept inward. The noise from below increased. The door wasn't completely open before Orin popped his head in and looked at her.

When he saw her sitting there, he stepped inside and closed the door behind him. "You're awake."

She didn't say anything as she eyed him warily while her fingers dug into the mattress. His gaze roamed over her before settling on her face; he rolled his eyes.

"You still think it was me?"

"Who else would it be?"

He glided into the room with the grace of a stalking panther. His body flowed with such mesmerizing grace that she almost forgot she wanted to kill him.

He may not have the same control over the shadows as Cole, but they coalesced around him in a way they didn't for others. The shadows were an ingrained part of him, and he was part of them.

Orin grabbed the small chair from the corner and carried it to her. It was one of the chairs from the pub. He turned it around and straddled it to prop his arms on the back while studying her.

"I'm not sure if you're aware of this, witch, but a fair amount of your kind don't like you in this realm."

"Witches can't control the shadows like you, and that thing was made of shadows… or something like them."

It had been so strong and relentless. Before, it only messed with and harassed her; last night, it sought to destroy her.

"What about warlocks?" Orin asked.

"They can have a darker side and be into darker magics, but they couldn't do that either."

His black eyes were intense as they studied her. "Couldn't they?"

"They'd have to embrace some *very* dark magic. That kind of magic isn't in a witches' nature, but...."

"Warlocks have done it before."

Sahira's gaze shifted to his closed shutters as she pondered his words.

"And what if more than one of them is in on it? What if they're lending their power to whoever was in your room?" he inquired.

Sahira's eyes shifted to him, but she didn't say anything. If they embraced darker magics, a warlock could do this alone, but...

"How did they get into my room? I had a protection spell on it. Unless it failed—"

"It didn't. A screeching sound started when I broke through the door, and I got hit with a lot of electricity when I tried to enter. It stopped once I broke through."

"It would," she muttered. "The alarm wasn't going off before that?"

"No."

"How is that possible? Only a shadow or something similar could have slipped past it."

"Could the warlocks or witches bypass it if they worked together?"

"No. They would have to break it, and since it worked when you entered the room, it was still intact."

And now that he'd brought it up, she recalled hearing the screech of the alarm while the thing was choking her. She hadn't made it loud enough to alert anyone outside this building, but it had gone off.

"I didn't want anyone else to know what happened last night, but I couldn't keep it from Belda. I broke your door and had to replace it. She's strict about the inventory here and would have known it was missing from storage. Besides, you're not in any shape to work today, and she needed a reason why.

"She won't tell anyone else, not even her pack. She's furious that someone attacked you in her pub. The rules are *very* clear about such a thing happening, and if she finds out who did this, she'll kill or banish them."

His black eyes riveted Sahira as they held hers. *Did he do this?*

CHAPTER THIRTY-NINE

She was so certain before, but he seemed so sincere. It could be part of his game. After all, she was in his bed, but right now he was more focused on learning the truth than getting in her pants.

"How do I know you're not sending me down some rabbit hole of misdirection?" she asked.

"You're always so quick to believe the worst in me. I'm the one who scared that thing away and took care of you while you were unconscious."

Feeling a little guilty about her words and her conviction that it was him, she bowed her head. "Thank you for that."

"You're welcome."

"But you have to admit, you haven't done much to make me believe the best in you. Ever since I arrived here, you've tried to manipulate me into doing what you want. You made it so you're the only person I can feed from in the hopes I'll sleep with you."

"And?"

Despite the discomfort in her throat and the throbbing in her forehead, a red haze clouded her vision. "*And?*"

"What is your point?"

If she believed she could get to him, she would launch off the bed and beat him into a bloody pulp. Even fueled by rage, she'd never land a blow against Orin.

He was far too powerful and fast. They both knew it, which was why he was staring at her with a bored expression.

"My point," she grated through her teeth, "is that I don't trust a thing you say."

"What's between us is a game, Sahira."

"I'm not a game!"

"But you are."

The casual tone of his voice only increased the red clouding her vision. She *really* hated him sometimes.

"You made yourself the challenge by declaring you'd never sleep with me, and I'm a man who likes to rise to every occasion. Like in chess, someone has to be checkmated. It won't be me."

"So, you're admitting you'd do anything to destroy me."

"I have no intention of destroying you, just winning the game."

"Don't you think I would be *disgusted* with myself for sleeping with you? Don't you think that would destroy a piece of me?"

He tilted his head to the side as he studied her. "I think you'll enjoy it too much to care. Besides, you can always continue to say no. That's *your* decision."

That was true, but still… "I hate you."

Unfazed by her words, he clasped his hands before him. "That will make the sex better."

He had no idea how maddening he was, or, more likely, he did and didn't care. She wanted to look away from his stare but couldn't break eye contact with him. If she did, he might see it as a weakness; to this man, any weakness was something to exploit.

"I at least hope you've cleaned the sheets since your last parade of women through here," she muttered.

He chuckled. "I have, and you inconsiderately interrupted my last parade."

"What?"

He unclasped his hands as he rose, turned the chair around, and settled into it with unmatched grace. "I'm waiting for you, Sahira."

She started to laugh but stopped at the seriousness of his expression. "What?" It was the only word she could form.

Grinning, Orin stretched his long legs before him. "I told you, I'm in this game to win it, and I have no doubt I will. There hasn't been another woman since you've entered this realm, and there won't be until I claim you; that's how much confidence I have in myself."

Unsure if that was infuriating or ridiculous, Sahira could only blink at him as his complete confidence that he would have sex with her sank in. "You must be hungry."

"So must you."

They stared at each other as the revelry downstairs ratcheted up. Orin was the first to break the silence.

"I know you don't think much of me, and I'm okay with that. There are very few, in *all* the realms, whose opinion matters to me, and they all share my blood, but I'm a lover of women. I worship their bodies and revel in their movements. I bring them great joy and only like hearing them scream in ecstasy… not pain or fear."

Sahira had to keep herself from shifting as his words conjured the memory of him in her room, with his hand between her legs. No matter how often she tried to ease herself, the memory still turned her on.

"I do not beat or choke them… unless they ask me to, and then it's only for their pleasure."

"I've seen you kill women before. I was involved in the war that put Lexi back on the throne too."

"Of course I've killed them before. Survival of the fittest, and we must do what's necessary to survive in war, but I would never do *this*"—he waved a hand at her face—"to someone. I know you don't think much is beneath me, but I would never exhibit this level of cowardice.

"I go after my enemies head-on; I don't hide behind shadows, spells, spirits, or whatever this thing is. And while you might continue to believe the absolute worst in me, deep down, you know it's true."

He was ruthless and freely admitted he'd do whatever it took to get his way. He'd revealed tonight that he was ravenous and waiting for *her* to feed, in the hope she couldn't control her lust when it happened. It made sense he would try to speed things up.

But he wasn't trying to take advantage of this situation, and he could. Whatever happened in her room could be a whole new game to him.

She hated that she couldn't trust him or anyone else in this horrible realm.

When the pounding in her head kicked up again, Sahira winced and lowered her head to press her fingers against her temples.

Why was someone doing this to her?

Besides the obvious answer of Orin getting her in bed or the witches and warlocks hating her mixed vampire heritage. Was either of those things enough to torture her like this? And how had they gotten past her security system?

Tears burned her eyes, but they weren't ones of frustration and anger this time. She was so tired, battered, and bruised.

She'd spent her entire life being looked down on and disliked by those who didn't know her for something she had *no* control over. Her parents made this choice, and while she was extremely glad she existed, shouldn't they be paying the price and not her?

Her father was dead, but her mother lived securely nestled and protected with the witches and had for years. Sahira had found her place of acceptance with Del and Lexi; they were family who loved and protected her.

She'd discovered a great friendship with Kaylia, a woman who had hated vampires more than most. When they first met, Sahira never would have believed they could become friends; they had, but that didn't matter here.

She was on her own here, and the only one seeking to help her with this was the one who would do everything he could to break her.

CHAPTER FORTY

WHEN SAHIRA'S TIRED, sad eyes met his again, something close to pity tugged at his heart, but Orin wasn't one for that useless emotion. However, he didn't like that this had battered her so much.

But then, whatever that thing was, it had tried to kill her tonight. If he hadn't woken, she'd be dead now.

Whatever did this to her had only two goals: tormenting and destroying her. And since she was *his* to play with in this realm, he wouldn't let them succeed.

"Has this thing been entering your room every night since you came here to accuse me?" he asked.

"Most nights, but though it's there, creeping in the shadows and touching me, tonight's the first time it attacked."

"I wonder what changed tonight."

"I think it's been playing with me, trying to scare me, but it's growing tired of that. It's always planned to kill me and has decided it's time."

"I asked Belda tonight," he said. "There are thirty witches and warlocks in this realm; would that be enough to get past your protection spell without setting it off and do something like this?

They'd also have to do it without weakening themselves so much that we would notice something. I checked out all the ones who came here tonight, and they all look strong and healthy."

Sahira's jaw tightened a little. "Half that number would be enough."

His teeth ground together as a muscle in his jaw ticked. "Cowards."

And he *abhorred* a coward. He didn't have time for someone who wouldn't fight their battles face-to-face. Any of the witches or warlocks could have called her out for a fight in the pit.

And she could have told them no, which would have stopped it right then.

His hands clenched until his knuckles turned white. Only half of them would be enough to do this to her, but which fifteen or so was it?

"They could probably use less," Sahira murmured. "Depending on how strong they are."

That narrows things down, he thought sardonically.

"Is there some way to find out who's behind this?" he asked.

"I don't have that kind of power, especially not against what could be so many of them. If they're grouping together against...."

Sahira gulped before lifting her chin to meet his gaze. In her eyes was the steely gleam he was familiar with.

"If they're grouping together against me, then they're protecting themselves from anything I could do to locate them. And I don't know anyone in this realm with the power to locate them."

When he rested his hand on her knee, her warmth reminded him how much time had passed since he fed. If he wasn't careful, he would weaken himself too much, and now that this new danger lurked in the realm, it could be a problem.

He wasn't ready to seek out someone else to warm his bed; that would be admitting defeat, and he *refused* to be defeated by this woman. He'd determined she would be the next one he fed from and would follow through on that... for now. It would have to change if he started to feel too weak.

And damn if he wasn't starving. He'd been controlling it, but touching and smelling her had awakened it.

But as his cock stirred, his gaze shifted to her bruised face and the finger marks encircling her throat. She was a game to him, but they were also allies outside this realm.

They'd worked together to take down the Lord, and though she'd adamantly deny it, they each had a devious side. They were also willing to do whatever it took to protect their loved ones.

She'd never admit it, but they were alike in some ways and connected by their relatives. No one else in this realm was going to fuck with her.

His sense of right and wrong was a little twisted, but he liked his moral code.

Sahira's eyes fell to his hand, and she didn't move for a second. He detected the increased beat of her heart as her scent intensified. She gulped before her dilated eyes met his again.

They held each other's stare before she shifted her leg. He didn't fight her on it this time as he released her. He was an asshole—he freely admitted it and would happily screw her until she couldn't walk—but he wasn't about to push himself further onto her when she was bruised and battered.

Orin sat back in his chair and rested his hands on his belly while studying her. "Whether you like it or not, we're allies in this realm. We're allies out of this realm too."

"Are we allies, or am I just a game?"

"Why can't you be both?"

"Because I can't trust someone who freely admits to toying with me."

"Why not?"

The incredulous look she gave him made it clear she thought

he'd lost his mind, but it was a legitimate question. He waited for her to say something; when she didn't, he continued.

"It's rare for the dark fae to consider anyone an ally; that should tell you something. However, you know we enjoy our games, and of course, since there's little else to do here, I'm going to play them."

"I don't want to be your game."

"Then be happy you're more than a game; you're also a beautiful woman I want to fuck. I have for a while now."

Color stained her cheeks, and he sensed her rising desire instead of uneasiness when she shifted on the bed. This stubborn woman knew how good it would be between them and would cave soon.

"You might as well have fun with life; we never know how long we have here," he said. "And look at where it's led us."

Sahira ran a hand in front of her face and down toward her throat. "I'm having a blast."

He patted her knee before rising, but the desire she'd awakened wasn't easily buried as he strode toward the door. Walking away from her proved to be more difficult than he anticipated, and not just because of his erection.

He didn't like leaving her behind and unprotected when something out there sought to destroy her, but he couldn't stay. Belda agreed to let him check on her and expected him back at work soon.

"I don't know if that thing can find you in here, so stay awake until I return," Orin said.

"And then what?"

He turned to look at her; she remained on the bed with her hands clasped in her lap as she stared out the window.

"We'll return to your room. Except, when you enter, I'll follow enshrouded in shadows. Hopefully, whatever or whoever it is will never know anyone else is there, and we'll destroy it."

When she didn't respond, he left the room.

CHAPTER FORTY-ONE

SAHIRA WOULD GET up and leave if she had the energy. She couldn't rely on or be indebted to Orin for anything. He'd only use it against her.

But she didn't have the energy and desperately wanted answers about what was happening. The idea of having Orin in her room caused a clammy sweat to coat her body as her fingers twisted together.

Letting him in even a little could completely backfire on her. He always took an inch and tried to turn it into *miles,* but she didn't have any other options, or at least not ones she could see.

She could challenge the witches and warlocks to the pit one at a time and try to take them all out. Her ability to teleport would have made this easier to do, but this realm had stripped it from her. So, she'd have to be sneakier in battle if she were to win.

Her first challenge would expect her to try to use her powers against them, but she wouldn't. She'd use her dagger and go in for the kill.

It would work well against her first opponent but not for any of those who followed. Which meant she'd most likely die before she got through all thirty of her possible attackers.

The overwhelming helplessness of her situation wasn't lost on her. When the enormity of it bared down on her shoulders, she almost allowed herself to become buried beneath the tumult of despair.

It would be so easy to give in to the sorrow trying to choke her, but she couldn't. She had to stay strong, or she'd never get through this.

And she had to get *out* of this town.

Even if they discovered who was behind this—and she still wasn't completely convinced it wasn't Orin—there were too many witches and warlocks here to contend with. And more of them could arrive at any minute.

Each of those new arrivals could become a threat to her.

Besides, she couldn't stay here and rot for eternity. She had to escape or at least try it.

Rising, she walked toward the window as her body protested every step and her head spun a little. Still, she compelled one foot in front of the other until she stood before the window.

With awkward movements, she opened the shutters and secured them before gazing out at the town that didn't want her here but was determined to keep her. It rained sometime during the night, or maybe it was during the day.

It was the first time since her arrival here that rain had fallen, and its ozone scent against the sandy earth was a familiar, much-missed aroma from home. It, and probably her exhaustion and battered body, brought tears to her eyes that she blinked away.

Her gaze shifted toward the direction of the pit. She couldn't see it, or what lay beyond, from here.

Sahira didn't know if she was right, but she suspected she had to go that way to get out… or die.

But first, she had to heal, gather supplies, and prepare for what sounded like a treacherous journey. She also had to deal with whatever attacked her tonight; she couldn't leave this pending guillotine looming over her head.

And she didn't know if whatever or whoever was behind this could follow her from the town. She shuddered at the possibility of having this thing trail her through the Barren Lands.

Sahira turned away from the window and retreated to the chair. There was no way she was climbing back into Orin's bed, especially not when her skin still crackled from the energy his touch created.

CHAPTER FORTY-TWO

WHEN THE PUB closed for the night, Orin returned to his room. Sahira was still up, waiting in the chair for him.

She'd spent the past few hours listening to the revelry below and contemplating her choices. They remained as bleak as before.

"Are you ready?" Orin asked.

Sahira rose and turned to face him. "What do we do?"

"The pub is empty, but you're going to stroll into your room as if nothing happened. Cloaked in shadows, I'll follow. I don't know if whatever this is somehow watches you in the daytime, watches over you, or is capable of doing such things, but we know it comes at night.

"So, you're going to sleep while I watch and wait. It might not come tonight since I interrupted it last night. I might have chased it off, but I think it will try finishing what it started."

"Lovely."

Despite being unconscious most of the day, the idea of going to sleep and letting that thing come at her again wasn't as horrible as it sounded. She was exhausted.

The emotional and physical stress of all this had taken a toll on her. Not to mention her lack of sleep and blood over the past week had really beaten her down.

"Are you ready?" Orin asked again.

"Yes."

As she walked toward him, he drew the shadows around him and vanished. She studied the place where he'd stood but wasn't sure if he was still there. He could have slipped away while cloaked in the embrace of darkness.

"What do the witches and warlocks think happened to me today?" she asked.

"The only one who asked about you was Zeth, and I told him you'd taken the day off. Belda agreed to tell anyone who asked that you'd asked for the day off work to do some research. Whoever did this to you knows it's a lie, but anyone else would accept it."

Sahira somehow managed to keep herself from jumping when his voice came from her right; she'd last seen him to her left. "I have to use the bathroom before I go to my room. Don't follow me in there."

Orin's chuckle set her teeth on edge. "That's not one of my kinks, witch. You're on your own in there, but don't talk to me again once we leave this room."

She tried not to let her unease show as she opened the door, left the room, and strolled down the hall to the bathroom. Unsure if she believed him or not, Sahira used her body to block the entrance to the bathroom as she entered and locked the door behind her.

She was almost positive he hadn't entered behind her but wasn't taking any chances. She used the toilet faster than ever before, washed her hands, and splashed water on her face before studying her complexion.

The knot on her head had faded and gone down. Now all that remained was a purple bruise. The finger marks on her throat were also fading, but she could see their imprint against her skin.

She looked exhausted, haggard, and shadows rimmed her bloodshot eyes. She was paler than normal, her cheekbones more visible, and she'd lost weight.

Not only did she have to put an end to whatever was happening in her room, but she had to feed. She couldn't keep pushing herself without the proper nutrition, and her meat-and-bread meals weren't cutting it anymore.

She needed blood before she collapsed or became a threat to everyone around her. That was a problem for tomorrow; tonight, she had to survive.

When Sahira left the bathroom, she resisted her impulse to look for Orin. She had no idea where he was, but he wouldn't be far behind when she entered her room.

Opening her door, she slipped inside and stopped to light the candle on her bureau. As the wick caught, she set the flint down.

Sure that she'd given Orin enough time to enter behind her, she closed and locked the door. When he didn't start banging on it, she knew he was somewhere in the room with her.

The hair on her nape rose; she tried to tamp down the feeling of being watched, but someone *was* watching her. Acutely aware of his eyes on her, she set the candle on her nightstand and looked at the shutters. She yearned for fresh air but decided to keep them closed.

She would love to change her nightgown. She'd been wearing it for far too long and associated it with some bad memories, but there was no way she was getting naked in front of Orin.

Although, it would be fun to torment him for a change. Had he been telling her the truth when he said he was waiting for her to break and hadn't been with other women?

Everything to Orin was a game, and it could be a lie, but she didn't understand why he would lie. He had nothing to gain from it.

She didn't think better of him for it, and it certainly didn't make her want to hop in his bed. For him, it was simply a matter of pride. He'd decided he wouldn't have anyone else until her and wouldn't cave.

He had to be ravenous, too, but he wasn't showing it as much as her. Someone hadn't been sneaking into his room to try to kill him, so that was probably why he looked a lot more chipper than her.

She glanced around the room but decided against redoing the protection spell. It wasn't working, and she couldn't have Orin accidentally triggering it.

She went to the bed, pulled back the sheet and blanket, and slipped beneath them. Exhaustion tugged at her eyelids, but sleep was difficult as she strained to hear any sign of Orin's breathing or movement toward her.

She didn't detect anything, as the man proved to be as elusive as the shadows cloaking him. Opening her mouth, she almost called out to him—she'd love to know *where* he was— but she bit it back.

If that thing had figured out a way to monitor her, it couldn't learn Orin was in her room. As much as it irritated her, she'd have to sleep without knowing his location.

As she snuggled beneath the quilt and her sore, aching muscles eased a little, she realized she wasn't worried about Orin trying to do something while she slept. Did she actually have a modicum of trust in him?

The possibility was almost as unnerving as the return of whatever stalked her. It kept her up as her mind continued to contemplate the possibility.

She wasn't sure how long it took, but eventually, she fell asleep.

CHAPTER FORTY-THREE

THOUGH THE ONLY ONE who could detect him in the room was a stronger dark fae—so, only Cole—Orin didn't move and barely breathed as he stood in the corner while Sahira finally slid into sleep. Her breaths were the only sounds in the room.

He glanced at the dwindling candle and the closed shutters. It was impossible to tell what time it was, but it must have been at least a couple of hours since he finished work.

Would this thing arrive before dawn or after it? Daybreak was still at least half an hour away, but he suspected it was more of a night creature.

He was beginning to think it wouldn't arrive, and the candle had nearly burned out when the shadows to the right of her bed shifted. Almost no one else would have noticed this subtle change, but like all dark fae, he had an affinity with the shadows.

The shadows were a part of him, and he was closer to them since he was stronger than almost every other dark fae. And this wasn't another dark fae.

The possibility of it being such had crossed his mind. He didn't mention it to Sahira because she would have jumped at the option, even if he believed it was a long shot.

The dark fae had no reason to try to kill her. They weren't known for their kindness, but they didn't randomly attack other immortals, and Sahira hadn't done anything to give them a reason to attack.

They would have come to him if she had. He was a dark fae prince with no authority in this realm, but a couple of them had still come to him to air their grievances like he gave a shit.

He'd told them to take it up with Belda. They still looked to him as their leader and wouldn't attack someone with a faint familial connection to him; they would come to him first. He was certain of it.

And he was just as certain the witches and warlocks had something to do with this. He'd told Carmella to make sure they left her alone, and as he'd suspected, most of them glared at him but remained mute.

The only ones who didn't care were Radagast and Elsa, but the warlock acted as if everything was beneath him, and Elsa mainly stuck to herself. He'd warned the witches, but they hadn't heeded it, and they would pay for that.

The shifting coalesced into a figure that rose from the ground beside Sahira's bed. The shadows... no, they weren't shadows.

These things were something else, something used to disguise whatever had come into this room... or they *were* the thing.

He'd never heard of or seen anything like this, but this realm contained *many* mysteries. It wouldn't surprise him if it held countless unknown creatures too.

This thing didn't have a mouth, but a parting within the darkness around the being created a gap resembling one. When it opened its mouthlike thing wider, it revealed the wall behind it.

The thing was more of a disembodied face than something with a torso and legs. Like its mouth, its eyes were two openings that revealed the space beyond, but there were no eyeballs.

Foot-long, hooked fingers inched toward Sahira. Excitement

emanated from it; this thing would drool in anticipation if it had a mouth. Fascinated by it, Orin tilted his head to examine its floating approach toward Sahira.

It was almost to her when he pulled free the weapon he always wore strapped to his side. The small sword had a thick blade but was lightweight and easily maneuverable. He spent many hours honing its lethalness; it could cut through tendons and bone as easily as scissors through paper.

He didn't shed the shadows enveloping him as he crossed the room with so much speed the creature only gained a few inches on her before he was almost on it. Leaping onto the bed, he closed the distance between himself and the beast.

With the shadows still cloaking him, the creature couldn't see him coming, but the bedsprings creaked, and the bed shifted beneath his weight. The strange, free-floating head turned toward him a second before he crashed into it.

That was when he proved it wasn't some floating, unknown creature. It was a living, breathing immortal who would die.

∿

SAHIRA WOKE with a gasp as a loud bang resonated through the room and something metal clattered against the wood. She bolted upright in time to see the fingers stretching toward her throat before jerking away.

She scrambled back across her bed as a shadowy figure hit the ground with a thud that rattled the floor and walls. At first, she had no idea why it was on the floor, thrashing like it was trying to kill someone while its grunts filled the room.

The lingering remnants of sleep dissipated, and she recalled the events of last night. Orin was in her room when she went to bed; he was cloaked in shadows and still was.

Heart racing, her breath came in rapid pants as she removed the dagger from beneath her pillow and leaned forward to see more of the fight. Because shadows blocked half the figure, Sahira could kind of tell where Orin was, but while he remained cloaked in shadows, she couldn't be certain.

It was tempting, but she couldn't try to kill whatever else was in the room with them without being sure where he was. She couldn't accidentally stab Orin… at least not this time.

Bracing herself on the edge of the bed, she kept her knees apart and the dagger's hilt clasped in both hands while waiting to end whoever had tormented her. She'd gladly plunge her blade through their black heart when she got the chance.

In the corner, almost hidden by shadows, she spotted the silver hilt of a small sword. She didn't know if it was Orin's or the intruder's.

Thuds, grunts, and a cry sounded as Orin unleashed a series of unseen blows on the thing. Or she assumed it was him doing the beating, as it didn't sound like him making all the noise.

Perched on the edge of the bed with dagger in hand, she thirsted for blood and answers as the shadows dissipated enough to reveal Orin. When he shifted to the side, Radagast's face appeared as whatever spell he'd used to cloak himself fell apart.

CHAPTER FORTY-FOUR

Sᴀʜɪʀᴀ ᴀʟᴍᴏsᴛ ᴛᴜᴍʙʟᴇᴅ off the bed when she spotted the refined warlock beneath Orin. She hadn't talked to him much since the night they all got drunk together, but they'd exchanged some pleasantries, and unlike some of the other warlocks and most of the witches, he *never* had a problem with her.

He'd *intervened* when Blair was being a complete bitch. He'd sat at a table and drank with her, all while plotting to *kill* her. And he'd most certainly been determined to kill her last night.

Betrayal twisted like a knife in her gut and sliced upward like it would cut her in half. She didn't know why she was so astounded or wounded by this; her own mother abandoned and turned her back on her after she was born.

However, seeing Radagast, a man who'd only ever been kind to her, lying on the floor, sucked the air from her lungs. *Son of a bitch!*

She had no idea how the warlock slipped past her protective barrier without setting it off; even if he was older and stronger than her, he wouldn't have known the right words to break through. He'd avoided the traps because he was wearing boots and could see them, but the spell stumped her.

Radagast clawed at Orin's face, pushing his chin upward as the heavier warlock sought to break free of his grip. Pulling his fist back, Orin delivered a bone-crunching blow to Radagast's too-perfect face.

Blood sprayed outward, but his newly flattened nose didn't break Radagast's hold on Orin. Sahira smiled as Orin repeatedly punched him until blood soaked Radagast's clothes and the floor.

The coppery tang on the air pricked her fangs as hunger hammered at her, but she wouldn't drink this foul creature's blood. She'd drink Orin's before she ever sank that low.

Her hand clenched on the dagger's hilt as she searched for an opening to ensure Radagast died. Unfortunately, she didn't get one, as they remained entangled in one another.

Planting his feet on the floor, Radagast lifted his hips and tried to throw Orin off. When that failed, the warlock, unable to get a good blow in against him, threw his head forward and smashed it into Orin's face.

The sickening bone-on-bone crunch reverberated around the room. Orin had to be seeing stars, but he didn't let up on his pummeling of Radagast.

The warlock hooked his fingers into Orin's shirt and yanked, pulling Orin over the top of him. Orin flipped over and started to twist away, but Radagast spun and landed on his chest.

For a disconcerting second, Orin's head and Radagast's hands sank into the floor and vanished. She blinked at what she was certain was a mirage, but it didn't dissipate as Orin's hands clawed at Radagast's face while the warlock clung to him.

When her eyes finally registered what they were seeing, she realized there was a hole in her floor. Radagast got around her protection spell because he'd found another way into her room.

Sahira shoved aside the horror curdling in her belly. There

was plenty of time to figure this out afterward, but with his head in a hole, Orin was at a disadvantage.

Radagast took full advantage of that as he lifted his hand and weaved his fingers to cast a spell.

No!

Leaping off the bed, Sahira closed the few feet separating them as she lifted the dagger above her before plunging it down, through Radagast's back and straight into his heart. The blade's tip burst out the other side of his chest and sliced open Orin's shirt.

Blood trickled from the scratch she'd left on his chest. Whereas her revulsion of Radagast had tamped down her ravenous appetite earlier, the scent of Orin's blood caused her fangs to lengthen and saliva to flood her mouth.

She staggered a couple of feet back and sank onto the bed as she strained to get her hunger under control.

~

WITH A GURGLED CRY, the warlock stiffened, his back arching as his body went still. A plume of blood erupted from his lips and sprayed Orin's face as Radagast's deep purple eyes bulged before falling to the dagger protruding from his heart.

The blade's tip scraped Orin's flesh and caused blood to bead on his chest. If the warlock fell forward, the dagger would pierce him too.

Hooking his legs around the back of Radagast, he lifted himself higher as he pulled himself from the hole and flipped the warlock over. The movement propelled the dagger farther through Radagast's heart.

Orin released the man and, rising, kicked the warlock over and ripped the dagger from his back. He twisted the silver metal before him while glancing from it to Sahira.

At first, she wouldn't look at him, but when she did, all the color was gone from her face. He'd seen her kill without remorse before, so driving a dagger through this asshole's heart shouldn't have upset her, but it had.

Then her gaze fell to his chest before darting away. Her knuckles turned white as she gripped the bed, and the truth hit him.

She's hungry. At any other time, he would have taken full advantage of it, but unfortunately, this wasn't the most opportune moment.

He held up the dagger. "This is fae metal."

It took a couple of seconds before she replied. "Of course it is. I wasn't going to take anything less than the best with me on my hunt for you."

He realized her fangs had descended when her words were a little slower in coming. "You could have accidentally stabbed me with it when you took him out."

He waved the dagger at the mark on his chest, directly over his heart. She regained more control over herself as her eyes shifted to him, and some color returned to her face.

"But I didn't," she said.

"You could have."

She shrugged. "Sometimes there are casualties in war. I can accept that."

The flippant answer, so close to one *he* would have given, irritated as much as amused him. "Funny."

The flash of her smile revealed her lengthened fangs before her attention shifted to Radagast. He lay, bleeding on the floor, with his hands clawing at his chest and his eyes rolling as gurgled sounds issued from his bloody lips.

The dagger could prove lethal to the warlock if he didn't get a chance to repair his wound. Fae metal to the heart wasn't an automatic death sentence for other immortals like it was to the fae.

Orin wasn't going to take the chance that Radagast might

heal himself. Belda probably would have preferred if they solved this in the pit, but he didn't think a pit fight was necessary when Radagast had entered Sahira's room and tried to kill her.

With the dagger in hand, he planted his foot on Radagast's chest. The warlock gazed at him from hooded eyes and a face splattered with blood.

When his fingers started to move in the rhythmic dance of a spell casting, Orin kicked his hand aside. "I don't think so." To ensure Radagast couldn't try anything else, he stepped on the bastard's wrist while grinning at him. "Did you really think you'd succeed in this?"

He must have, as he'd been ballsy enough to return the *night after* Orin interrupted his attempt to kill Sahira. The man had balls as big as mountains, something Orin normally admired, but not today.

He was going to cut off those balls.

CHAPTER FORTY-FIVE

RADAGAST DIDN'T REPLY, and Orin hadn't expected one. When the warlock tried to bring his free hand to his chest, Orin bent and snapped his wrist.

The blood pooling in his mouth choked Radagast's scream; it made Orin smile. Holding the dagger before him, he admired the expertly crafted blade as the candle's flame gleamed on its shiny surface and blood dripped down it.

"It's a magnificent piece, but I'd expect no less from the fae."

He bent and went to work carving Radagast's heart from his chest. While working, he ignored the man's whimpering cries and hummed a fae folk song.

Radagast's struggles didn't last as his eyes rolled back in his head, and Orin broke through his rib cage. When the hole was big enough, he reached in, tore out the warlock's still-beating heart, and dropped it on his belly.

There would be no coming back from that.

"Shouldn't we have asked him if anyone else was in on this?" Sahira inquired.

He expected to see revulsion when he looked at her, but his cruelty hadn't fazed her. Her fangs had retracted to the slightly longer, sharper points of all vampire fangs in their resting state.

Orin bent and wiped the blood from the blade on Radagast's pants. "Do you think he would have told us the truth?"

"No."

"Then why waste our time?"

She didn't answer as her gaze shifted to the hole in the floor. "Now I know how he got through my protection spells. I didn't realize there was an entrance in the *middle* of my room; I only secured the perimeter."

"I'm curious to know if anyone else is aware of it."

"I searched this entire room my first night here and never noticed it."

When they finished here, he'd tear his room apart again. He'd gone through it soon after moving in and then again after doing some redecorating, but now he would examine every floorboard on his hands and knees.

Sahira held her hand out to him. "My dagger."

Orin gave it to her before turning his attention back to Radagast. "Asshole."

"I should have known it was too good to be true when he was kind to me."

"You're not to blame for this."

"I know, but I should have seen it coming."

She rose and walked over to the opening in the floor. She knelt beside it while he grasped Radagast's ankles and dragged him farther away from the hole.

"What do you see?" he asked.

"Stairs."

Before he could question her further, she stretched out her leg, stepped onto something, and disappeared into the opening. Orin walked over to the edge of the hole and peered into it.

The wooden slat Radagast removed to enter the room hung on hinges inside the pit. The hinges had no rust and looked brand-new; no wonder he never heard the thing open.

He'd expected wooden stairs, but these were made of stone. Chunks of rock were missing from several, but they were in good condition.

As he examined the stairs and the small stone space below, he decided Radagast didn't build it. The pub was designed around this.

Besides, Belda would have noticed him hacking away at stone and carving into her pub. She would have lost her shit... unless she knew he was doing it.

But he didn't think that was likely either. This wasn't Belda's or any other lycans' style. Emotions ruled them, and they went at things head-on. Plus, he didn't see her setting Sahira up like this.

The warlock hadn't struck him as the type to get his hands dirty with anything requiring hard labor. He'd intended to draw out his torture before finally ending it.

At the end of the stairs, he discovered Sahira standing in the shadows of the small square room. The glow from the candle above barely illuminated the space, but he saw enough to know it was empty.

Sahira ran her hands over the stone wall as she searched for something to reveal the entrance. Orin joined her, and after ten minutes, his fingers found a small divot in the wall.

He pushed on the divot, and with a click, a door swung open a few inches to reveal the space behind the pub. He gripped the thick stone door with a steel interior and pushed it out enough to step outside.

The closest building was the large storage barn fifty feet away. Morning was approaching, but everything remained dark, and since no homes were beyond the pub, no immortals were anywhere near.

Orin turned to examine the other side of the open doorway. On the inside, the door was stone, but the outside was the same wooden facade as the pub.

"Can you close the door?" he asked her.

She stepped outside and swung it shut. He should have told her to keep it open, but if Radagast had gotten inside, they could too. They stood side by side, studying the wall, but he couldn't see any difference between the closed door and the pub wall.

"There's no difference," she murmured.

"If I didn't know it was there, I would never know it was. Whoever built this did a fantastic job."

"Yippy for me."

"Come on; I have plans for our friend."

It took some time, but Sahira found the small knot in the wood that was a button. The door swung silently open, and they both entered the room again.

Once they were back in Sahira's room, Orin lifted Radagast's heart before slinging the warlock over his shoulder. He carried the man downstairs and dropped his body on the table with a loud bang. The table rattled but remained firm beneath Radagast's limp body.

He went to the storage area behind the bar, found a piece of rope, and returned as Sahira emerged with a bucket of water and cleaning supplies. She stopped to watch as he tossed one end of the rope over a beam and pulled it down.

He wrapped that end around Radagast's throat, shoved his heart into his mouth, and lifted the asshole until his toes dangled above the table. He made sure Radagast's heart and the giant hole in his chest were clearly visible.

"Belda won't be happy when she sees that," Sahira remarked.

"I don't care. There's a chance she knew about that entrance into your room, which means she kept this detail to herself when I told her something attacked you. Also, even if she didn't know, I *will* make it clear that no one is to fuck with *either* of us again."

Once he finished, he sat in one of the chairs and leaned back as he folded his hands and rested them on his belly. He plopped his feet on the table and tipped his chair back as he smiled at Radagast.

CHAPTER FORTY-SIX

BELDA WAS *NOT* THRILLED to discover Radagast's body hanging from one of her beams. She promised to exile Orin as he remained sitting in the chair, smiling and twirling his thumbs while listening to her rant.

The lycan's face got redder, her voice louder, and her eyes flashed silver as the wolf inside sought to break free. Belda would kill him, or the top of her head would blow off. Other immortals looked on in horror and disbelief as they crowded the doorway and spread around the room.

Belda's pack stood a few feet behind her, arms crossed over their chests. Like all lycans, they were tall, broad, and extremely powerful; they were also extremely intimidating, though Orin didn't think so.

Sahira looked from Belda to Orin and back again while Belda ranted. Only bats could probably hear some of the octaves the lycan hit.

And Orin never tried to defend himself. The entire time, he sat there with a smirk, and his eyebrows quirked in a way that only made him more handsome—something she hadn't believed possible.

When Belda finally calmed down enough to stop shouting, she pointed at Boris and some of her pack. "Take him out of here. He's no longer welcome in this town."

Orin rocked back in his chair but didn't look fazed when a couple of the lycans started toward him. When they were only a few feet away, Orin spoke.

"If any of you touch me, I'll string you up like Radagast, but I'll hang you by your balls and shove your cock in your mouth. You won't be dead when it happens either."

"Are you threatening me?" Boris growled.

"It's more like a promise, but you can call it a threat if it helps you sleep at night."

"Fuck you, fae."

Orin ignored him as he focused on Belda. "We have to talk… alone."

"I'm not—"

"If you want to know what happened here, and you do, you'll send them out so we can talk. If you still think I didn't have a good reason to kill him, I'll leave and never return afterward."

Belda looked from him to Sahira and back again. She jerked her head at one of the lycans, who gave her a disgruntled look before retreating to the door.

"Do you want me to stay?" Boris asked.

"No," Orin answered.

"I don't take orders from you."

Orin and Belda locked gazes for a minute before she turned to her beta. "Get everyone else out of here. I'll join you soon."

"I don't trust him."

"Neither do I, but he won't attack me."

"No, I won't," Orin said.

"You better not be fucking with me on this, Orin," Belda told him.

"I would never."

Boris ushered the rest of the immortals out and closed the door behind him. When a hush descended over the pub, Orin set his feet down and rose.

"I have something to show you," he said.

He didn't wait to see if Belda was following him before climbing the stairs. Sahira attributed that to his royal heritage. As a prince, he was used to saying something and having others obey him.

As an alpha lycan unused to obeying anyone, Belda hesitated, but her curiosity won out, and she followed him upstairs. Sahira trailed after her.

She'd brought cleaning supplies up but hadn't cleaned yet. Orin had told her to leave the mess so Belda could see the full extent of what happened here.

The lycan paused in the doorway as she gawked at the blood splatters. She pointed to the hole in the floor. "What is that?"

"A trapdoor," Orin stated.

"Did *you* do that?"

"No. I was wondering if *you* did."

Belda glowered at him. "No."

"Did you know about it?"

"No."

"Radagast did."

Belda's brown eyes narrowed on him. "What happened?"

Orin filled Belda in on the events of last night. When he finished, Sahira took over and explained what had happened over the past week. When she pulled down the collar of her shirt to reveal the bruises and welts, Belda's jaw clenched, but she didn't say anything.

"Orin told me something attacked you, but I wasn't expecting anything like this," Belda murmured.

"What were you expecting?" Orin asked.

"A spell from the witches or something similar. I couldn't do anything without proof it was them and figured they'd leave you alone after Orin interfered, but...."

"Radagast was too arrogant for that. He believed I wouldn't interfere again, or he could kill us both."

"Yes." She pinned Sahira with her intense gaze. "Do you think the other witches are in on this?"

"I don't know. When I believed they were sending something into my room and somehow bypassing my protection spell, I was sure there had to be at least a dozen involved, but Radagast didn't need anyone else for this. It wouldn't have taken much power for him to mask himself as that shadowy creature."

A muscle twitched in Belda's cheek as she studied her before striding forward and vanishing downstairs to the room below. Orin and Sahira exchanged looks, but neither followed her; she returned a minute later.

"Radagast stayed in this room when he first arrived," Belda said as she pulled the trapdoor into place. "It was once mine, too, but I never knew that was there."

"He must have found it somehow," Sahira said.

Belda stepped back to examine the floor now that the trapdoor was secured. It fit so perfectly into place that Sahira couldn't see a difference in the floor panels.

Whoever designed this did a spectacular job. Her brother, a man who loved to build tunnels and secret entrances, would have hammered them with questions about their technique.

"It's impossible to see," Orin said.

"So it is," Belda murmured. "Okay, so we have some cleaning to do, and you're going to cut that asshole down. Get him *out* of my pub. No one can know about this trapdoor or the other entrance; I won't have immortals tromping in and out of *my* pub when I don't know about it. We'll tell them he came in through the back door and attacked you last night. They don't have to know it's been happening for a week."

"What if the other witches and warlocks already know about it?" Sahira asked.

"It's possible," Orin said, "but I don't think he told them. This was his secret space, one he discovered when he lived here, and one he kept to himself because it would have made him feel superior."

"I agree," Belda said. "But in case we're wrong, can you put a spell on the outside door that would alert me to someone entering, even if I'm not here?"

"I can make it so an alarm sounds, but it would alert the whole town."

"Any other options? I don't want anyone else knowing about this."

Sahira believed her when she said she didn't know about the trapdoor; she'd been shocked to see it and wanted to cover it up. Besides, Belda had no reason to lie about this. She was determined to keep this town as peaceful and fair as possible and had done an amazing job.

"No, but I can make it so an alarm goes off in this room. I can keep it quiet enough that no one will hear it below; if it goes off, I can tell you about it, and if I move out, you can come up and check it daily."

"You're going to stay in this room?" Orin asked.

"The devil you know," Sahira said. "All the rooms could have something like this."

"That's doubtful," Belda said. "There's not much empty space in this pub."

"Did you think there was any before this?"

"No," she admitted.

"Now that I know it's there, I can set a proper protection spell and an alarm on the outer door. I'd feel safer here than anywhere else."

"Understandable."

"There will be those who won't believe the story about Radagast breaking in to attack me," Sahira said. "Mainly the other witches and warlocks."

"At least now they'll have a *real* reason to dislike or distrust you."

And I have one more reason to get out of this town.

CHAPTER FORTY-SEVEN

ORIN STOOD behind Sahira as she sat in watchful silence while the witches and warlocks stormed the pub to demand answers about Radagast. Belda wanted her to stay in her room until it blew over a little, but Sahira refused to retreat.

Instead, she sat with her hands in her lap, her shoulders back, and her chin held high. The marks on her neck were on full display, and her face was blank as the witches and warlocks accused her of murdering Radagast.

After half an hour, Zeth slipped inside the pub and strode over to join her at the table. Orin almost told him to get out, but he bit the words back. Sahira needed all the support she could get right now.

The witches and warlocks had to see Sahira had more than him, Belda, and the pack on her side. Over time, some vampires, drawn by the commotion and the rumors running through town, braved the sun with blankets over their heads as they bounded into the pub.

Many shook the blankets off without harm, and a couple came in with their fingers or feet smoking. Others soon smothered their tiny fires.

At first, they hung off to the side, listening as the witches and warlocks demanded justice while gathering the details. Eventually, a few of them broke away to stand behind Sahira.

The witch Elsa also ducked into the building. She glanced around before giving a small wave to Sahira and vanishing out the door again.

After an hour of listening to the witches and warlocks whine like spoiled children denied a toy, Orin had enough. "I'm the one who cut out his heart, so I'm the one who killed him. If you'd like to resolve this issue, I'll gladly meet any of you in the pit."

Not surprisingly, no one took him up on his offer.

When they demanded to know if Belda would do something about his breaking the rules and killing outside of the pit, Belda told them, "Radagast broke into *my* pub and into *her* room, where he attacked her. *He's* the one who broke the rules by not taking it to the pit. Justice has been served."

"Justice would have been served if *she* had been the one to kill him. Instead—" Carmella smiled smugly at him before shifting her attention back to Belda. "—*Orin* did it. He wasn't the one under attack."

"He had every right to defend a member of his family; you all would have done the same," Belda said.

"They're not family," a witch grumbled.

"Not by blood, but the marriage of our family members will unite us as such," Orin said. "And I protect mine."

The witches and warlocks crowding the pub weren't thrilled to hear this. If they decided to go against the rules and come after him, he'd have a problem defending himself against that amount of power, but he wouldn't be alone.

Belda and her pack weren't about to let that happen, and a growing number of vamps were gathering behind Sahira. They also had the demon.

The witches and warlocks were powerful, but they'd have a

bitch of a time against so many, and Orin would ensure they lost. And when they did, he'd slaughter every one of them.

They were a threat that had to be eradicated before they tried to overrun Belda's hold on this place. Until Radagast decided to be a complete douche, there was no reason to question the ways of this realm.

A few immortals had balked against Belda's rules when they arrived and paid for it, but everyone else accepted them. What else was there to do? And things ran smoothly, so why change it?

Now the witches and warlocks believed they had a reason to change it; they saw themselves as the wronged party, though Sahira's throat clearly bore the marks of a coward. It took some time, but eventually, the calls for vengeance subsided.

Some witches and warlocks continued to glower at him and Sahira, but most retreated. When they did, the vampires also began to disperse.

A few of them clasped Sahira's shoulder as they walked out the door. Ahmar, who had become the unofficial leader of the vamps—a ruler wasn't something they typically had, but they'd grouped together to keep themselves safer from the witches and warlocks here—rested his hand on her.

"You let us know if they bother you again; you're part of us too," Ahmar said.

Sahira rested her hand over his. "Thank you."

Ahmar squeezed her shoulder before leaving the pub. Orin didn't like all these men suddenly paying more attention to her, but he was grateful for the help against the hex-casting crowd.

This support for Sahira would help keep the witches and warlocks in check. They wanted revenge for their friend, but none were stupid or brave enough to risk their lives for it… yet.

Things were about to become much more tense and unpleasant in this realm.

CHAPTER FORTY-EIGHT

As the night progressed, Sahira finally relaxed enough to talk with Zeth. Orin couldn't hear what they said as they sat with their heads close together, but after a while, Zeth patted her hand, and she rose.

Orin kept his eyes on her until she was securely in her room with the door locked. Things remained quiet as the night dragged on, and eventually Belda kicked everyone out for closing.

After the last one left, Orin turned off the lights as he relished the familiar hush that descended on the pub. This was his favorite time of night.

He climbed the stairs to his room and paused outside Sahira's door when he saw the light filtering out from beneath it. He hesitated before knocking, but the light wouldn't be so bright if she were asleep.

However, someone had tried to murder her this week; she probably preferred to sleep with a lot of candles lit. He listened for any sound coming from within but heard nothing; if she was asleep, he hadn't woken her.

He was about to retreat when the door opened to reveal Sahira in a dark green nightgown that covered her feet and grazed the floor a little. Her thick mahogany hair tumbled around her shoulders as she stared at him from eyes still rimmed with dark circles, but she hadn't been sleeping.

He'd never seen her with her hair down before; his fingers twitched with the sudden urge to touch its shiny waves. It was as soft as it looked; he was sure of it.

Does she know how beautiful she is? He had no idea where the thought came from or the tenderness accompanying it.

Of course he recognized beauty in women; he'd fucked some of the most gorgeous women in all the realms, but he'd never really taken the time to notice.

Now, he realized it was more than her striking features and gorgeous eyes; it was also her unwavering strength. She refused to hide when Belda asked her to and when she had every right to retreat from the world—she wouldn't bend to the witches' and warlocks' wrath.

She also defended those she loved with everything she had. She was proud, courageous, and loyal.

He highly respected those traits in others even if, like with her, they went against what he was determined to have—*her*.

His gaze roamed over her body, but the baggy gown hid most of her curves. He could still picture them, though, and his shaft hardened as the images flooded his mind. Now that she looked better and less shell-shocked, she was fair game again.

Orin leaned against the doorframe as he crossed his arms over his chest. "Are you sure you want to stay in this room? I spent a lot of time today looking for possible other dead spaces in this building that could hide another secret passage. There aren't any."

"I'm still not taking any chances. I have protective spells in place, and now that I know what to focus on, they'll work."

Looking over her shoulder, he spotted books lying on the trapdoor; she'd also established a backup alarm system. No one would get in here again without her knowing.

"Did you get everything cleaned up?" he asked.

It was a dumb question considering he didn't see any blood on the floor and the furniture was back where it belonged, but he wasn't ready for bed yet and enjoyed looking at her. This image would serve him well when he was jerking off later, something he was growing increasingly tired of doing.

Something had to break between them soon.

"I did. It gave me far more laundry than I wanted. I've been putting off doing it, but I'll have to go to the river and do some washing tomorrow."

"I haven't been in a while either. I'll go with you."

She gave him a disbelieving look. "I can go alone."

"You can, but I have a whole basketful to do too. Besides, it's probably best if you don't go alone anywhere so secluded for at least a little while."

Her jaw tightened, and her eyes sparked with anger, but she didn't protest his words. She might not like what he said, or the constraints on her, but it was the truth.

The witches and warlocks had always looked down on her and liked her less now. Sure, she had other immortals to help keep her safe, but that wouldn't do her any good if she went to the river alone and they sought revenge.

He couldn't help her if she was dead.

"But by the time I get done at the library tomorrow, you'll have to be on the bar," she said.

"Tomorrow is my day off. I'll meet you at the library when your shift ends."

Before she could protest, he unfolded himself from the door and rose to his full height. "Good night, Sahira."

He started to walk away, but her next words stopped him. "Orin." He turned back as she stepped into the doorway. "Thank you for helping me last night."

"How much did you *hate* saying that?"

She scowled at him. "A lot more now."

Orin grinned as he waved and walked a few steps backward before turning and retreating into his room. He shouldn't care what happened to the witch—she was strong enough to fight her own battles—but he didn't like bullies, and that's what the witches and warlocks in this realm had become.

He couldn't let her go anywhere she might be vulnerable to them, at least not for a little while. Eventually, things would settle down again, but he'd never trust them around her.

He kept telling himself he only cared because they would technically be family soon, and Lexi would have a dragon fry his ass if something happened to her aunt, but that wasn't entirely true.

Truth be told, he'd grown to like Sahira a little, and there were so few immortals he liked. He didn't want to see something happen to one of them.

Besides, it wouldn't be any fun if she died before he got the chance to fuck her.

CHAPTER FORTY-NINE

SHE WASN'T EXPECTING Orin to show up, and she definitely wasn't expecting him to arrive with a laundry basket tucked under his arm. As he sauntered down the street, nodding greetings to some and grinning at any witches and warlocks he passed, she couldn't help admiring the confidence he exuded, even if his arrogant attitude often grated on *all* her nerves.

She also couldn't stop admiring how the dark fae's green pants hugged his thighs and revealed an enticing bulge. Shifting her gaze away didn't help, as she was confronted with the carved muscles in the forearms bared by his black tunic.

She'd never known arms could be so hot and resisted fanning herself when he waved at a witch. Hunger had become an ever-increasing, festering part of her, but he remained unfazed. He still looked great even if what he said about not being with other women since her arrival was true.

Hell, he had a *spring* in his step. He looked carefree, and she felt like someone had settled the world onto her shoulders and told her to carry it.

Maybe he'd lost a couple of pounds, and if she looked closely, she could see it in his face, but he didn't look like he was about to jump on the next woman and start screwing her. She was getting close to a point where she might jump on someone and start feeding on them.

Tugging at the collar of her shirt, she tried to deny that she was heading toward desperate times as she turned her gaze to the gardens, but it was true. Food had stopped being enough to keep her sated; she required blood, and soon.

Tearing her gaze away from the gardens, she focused on Orin again. She hadn't expected to see him carrying a laundry basket, never mind *washing* the clothes in it.

Then a sinking feeling settled in her stomach as he reached the porch steps. Resting his foot on the first stair, he gave a small bow and waved his hand elegantly at her. The man was in far better spirits than her.

"Good afternoon, witch."

"I'm not washing your laundry for you."

He straightened up as his head tilted to the side. "You don't think I can do it myself?"

"You definitely can, but are you going to?"

"Of course. Come on now, cranky pants, let's clean us some clothes."

Unsure of how to react to his playful demeanor, and more than a little convinced he would try to get her to wash his clothes, she lifted her basket from where she'd set it beside her. She eyed him warily as she walked down the stairs to join him.

He was still smiling as he sauntered behind the library with her at his side. She couldn't stop staring at him as she tried to figure out his game.

"How was your day?" he asked.

"Fine. Yours?"

"Great."

Sahira rolled her eyes as they walked around a home where the backyard ended on a hill. The hill was mostly rocky, but dirt kicked out from beneath her feet as the ground shifted while she descended.

Altering her hold on the basket, she rested her fingertips on the ground to help keep her balance on the steep hill. Beneath her hand, the dirt pulsed with the life flowing through it; its presence helped soothe her.

"The ground here feels different than other outer realms," she murmured.

Orin glanced back at her. "Why is that?"

"In other outer realms, there's not a lot of life in the earth, and sometimes, there's not *any,* but there is here."

"Which is why they can grow crops and keep livestock alive."

"Which is also why it's not really an outer realm."

"What is it, then?"

When they made it to the bottom of the hill, Sahira surveyed the rocky, sandy land with all its many surprises. "I have no idea."

She hated admitting that. She'd been here long enough that she should have discovered some answers, but all she had were more questions.

"Perhaps this is the way this realm is, and we're seeking answers that aren't there," Orin suggested.

"Maybe."

"You don't want to believe it?"

"I don't like not having answers."

"But that is your answer. It's just not the one you expected."

Her grip on the basket tightened, and she met his steady gaze. "Are you beginning to think we'll never escape?"

"Fuck no. One way or another, I'm getting out of here."

Sahira didn't reply as they crossed more rocky terrain, but after a hundred feet, dozens of trees started springing up, and the inhospitable earth gave way to tall, thick grass that brushed her waist.

Grass! She hadn't realized how much she missed live plants and color until she stood amongst the green grass. *This* was where Zeth came for food for the animals.

She stopped walking and closed her eyes to listen as the wind soughed through the tall blades. They brushed against her skin in the most delightful ways.

When she opened her eyes again, Orin had stopped walking. He studied her with his head tilted to the side again. All his carefreeness had vanished; his eyes gleamed with something she didn't understand, but the set of his jaw and the tenseness of his face finally revealed his hunger.

And it was directed at her. It should be illegal for any man to look at a woman like that, never mind one as handsome as him. Sahira's heart slammed against her ribs as her mouth went dry and unexpected desire bloomed in her belly.

Sahira gulped and straightened her shoulders before striding forward again. She was here to wash clothes, and that was *all*.

She told herself this, but that look had awakened another hunger inside her. It was one she'd have to keep under control... somehow.

CHAPTER FIFTY

HER FINGERS BRUSHED one of the branches on the trees, and she felt a small stream of life flowing through their leafless limbs. She didn't know if it was from the tree or the earth it was rooted in.

The trees weren't tall. Most were only five or six feet, but some were only three or four. Their branches didn't stretch to the sky but bent toward the ground like a weeping variety. Their roots ran above the ground, creating a tripping hazard in the thick grass.

"If Lexi was here, she might be able to wake them," Orin said.

The mention of her niece was an unexpected knife to Sahira's chest. For a minute, the reminder of her family nearly brought her to her knees as she stopped breathing.

Since arriving here, she hadn't allowed herself to focus too much on Del or Lexi. She couldn't think about how they were doing, fear they might be in trouble, or let herself miss them.

If she did, she'd realize there was a chance she'd lost them forever. She might start sobbing and never stop. But his casual

244 BRENDA K DAVIES

reminder of all she was missing was so unexpected she hadn't prepared for the blow of grief.

"Are you okay?"

Sahira couldn't respond as she tried to breathe through her sorrow. Eventually, she felt strong enough to meet Orin's curious stare, but more than curiosity shone in his crow-black eyes...

So did *concern.*

Is it real? And that was the question. Even after he helped her with Radagast, it was *always* the question with him.

He'd told her that she was nothing more than a game, one he intended to win, so she had to question *everything* he did. She hated this whole dynamic between them. Not being able to trust him sucked.

"I'm fine," she said.

"You miss her."

"Of course I do; don't you miss your family?"

"I do."

Though he played many games, that was true. He was... complicated, to say the least.

"Why did you fight against your father and brothers in the war?"

She hadn't expected to ask that question; she was curious, of course, but it had popped out before she thought of voicing it. When Orin started walking again, she fell into step beside him.

Careful to avoid the roots she could barely see through the grass, Sahira tried not to faceplant as she waited for an answer she doubted was coming. He surprised her when he replied.

"Because we needed to make a stand against the Lord."

"But Cole, Brokk, and your father were secretly fighting against him; I now know Del was too."

"That wasn't enough for me."

"Is anything?"

He stopped walking and tilted his head in that cute yet soul-penetrating way he had of studying her. It was as if he somehow saw more of her than anyone else, but that couldn't be possible.

"Not yet."

With that, he started walking again. She stared after him before following; she'd never been curious to learn more about Orin, but she was suddenly fascinated by this gorgeous, enigmatic, exasperating, and mostly soulless man.

"That must be a difficult way to live," she said.

"I've enjoyed it for the past six hundred and thirty-seven years."

"Do you ever plan to settle down?"

"And what? Farm in the Gloaming? Raise a family? Build a house and live in one place? Do you honestly see me doing anything so mundane?"

"You don't have to farm or raise a family, but you could stay closer to yours for a change."

"I have stayed closer to them since we came back into contact with each other. I wouldn't be here if it wasn't for trying and failing to find the crudue vine."

"Neither would I," she muttered.

"What about you, Sahira? Do you have grand plans of settling into a mundane life with babes clinging to your skirts and boredom your constant companion?"

"I'm sure it's not as awful as you think. Cole's happy to have settled down."

"Cole's always been the more responsible one; that's not my life."

She couldn't argue with him.

"So, do you have plans for babies and a husband?" he asked.

She couldn't be sure but believed she detected a slight edge to his voice. It had to be her imagination, as there was no reason for it to be there.

"My only goal is to return to my family. After that, I'll see where the realms and life take me. Once Lexi and Cole establish a firm hold over the realms, there will always be those who will seek to take it from them."

"Too true."

The sound of running water caught Sahira's attention, and she smiled at the familiar, cherished ripple of water over rocks. It had been far too long since she heard the calming, musical rhythm.

"It's not completely awful here," she said.

"The sound of running water and grass makes you suddenly like this place?"

"No, the life, the rhythm, and the stark beauty make me like this place. If we weren't stuck here, it would be a great place to explore."

"But we are stuck."

CHAPTER FIFTY-ONE

THE WITCH PERPLEXED HIM. The serene look on her face as she closed her eyes and inhaled was captivating.

"It's not completely awful," she murmured.

"It's not," he agreed, although he loathed everything about this place.

When she opened her eyes and their gazes met again, confusion emanated from her, but she couldn't be more confused than him. He'd bet she was a lot *less* confused than him.

Cursing himself and her, he turned on his heel and stomped through the trees to the stream. He'd been in a good mood earlier; irritating every witch and warlock he encountered was great fun.

That good mood was gone. In its place was a whole lot of pissed off. He didn't know why, but he did know it was the witch's fault.

Except he couldn't blame her when all she'd done was find some joy in this soul-sucking, bleak realm.

When he got to the river, he set his basket down and leaned back on his heels to study the water cutting through the rocks, trees, and grass. He supposed it was nice in a *look at me, I'm so pretty while you're stuck here and rotting* way.

If he could punch a river in the face, he'd punch this one.

The water disappeared around a bend a hundred feet to his left and only became visible fifty feet to his right. From experience, he knew it ran behind the pub and out into the Barren Lands.

He'd never followed it; he supposed he should have, but Belda once told him that she followed it, and a few hundred feet from the town, it vanished into a mountain. She never found it again.

Red-and-black rocks jetted up from the water flowing over them. The flow created small rapids in some spots, while in others, it was smooth as glass.

Some tree roots had been exposed and jutted into the water. Their branches created ripples from where they dipped to kiss the surface.

Occasionally a broken-off tree root or stick would float by, but no leaves or other debris marred the water. Because the riverbed's rocks were black-and-red, the water appeared dirty, but from previous visits, he knew it was crystal clear.

Sahira set her basket beside his. "When humans invented the washing machine, I'd hoped to never wash clothes like this again."

"You're a witch; can't you magic them into washing themselves or something?"

"Do I look like a cartoon mouse?"

"What?"

Sahira waved a hand dismissively through the air. "Never mind. It's a human thing."

He knew a lot about the human race; he'd visited their realm before and after the Lord's war. They could be a lot of fun—and they were also batshit crazy. In all his visits, he'd never seen a cartoon mouse.

"So can you magic them or not?" he asked.

"Is that why you decided to do laundry with me?"

"No, I offered to do this so you wouldn't have to be alone in a secluded place. You magicking them clean would be a bonus. But I'm glad you continue to think the worst of me."

He hid a smirk when she winced a little. It was good to know he'd hit a tender spot with that observation.

"I... don't think the worst of you," she muttered.

"That didn't sound convincing."

She crossed her arms over her chest. "What would you think about someone who had made it clear you were nothing more than a game to them?"

"I'd think it was going to be a fun game."

"Liar."

He chuckled as a broken root drifted by. "So, yay or nay on the magic?"

"Nay. I won't abuse my powers in such a way."

"What abuse? You're saving time, and we're getting clean clothes. It sounds like a win-win to me."

"Sometimes, we have to get our hands dirty to appreciate the things we have."

"Sounds like some witchy, earthy bullshit to me."

"Witches are a part of the earth and the world. Our powers come from the elements, and we have to respect them. Abusing them can take us to a dark place. I'm never going there."

"I'd certainly enjoy a trip on the dark side."

"Good thing you're not a witch, then."

"Having a little magic laundry won't turn you into an evil witch."

As he'd known she would, she bent and lifted the bar of soap from where it sat on a shirt in her basket. With her toe, she nudged the basket closer to the shore.

"Get to work," she told him.

"You're no fun."

When she gave him a mischievous smile, everything in him tensed as his body tingled with awareness. He was ravenous, and she was a delectable fruit that refused to be plucked.

It had to be soon, or his hunger would win, and he'd have to find someone else. He wouldn't give up on her after, but he'd consider it a bit of a personal loss, and he didn't lose. *Nope, it's never going to happen. She'll cave first.*

With that thought firmly in mind, he joined her at the river's edge. They didn't speak as they scrubbed their clothes with soap and beat them against the rocks jutting out of the water.

CHAPTER FIFTY-TWO

SAHIRA WORE a resolute expression and didn't complain, but the set of her jaw told Orin how much she disliked doing this. It served her right for not magically washing their clothes.

They could be lying on the riverbank, soaking up the sun, while watching their clothes wash themselves. Instead, his magnificent hands were getting pruned.

After about twenty minutes, she spoke again. "I didn't expect you to know how to do this."

"Why's that?"

"Because you're a dark fae prince who I'm sure never worked a day in your life. You grew up having servants do this for you."

"You don't consider training for war, and fighting in wars, work?"

"It is, but not the domestic kind and certainly not the kind royalty does. Even before the Lord attacked the human realm, when I had a working washer and dryer and all the electricity required to run it, I still hated doing laundry, but I didn't have servants to do it for me. I doubt your father ever made you wash your clothes."

"It would mortify him to see any of his sons doing such a thing, but I became an outcast who hid away in a prison on an outer realm. I may have had followers, but I had to fend for myself. Besides, *no one* in this realm cares about my royalty status or that I could make them very wealthy if we ever escaped. They've all given up."

"True."

His dire words put a damper on the conversation, and they didn't speak again for a few more minutes. Eventually, his curiosity about her won out over the reminder that immortals who had been here far longer than them had given up hope of leaving.

"Did your father expect you to do your laundry?" he asked.

"From the time I was ten, I would take my laundry to the lake and wash it while he and Del did theirs."

"Del didn't try to make you do his laundry for him?"

She laughed as she used the back of her arm to wipe the sweat from her brow. "He tried but failed miserably." A far-off look came over her face as she gazed across the water. "We beat the shit out of each other that day."

"Siblings—you can't help loving them even when trying to kill them."

"So true. We didn't fight often. That was one of the rare times we did, and my father stopped it. He was determined that we get along and love each other."

"He succeeded."

"He did."

Orin draped his freshly rinsed shirt over a nearby tree. "How did you come to be, Sahira?"

He'd been curious about it since learning of her heritage but never asked. Most would probably consider it rude, but he didn't care.

∿

SAHIRA KEPT SCRUBBING her nightgown while refusing to look at him. She gave him credit, he'd asked what *no one* else had before, but she knew everyone who learned of her improbable existence was dying to learn the answer.

All the others whispered about it behind her back. They speculated, guessed, and made answers up, but none of them knew the truth.

How could they when she didn't either?

"Is it time someone explains to you what happens when a man and woman come together?" Sahira asked.

His eyebrow quirked in that endearing, annoyingly charming way he had. "Honestly, little witch, I'd love to hear you tell me every exquisite detail of exactly what happens when a man and woman come together."

Sahira rolled her eyes before dunking her nightgown in the river again. She'd been having an enjoyable afternoon with him. Now, she had to fight against her impulse to run away.

"But we both know that's not what I meant," he continued. "How did your mother and father end up together?"

CHAPTER FIFTY-THREE

WITH AN EXASPERATED SIGH, she turned to face him. "How did your mother and father get together?"

"That's easy. He was a dark fae king, and she's from a prominent dark fae family. He needed to feed, she was more than happy to screw him, and after a few months, I was conceived. According to them, I was planned. My father would never love or marry again but wanted more children.

"After my birth, she stayed in the palace for a while. As I got older, she decided to return to her home and family. She wanted to take me with her, but my father refused. He didn't think I was old enough to be away from his protection.

"Her family, *my* family, would have done everything to keep me safe, but the dark fae palace is a special place that protects its own. My father made sure I could take care of myself."

"Were you allowed to leave the palace?" The possibility of a child being locked away like that horrified her.

"Of course, but I always did so with an army of guards and usually Cole or my father until I was strong enough to protect myself. The Gloaming was a safe place, and few there would have tried to harm me, but there were always those who had an issue with my father, and the only way to hurt him was through his family. Also, strangers sometimes arrived, and my father could never truly know their intentions."

"What happened to your mother?"

"She came to visit often, and once I stopped aging and was strong enough to take on anyone who dared to attack me alone, I would visit her home and the rest of our family often. Sometimes I would spend weeks or months there before returning to the palace."

"Why would you stay away for so long?"

"I didn't have the same expectations on me as Cole. He was the firstborn and had it the worst, but there were still pressures and duties in the palace that I didn't feel like handling. I was content to let Cole deal with all the bullshit of being a dark fae prince.

"There was no guarantee that one of us could take over the realm if our father died, and I doubt few believed we could. Cole is only half dark fae, and I didn't take any of it seriously enough to try. None of my other brothers were interested in ever being king either… including Cole."

"He didn't have a choice."

"I know, but despite no one thinking any of us could one day rule, there was still a lot expected of us. We were all expected to attend commission meetings, and there were other prominent families, such as my mother's, who were always asking for something.

"There was also my father. He loved all my brothers and me equally. That might sound impossible, considering how much he loved Cole's mother, but he loved us all the same. We were all vastly different, and he cherished those differences but was also very demanding. He expected the best from us, and sometimes…."

He looked away as if he'd been about to say something he'd regret.

"Sometimes?" Sahira prodded.

Orin shrugged and dunked a pair of pants in the river. "Sometimes I needed a break. I found that with my mother and our family."

"What became of her?"

"She's still alive. When I decided to go against my father in the war, I tried to get her to leave the Gloaming before announcing my decision. She refused. It was her home, and she was right in believing my father wouldn't hold my choice against her, but I worried the Lord might.

"Thankfully, the Lord didn't go for her either. I'm unsure if he didn't have the time or was just waiting until he could level the entire Gloaming. She vacated the Gloaming during that attack, and for a while, I didn't know where she went, but I found her last month.

"She returned to the Gloaming when Cole started rebuilding it. She and her husband still don't have a home for them or my sister. They're traveling back and forth between the Gloaming and Dragonia now. I found them a home in Dragonia where they can stay until their new home in the Gloaming is built."

"You have a sister?"

She hadn't expected it, but he smiled at her as his eyes gleamed with what could only be called love. When he spoke of his brothers, it was obvious he loved them, but his whole face lit up at the mention of his sister. It was like looking at a completely different man.

"Her name's Elira. She's three years old and the cutest little bundle of trouble you'll ever meet."

Sahira didn't know what to say or make of this sudden, vibrant change in him. It warmed her heart in what could only be an extremely dangerous way.

"My mother and stepfather have been married for ten years now. He's a good man, makes her happy, and is a great father to

Elira. But he knows if he hurts either of them, I'll cut off his cock."

His switch from loving older brother to murderous stepson was far more expected than how his face lit up over his sister. "That knowledge would keep a lot of men in line."

Orin chuckled, but it died away as his attention shifted back to her. All signs of amusement and love were gone as he pinned her with his stare.

"So, witch, how did *you* come into being?"

CHAPTER FIFTY-FOUR

SAHIRA KEPT her attention on her shirt as she scrubbed it on one of the rocks. What he didn't understand was... "I don't know."

Water ran from the shirt to spill back into the stream as she held it over the water to examine it. She kept waiting for him to say something more, but he remained quiet, though she could feel his eyes on her. Unable to stand the silence, she continued.

"You've met my mother; you know we're not close. She'll never tell me what happened, and my father never did."

"Did you ask?"

"Once I realized how rare my heritage was, and how much some disliked me for it, I asked him. I had to know why some immortals hated me simply because I existed."

"People hate me because I exist."

"They hate you because they got to know you."

He slapped his hand over his chest as he smiled at her. It was so out of character for him, but she got the sense he was trying to make her feel better, which was even *more* out of character for him.

"Ouch. Straight to the heart, witch."

Sahira fought the smile tugging at her lips. "You're such an ass."

"So I've been told." And then he switched back to being serious. "What did your father say when you asked?"

"Sometimes in life, things happen that don't make sense."

"That they do, but a vampire's dick doesn't often fall into a witch's twat."

"You're disgusting."

But she wasn't as repulsed by him as she used to be. She was either getting used to his vulgarness or... Hecate forbid... she was starting to *like* this man.

"I've never denied it," Orin said. "So, what do you think happened between them?"

"I don't know. My father never married Del's mother. He said he cared for her but never spoke of love when it came to her, so I don't think they shared anything like that. They were raising Del together when she was killed by lycans when Del was two.

"Two years later, I was born. What occurred for that to happen is something I'll never know. Only one immortal can tell me, and she never will."

"Do you think it was rape?"

Sahira yanked her shirt from the water as she spun to face him. Beads of water sprayed off it as she turned, splattering his face. He wiped away the drops.

"My father was no saint, I'll never tell you he was, but he was a good man and loved Del and me. Saint or not, he would *never* do that!" she snapped.

Orin flicked away some of the beads of water as he studied her. She could tell he doubted her conviction, and she didn't care. Her father was a great man; he wouldn't have done something so awful to anyone.

"You didn't know my father. I did. Their relationship was consensual," she insisted.

"That's all you had to say. You didn't have to splash water all over me."

She scowled as she tried to ascertain whether he was telling the truth. When he said nothing more, she returned to scrubbing her shirt.

Not for the first time, she wished her father had told her what happened. She truly believed he hadn't hurt her mother, but...

"He hated talking about her," she admitted. "I think it was painful for him, even if he never admitted it. I think he cared about her."

Orin didn't say anything.

"She left me a book of shadows before she abandoned me. Other than life, it's all she ever gave me, but I was lucky enough to have my father and Del. They kept me safe and loved me. I had a wonderful childhood; I didn't know I was an oddity until I was older. They never treated me as such."

She felt Orin's gaze but didn't look at him again. She didn't have anything else to say on the subject.

"I met your mother. She's a bitch. You were better off without her."

Sahira didn't know how to reply, and they didn't speak again. When they finished washing their clothes, their baskets were full of damp clothes they'd hang on the line behind the pub.

Sahira settled her last pair of pants on the pile as Orin rose and extended his hand to her. Unsure of what to do, she stared at it.

She'd prefer not to touch the dark fae; he unnerved her but also made her feel more alive than anyone she'd ever met. His touch did things to her that were best avoided.

However, he'd helped destroy Radagast and come here to protect her; she couldn't be rude. Reluctantly, she slid her hand into his and almost yanked it away again when an electrical thrill ran through her.

She'd never admit it, but she loved the feel of his hand encircling hers. The strength of his fingers and the way they fit into hers made her knees weak.

Something flickered in his eyes; he'd felt it, too, or at least he'd felt *something* as his eyes held hers and his thumb caressed the back of her hand.

CHAPTER FIFTY-FIVE

A SHIVER RAN down Sahira's spine. It had been too many years since she'd had sex with anyone. She'd willingly locked herself away to keep Lexi safe and didn't regret it.

She wouldn't have anyone tromping through the manor with the last arach child underfoot. And while she could have traveled to a different realm and found someone to scratch her itch, she worried she wouldn't return in time to make Lexi's potion.

She was also concerned that something might happen to *her*. She was powerful, but they might attack her if she stumbled across the wrong immortals in another realm. Sex wasn't worth having her niece grow up without her.

They weren't related by blood, but the second Sahira saw the tiny bundle cradled in Del's arms, she loved Lexi. And Lexi had loved her deeply too. Because of that, she avoided anything that might be a risk to herself or that beautiful baby.

Besides, there were human men to keep her occupied. They were far less dangerous than any immortal. Sure, they weren't as satisfying as immortal men and struggled to keep up with her, but they were good in a pinch.

And Sahira had used human men a time or two, but it wasn't

that satisfying when she didn't enjoy it as much. So, it had been almost two decades since she last shared her bed with a man.

Now that things were calmer in Dragonia, she'd planned to change that but hadn't found the time. That's why Orin's touch was far more pleasing than it should have been and why she kept reacting to him this way... or at least that's what she told herself.

Deep down, she knew it was a lie. It was the man himself. She hated him... but she didn't, not anymore.

She still didn't trust him—she couldn't when he'd declared her a game—but he wasn't as repulsive to her as he once was. Maybe that was all part of his game too; she didn't have it in her to care anymore.

She was too tired and too famished to continue fighting *everything*. He'd become almost a friend in a realm where she didn't have many, and game or not, he'd helped her with Radagast and was here to help keep her safe.

With a gentle tug, he pulled her a little closer, and she didn't try to resist. His thumb stroking the back of her hand caused the hair on her arms to rise. Excitement pulsed through her veins, and her mouth went dry.

She was still sore and exhausted both emotionally and physically from Radagast's attack, but she couldn't tear her eyes away from his.

This is Orin. Get away from him!

The warning blared like a siren through her head, but she couldn't resist how amazing his touch felt. She'd never been with a dark fae in all her four hundred and fifty-three years, but she'd touched a few of them. She didn't recall anything like this happening with them; it would have been impossible to forget.

While her brain pummeled her with every reason why she shouldn't get any closer, her heart *yearned* for this connection with him. She could no more stop this than she could a runaway freight train.

A muscle twitched at the corner of Orin's clenched jaw. His arm slipped around her waist as he pulled her closer.

She opened her mouth to protest or moan as his chest pressed against hers, but no sound issued before his mouth descended with the ruthlessness of a conqueror who wouldn't be denied. And it was quite clear she was the conquest he sought.

When he released her hands, she planted her palms against his chest, but as her brain said to push him away, her fingers bit into his thick muscle. Like all pure dark fae, his build was slender, but every inch of him felt like chiseled rock.

He was so warm beneath her hands, so familiar yet unfamiliar. His heartbeat pounded in her ears as hunger tore through her belly like a knife through flesh.

She almost whimpered but restrained herself enough to keep that much of her dignity intact. She couldn't stop her fangs from descending.

She tasted blood when they scraped his bottom lip and nearly threw herself into his arms as that sweet ambrosia hit her. Orin's hand on her waist bunched in her shirt as he pulled it up until warm air brushed against the curve of her back.

The fresh air against her overheated flesh only made her desperate for more as his elegant fingers cupped her ass. Her breasts ached as an almost painful need spread between her thighs. His erection prodded her belly, and her shirt moved higher as she melted into his kiss.

Conquered.

She'd been conquered. And here, at this moment, she was okay with it.

CHAPTER FIFTY-SIX

SHE TASTED and smelled better than Orin imagined as her silken skin slid against his palms and her honeyed scent filled his nostrils. Hunger twisted in his gut and spread out through his limbs.

He'd been doing okay, surviving on food and nothing else, but his hunger had grown. Now, it was an undeniable, flaming-hot poker burrowing deeper into him.

He had to feed, and she was finally bending. The satisfaction he'd expected to experience over breaking her didn't come; it couldn't when she fit so perfectly in his arms and felt so good against him.

He hadn't expected this strange sensation of rightness, but had anyone's kiss ever tasted or felt this good? He tried to find an answer, but the feel of her had buried his past.

Gripping the backs of her legs, he was about to lift her, lower her to the soft riverbank, and sate himself between her pretty thighs when something crunched nearby. He was so determined to feed that he didn't acknowledge it until Sahira shoved against his chest and twisted her head away.

With the kiss broken, his lips found her neck as another crunch sounded. This time, the noise pierced the ravenous haze enshrouding him.

He was hungry, and someone had arrived to take away the feast he was about to enjoy.

The sound he issued wasn't something that came from him often, but his enemies heard it shortly before they died. Sahira's head, which had twisted toward the woods, turned back to him.

Her wide eyes met his as they stared at each other for a second before she pushed at him again, and he reluctantly released her. It was already too late to separate before someone saw them.

From amongst the deadened trees, Carmella stared at them with evident disgust. "Slumming it now, are you?"

When he stepped toward her, Sahira grasped his arm. "Not worth it," she whispered.

"But it is."

"It will only cause more problems for *me*."

Orin debated this before relaxing. She was right; even if he was the one who took Carmella to the pit, the witches and warlocks would blame her.

Besides, was he really considering a pit fight because of something Carmella *said*? Sure, it had been about Sahira, and he kind of admired the annoying, stubborn woman, but that was no reason to fight someone.

It's because you're starving, and she interrupted feeding time.

Yes, that was the *only* reason he was primed to kill.

Sahira's grip on his arm eased before she released him. Without acknowledging Carmella, she lifted her basket and walked into the trees.

Orin smiled as he lifted his basket and strolled toward the witch. "I've been with a lot of women, Carmella. So many I can't even begin to count them." Her head tipped back to look at him as he stopped before her. "But you're the only one I regret."

"I can say the same to you, Prince Orin."

"Stay away from her, or you'll be the next one hanging from a beam."

"You don't frighten me."

When he leaned a little closer, apprehension flashed through her eyes, and they flickered away before returning defiantly to his, but it was too late. "Yes, I do."

She stepped away and shifted her laundry basket so it was between them. "You do something to me, you risk the wrath of all the other witches and warlocks. You'll also turn Belda against you."

"See, here's the difference between us: when I say you and your little friends don't scare me, I mean it. You know better than to fuck with me, Carmella."

Orin waited for her to say something more, but she shifted her gaze to the river before walking away. He watched until she disappeared around a bend before focusing on the woods again.

He could catch up to Sahira but decided against it. Not only did he need a minute to control his lust and anger, but he also required time to think about what just happened between them.

Besides, she should be back by the library and safe in town by now. No one would bother her when she was out where everyone could see her. Plus, the sun was setting, so the vamps would be out soon; they would watch over her.

He'd expected the witch to be fiery and delectable, but he hadn't anticipated how she warmed his cold heart. He hadn't felt so detached while holding her.

His entire life had mostly been one of indifference to so many things. He'd only ever truly cared about his family; they were the only things that made him feel *something*.

But now the witch had made him feel something, too...

something more than famished and horny. Something more than a desire to screw and move on.

She'd awakened something inside him; he wasn't sure what it was, but it almost felt *good*.

And he didn't like it.

CHAPTER FIFTY-SEVEN

SAHIRA DIDN'T SEE much of Orin over the next three days, and she was fine with that... mostly. Not having to deal with the infuriating man, and *that kiss,* made it a little easier to get through every day, but her malnutrition was becoming a *big* issue.

She'd never gone this long without feeding before, and her body reminded her of that as her veins burned, her heart lumbered to pump, and every time she swallowed, it felt like she was eating glass. No matter how much water she consumed, she was constantly thirsty.

She was also always hot or freezing. Last night, she woke with her teeth chattering and soaked in sweat.

Her lack of blood was becoming a dire situation, but she hated asking Orin for anything, especially after that kiss. She mentally kicked herself for the thousandth time for letting it happen and enjoying it so much.

What were you thinking?

She hadn't been thinking, and *that* was the problem—well, at least she hadn't been thinking with her brain. Her body was the one running that show, and not very well.

She had no idea what Orin would say when she finally broke down and went to him for blood. Would he laugh at her or try to use it to his advantage?

Sahira shuddered but wasn't sure if it was because she was curious what that advantage would be... or because the idea terrified her.

And if she was honest with herself, it also intrigued her far more than she would have liked.

Closing her eyes, Sahira took a deep breath while trying to calm her heart's riotous beat. She didn't think a vampire could die from not feeding, but it sure felt like her heart would explode out of her chest, which would kill her.

Huffing and puffing far more than normal, she finished ascending the stairs to the second-floor library balcony. Eyeing one of the ladders going back and forth between the stacks, she questioned if it would be safe to climb it in her condition.

Falling from it wouldn't kill her, but the idea of passing out and crashing onto the floor below wasn't appealing. She'd require blood to help her heal afterward.

Bending, she rested her hands on her knees and inhaled a tremulous breath. She had no idea how she would get through her shift at the library and her following one in the gardens, but she had to do it.

After returning her clothes to the pub, she'd hung them on the line and went to find Belda. They'd discussed her options and decided she could have more supplies if she worked extra hours in the gardens.

After what happened with Radagast and that kiss, she couldn't stay in this town. She had to get out of here and this realm or she would die, and probably far earlier than she should.

It was only a matter of time before the witches and warlocks came after her again. With how she felt, if one of them came at her, she'd die before she could fight.

You have to feed.

She didn't like it, but she didn't have a choice. She was risking her life and making herself more susceptible to an attack by being stubborn.

She considered asking Zeth if she could feed from him, but after Radagast, she didn't trust anyone. She didn't trust Orin either, but at least he'd made his motives clear, and she didn't believe he'd do anything to put her life at risk.

After she finished here, she'd go to the gardens for a couple of hours, then talk to Orin. It was time, and she could feed without giving in to temptation.

Unbidden, the memory of the kiss she'd been trying to bury came rushing to the forefront. His hands burned into her skin as his tongue entwined with hers as if it were happening again.

This time, her heart wasn't racing from exertion but excitement as her fangs prickled and her body reacted as if he was truly touching her. Ducking her head, she strove to bury the memory and her body's intense reaction to it.

"Are you okay?"

Sahira looked up as Elsa strolled toward her with an armload of books tucked against her chest. The witch's pretty face scrunched with concern as she eyed Sahira.

"I'm fine," she managed to say.

Elsa didn't look convinced of this as her eyes roamed over Sahira. Sahira didn't know what to make of this woman; she was a witch but lived separately from the others and didn't belong to their coven.

She'd never been anything but nice to Sahira and was one of the few immortals who'd asked if she was okay after Radagast's attack. However, Radagast had always been kind to her, too... before he tried to kill her.

Elsa also worked in the gardens after her shift in the library. Sahira had no idea why and didn't ask; they talked about the plants and their care but nothing else.

She liked Elsa and wanted to trust her, but she couldn't. And that only made her hate this place more.

"Do you need a break?" Elsa inquired.

Sahira forced a smile she hoped didn't look as strained as it felt, especially since another one of those hot flashes was coming and sweat already beaded her forehead. "No, seriously, I'm okay."

Elsa didn't look convinced as she bit her bottom lip but eventually moved on. Taking a deep breath, Sahira ignored the sweat trickling down her nape as she gripped the ladder.

She rolled it down the bookshelves until she reached the section she sought. She made sure the books were tucked securely under her arm and was about to start climbing when, in the distance, a bell rang.

Sahira froze as the first clear ring echoed over the land. It reverberated around the walls as it announced the death approaching them.

Then, as the tolling of the bell faded into the distance, silence descended. At first, no one in the library moved, but the immortals below burst into action when the other bells started ringing.

They scrambled for the windows, and the metal shutters closed with a resounding bang that briefly drowned out the bells. Sahira released the ladder and stepped away as bars fell across the shutters, locking them securely in place.

Immortals scrambled away from the locked windows as a flurry of noise and motion came from the entrance. Others flooded through the archway and into the library as shouts came from the front door.

"Hurry!" Gromuck bellowed as more immortals poured into the library.

Light fae, dark fae, vampires covered in still-smoking blankets, lycans, dwarves, imps, and berserkers filled the space, along with witches, a warlock, and other assorted immortals.

She'd never seen the library so full, but they kept coming as they sought shelter amid one of the original buildings. Finally, the front door slammed shut with a bang.

A second later, something crashed off the side of the building and scratched across its surface. Something else skittered across the roof.

The hair on Sahira's nape rose. The Reaping was upon them.

Certain death had arrived.

CHAPTER FIFTY-EIGHT

ORIN SET the clean mug on the bar with a barely audible thud. Half the occupants of the packed pub spun to glower at him. A few feet away, Carmella shushed him but didn't tear her eyes away from the ceiling as dozens of scratchy feet scrambled across it.

He didn't point out that her shush was louder than he'd been. Speaking wasn't the best idea since everything had gone deathly silent following the toll of the bells, the rapid influx of immortals, and the shutters closing.

He'd never dealt with scarog beetles, but they supposedly had an insatiable thirst for blood and mandibles that ripped the flesh from their victims. He wasn't looking forward to this.

Were they all supposed to stand in the same spot until these things killed something and twenty-four hours passed?

That wasn't going to happen. It wasn't just him; most immortals in this room couldn't stay still for twenty-four hours, and that was *if* the scarogs killed someone in that time.

Judging by the number of immortals who flooded the pub at the tolling of the bells, he'd guess they'd packed all the original buildings, and most had gotten to safety. If that was the case, how did the scarogs finally kill someone?

He studied everyone crammed into the pub as he contemplated this. Did they eventually sacrifice someone to make the beetles leave, or were there a few who hadn't made it to safety and would get caught?

And if they sacrificed someone, what did that mean for Sahira? Some of the witches and warlocks had made it here, and he was sure some made it into the library too. She'd be the first one they sacrificed.

Orin's nostrils flared, and his chest constricted at the possibility. With the spike of irritation came a rolling wave of hunger. But then, everything made him ravenous lately.

He'd pushed himself to a breaking point. It had been a stupid thing to do, especially with The Reaping on the horizon, but he'd been so convinced she'd cave, and so determined to win, that he'd kept going until hunger had become his constant companion.

He was starting to see its effects in the shadows under his eyes and the gauntness of his cheeks. Clothes that used to fit him had to be belted into place.

And now, they were trapped in here. Orin scanned the crowd packed into the pub as he weighed his options. If they were in here too long, the mermaid and a couple of the lycans could be fun to revisit.

He hated that he would lose this part of his game, but it might have to happen. Until then, he would have to wait this out.

Gradually, the pub started coming back to life. No one spoke, but some of the occupants shuffled around as they found seats or consumed what remained of their drinks.

There weren't enough tables and chairs, so some settled against the wall. When a dwarf went to sit on the empty stool he usually occupied, Orin's dark look sent him slinking away. Whispers started through the crowd, but everyone remained mostly mute.

Belda looked at him and slid her finger across her throat. When he started working here, she told him that once The Reaping arrived, the drinks would end until it did.

She didn't want a bunch of drunk immortals crammed into her pub, and he didn't blame her. The last thing they needed was a fight breaking out, but they could always sacrifice the fighters and end The Reaping.

That sounded promising to him.

Belda had shown him the room of weapons in the basement, but the lycan hadn't made a move for them. He suspected she would wait until it was necessary before breaking those out.

Orin stepped out from behind the bar and settled onto the empty stool at the end. He stared at the shutters as he rested an elbow on the bar and tried to ignore the hunger pangs doing a number on his stomach.

Sahira must be experiencing the same thing, which meant she'd also probably weakened herself and was now trapped with immortals who would prefer to see her dead. He shouldn't give a shit—*she* was the one who'd done this to both of them—but he did care.

As much as she annoyed him, he didn't want anything bad to happen to the witch. Thankfully, he was shallow enough not to get too introspective about *why*.

He tapped his fingers on the bar as the feet scampered faster across the ceiling. As more of those things descended on the town, their wings created a buzz that set his teeth on edge. It had only been five minutes, and he already hated these beetles.

Their many legs scratching against the roof reminded him of skeletal fingers clawing at the insides of a coffin. Instead of trying to break free, these things were trying to enter the place they were determined to turn into *his* coffin.

That was *never* going to happen.

CHAPTER FIFTY-NINE

THE OCCUPANTS of the library had stopped resembling statues and come back to life as they carefully moved around. Gromuck left the main room and returned a few minutes later with some spears.

She handed one to Belda's beta, Boris, sitting in the corner, still reading through a book on the geography of the different realms. The lycan barely looked up before flipping the page.

Apparently, this wasn't his first Reaping, as he remained cool while others were crowding around Gromuck for weapons. She unceremoniously shoved five of them aside with one swipe of her arm.

They staggered back but didn't approach the orc again. Gromuck tossed a second spear to Elsa before looking up at Sahira and tapping another against the ground. She guessed that was her cue to get down and back to work.

Setting the books next to the ladder—she'd take care of them later—Sahira descended to claim the weapon. She didn't know how many Gromuck had, and given the number of immortals now filling the library, she'd take any weapon she could get.

Her dagger was strapped to her side like it was every day, but she'd never say no to more protection. Gromuck released the spear to her before thudding out of the room.

Two pixies flitted into the library. One left a silver trail behind her, while yellow followed the other. They settled onto a shelf and slid back until they nearly blended in with the books.

Hunger still thrummed through Sahira's veins, but she pushed it aside. She had to be at her absolute best to get through this, and she was determined to do that.

Cursing herself for letting things get this bad, she followed Elsa and Gromuck from the room. Before today, she had believed the threat Orin possessed was far more dangerous than the scarog beetles.

She'd been wrong. So very, very, *very* wrong.

A thick metal bar barricaded the front door. About thirty-five immortals had made it inside before it closed.

Gromuck and Elsa stood in front of an open door across the way. Immortals crowded around them as they tried to see what was inside, but Gromuck held them back.

Sahira pushed her way to the front of the crowd and stopped beside Elsa. She'd never seen this door open before but had been told it was a storage room full of food supplies and barrels of water.

More weapons were secured within, but Gromuck didn't take those out. On her second day here, Elsa informed her that those weapons would remain stored inside unless something major happened and the beetles somehow managed to penetrate the building.

It had never happened before, but there was a first time for everything, and they weren't taking any chances. They also weren't going to hand out weapons to a bunch of immortals confined in a small space; only the workers got those.

Thankfully, Gromuck was stronger and bigger than everyone else here, including the lycans. If they all decided to jump her at once, they'd take her down, but there was no reason for that.

And Sahira hoped things didn't get to a point where the other immortals might try something. So far, things had been well-ordered in this town, but situations like this brought out the worst in others.

Sahira's hand tensed around the spear as she met Elsa's gaze. The witch gave her a wan smile, but she sensed Elsa's unease as she looked over the crowd.

Gromuck removed a barrel and some glasses from the room. She set the glasses on a barrel with a spigot coming out the bottom.

The orc locked the storage room and made a show of putting the key around her neck; it hung from a thick chain. "Food later."

With that, Gromuck stomped back into the library. Sahira looked from the barrel to the locked door before also returning to the library.

Most of the immortals remained within. They settled on the floor, in the chairs, and browsed the shelves as they wandered the room. Boris remained at the table, engrossed in a book that would have put Sahira to sleep.

A small line was forming outside the bathroom, but at least they had one and they had supplies. That would keep everyone a lot calmer... or so she hoped.

Something crashed into the wall, and she nearly jumped out of her skin. A few other immortals released small squeaks and were startled, but most barely paid attention.

She hoped never to get that accustomed to this. Sahira gulped as something else bounced off the wall, and a beetle smashed into one of the shutters with enough force to rattle it.

Boris, never taking his eyes off the book, placed his hand against the shutter to stop the reverberations still rocking it. The walls rattled so much that something clattered to the floor.

A book must have fallen off a shelf or table, but the sound

sent the scarogs into a frenzy. Their wings hummed as they battered the walls with increased fervor.

The scarog's wings and feet scratched the walls and roof. Their feet clicked against the shutters as they sought some way to break in.

The interior walls are made of steel, she reminded herself. *They can't break through that.*

At least, she hoped they couldn't.

Sahira gripped her spear tighter as she stepped back. Everything in her screamed to run as her heart hammered, her palms grew sweaty, and adrenaline flooded her veins until she swayed from its rush.

She had to leave, but there was nowhere to go. They were trapped in this building and surrounded by creatures who would tear their skin off and devour every inch of them.

CHAPTER SIXTY

HER GRIP on the spear became slippery as the beetles scurried over and crashed into the building. More books rattled on their shelves, and another tumbled to the floor.

"Does this happen every time they come?" someone whispered.

"Yes," Gromuck grunted.

Something crashed off the wall and sounded like it would break the building. Sahira closed her eyes and counted to ten as she tried to control the panic spiraling higher inside her.

Focusing on Lexi and Del, she recalled how she loved standing in the doorway, watching them in their chairs, reading together in the library. When they played outside together, Lexi's laughter always made her smile when Del spun her in circles.

They were a small family, but love enveloped them and their home. She couldn't have asked for anything more from life, and she never did.

All Sahira wanted was to return to her brother and niece. She'd give anything to see them again, to feel their love, and hug them close. No matter what happened, she would survive this and escape this realm.

Tears burned her eyes, but she closed her eyes against shedding them. She would not cry in this place with those things crawling all over the building and witches and warlock here to witness her weakness.

Another bang sounded as something crashed onto the roof. Holding the spear against her chest, Sahira turned her back to the shelves and stepped into them so no one could attack her from behind.

The click of the beetles' feet, and maybe their antennae too, became louder as they swarmed the building like bees in a hive. When the building shuddered again, more books tumbled from the shelves to slam onto the floor.

The books on the second floor fared better than those on the first. But as the bangs shook more and more of them free from their secure places on the shelves, it was only a matter of time before more crashed.

Shit. Shit. Shit!

Elsa came to stand beside her. Her chocolate-brown hair hung in a braid over her shoulder, and her chestnut-colored eyes were full of concern.

"We can work together to enact a strong protection spell over this place," Elsa said.

Sahira glanced at where the three witches and one warlock stood near the front door. They'd grouped together away from the rest of the immortals.

"Don't you think it would be better if you worked with them?" Sahira asked.

"No."

Sahira glanced at the witches and warlock. All four were watching them. "They won't appreciate that."

"I'm not one of them."

Sahira wanted to believe that—Elsa had certainly worked to separate herself from them—but she was acutely aware that *nothing* in this realm was what it seemed.

Another loud bang rattled a dozen or so more books from the shelves.

A flurry of movement from the scarogs battering the walls and roof accompanied the books thudding against the floor. Every time some new sound came from inside, those things went crazy.

Sahira's heart hammered as the scarogs clambered and beat at the walls. If they could, they'd tear this place down around them, but it had held up for centuries against these things and would hopefully hold up for another year.

Elsa stepped closer to Sahira. "Look, I don't care what you are. We can work together to help ensure we *all* get out of this. A protective spell can help while everyone's inside."

She was right. Sahira rested her spear against the wall and leaned closer to Elsa.

The witch murmured a few words to her, and Sahira nodded. It wasn't the strongest protection spell, but without herbs, stones, or other ways of enhancing their magic, it would do.

Together, their hands moved as they recited the spell. Their fingers ebbed and flowed with the cadence of the words while the power swelled between them.

"Mother sun, father moon, we call you forth to lend your power and protect us during this dire hour."

When they finished casting the spell, power flowed from Sahira's fingertips. She could practically feel it dancing in the air as it weaved through the elements, solidifying and strengthening a protective bond around the building.

The spell laced around the edges of the building, climbed the walls, and spread across the ceiling. There were too many books for them to try casting a spell to keep them all in place; some of them would slip through.

In her mind's eye, all the colors it created swirled as they danced through the air. Pinks, oranges, yellows, and silvers were little starbursts illuminating the world around them.

Because they were the creators, only she and Elsa could see its power weaving around them, but the other witches and the warlock would sense it. The colors faded when the spell was firmly in place, but she felt its power pulsating around them.

"How long will that last?" one of the lycans whispered.

"At least a day," Sahira said. "Maybe longer. But don't open anything, and don't go outside."

The witches and warlock remained stone-faced where they stood by the door, but their disapproval radiated from them. They had to leave this building soon, but doing so meant someone had to die.

She couldn't stay in here with them.

"It sounds like it's calming down," an imp said.

"Always worse at night," Gromuck grunted.

Sahira repressed a shudder; how could it get any worse than this?

She learned they had a week's worth of supplies stashed in the library during her training. All the original buildings did.

But, no matter what, someone had to pay the ultimate price for this to end. Sahira tried not to think about that while she ignored the witches and warlock.

CHAPTER SIXTY-ONE

ORIN PROPPED his chin on his hand while studying the pub's occupants. Most remained quiet while some played cards, and others talked amongst themselves.

A few were not taking the stress of being locked down and the looming possibility of death well. They paced and sweated while their hands trembled. Others talked more loudly than they should, with faster voices than normal.

One of them was Carmella as she paced back and forth behind the bar. Another was a vampire who kept rising, then sitting, then rising again, only to sit without stepping away from his chair.

The third, and the one who concerned him most, was a berserker whose eyes kept rolling around the room as he paced to the door, turned, and stomped back the way he'd come. Every inch of him emanated malice.

"How long has he been here?" Orin asked Belda.

"About twenty years."

"Is he like this every time?"

"I don't know. This is the first time I've had the misfortune of being in lockdown with him."

"He looks about to explode. We might have to sacrifice him and shove him out the door."

"He's survived the last nineteen Reapings; he'll survive this one."

"I hope you're right, but if he decides to do something stupid, I'm shoving him out the door."

Belda scowled at him but didn't protest his statement.

"I'm not the only one watching him," Orin told her.

The berserker's irritating behavior had drawn the attention of many of the fifty-plus immortals in the pub. A few watched his every move with a calculating gleam in their eyes.

"We'll have a bigger problem if he starts a fight," Orin said.

"Then why don't you try to calm him down?"

"We both know I'm not the calming type. Besides, telling a berserker to relax would have the same effect as telling a woman to relax. I don't like playing with explosives."

And that was the kicker of it. If they tried to calm the berserker down, he'd most likely lose his shit, but if they kept letting him carry on like this, it could set off another immortal.

He had a feeling that, one way or another, things would get ugly.

～

ONLY A DIM GLOW illuminated the edges of the windows and the main door. With the shutters closed, it was impossible to tell if it was day or night, but the dwindling glow around them revealed night was coming.

And Gromuck had said things get worse at night.

Sahira settled with her back against a bookcase and a spear in hand while others scattered around the room. They all kept their backs to the walls and focus on the door or the covered windows.

Some had already fallen asleep, and a few read. Two lycans,

a vamp, a berserker, and a dwarf played cards at one of the tables.

Despite the constant noises of the scarogs and occasional falling book, they all relaxed a little. Sahira's shoulders were so stiff they hurt; the hunger had started creeping in again, and all the heartbeats surrounding her were annoying, never-ending drumbeats in her ears.

If the other occupants of this building had any idea how much her mouth watered at the prospect of their blood, they'd open the door and shove her out to keep themselves safe. They'd be right to do so.

It didn't help that she could still feel the witches and warlock staring at her. It wasn't as consistent as it was initially, but she felt it every time their eyes landed on her.

When she snapped, she'd eat one of them first. She almost smiled at the idea but was so famished that smiling wasn't possible.

Closing her eyes, Sahira kept her chin against her chest as she inhaled and exhaled. Those calming breaths weren't helping as much as they should.

If they were trapped here for a week, she had no doubt she'd lose it; her thirst wouldn't stay contained until then.

Take it one minute at a time.

But the seconds and the minutes kept getting longer; she was certain of it.

A resounding bang jerked her head up and doused her obsessive thoughts about blood as the building shook again.

More books clattered from the shelves. They created a cacophony that caused the beetles' wings to beat faster. Their feet scratched against the surface of the building with more speed as a loud hum reverberated through the air.

Then everything went quiet again.

Pages rustled as the readers returned to their books. Cards

landed on the table, but the sound of those things was much nicer than the noise the beetles created.

A few more minutes passed before a sudden shout pierced the room. The berserker jumped up, lifted the table, and flipped it over. The other occupants of the table all jumped to their feet.

"Asshole!" the berserker shouted.

In the blink of an eye, he leapt at a lycan who shifted into a wolf.

"Not here!" Gromuck bellowed as the lycan's jaw clamped down on the berserker's head.

Boris jumped up and ran toward the battle as the other lycans swarmed around the fight, seeking to protect their packmate. The sleeping immortals woke as anyone near the skirmish fled.

Elsa jumped to her feet, and though hunger had caused every muscle and bone in her body to ache, Sahira planted a hand on the ground and pushed herself up. She lifted her spear and held it before her as the lycan rolled and bashed the berserker into the ground.

Something flashed, and the lycan yelped as the berserker plunged a knife into the wolf's side. The other lycans howled, and another one transformed to attack the berserker.

"No!" Boris shouted. "This will *not* happen in here."

Outside, the scent of the blood or the noise sent the scarogs into a frenzy. Their wings, feet, and bodies battered the walls and roof until they drowned out the lycan's howls.

Freed from the lycan's jaws, the berserker, bloody and broken, scrambled back as another wolf lunged at him. Before it could recapture him, Boris's arm shot out. He caught the massive wolf and sent it flying into the bookcase.

Shelves splintered and fell apart; books toppled to the floor in a wave as the lycan hung suspended for a second before sliding to the ground. Boris had stopped the fight from continuing, but the berserker was going into full-on fight mode.

If he did so, he'd take them all out.

With his face turning red, the veins in his arms bulging, and the muscles in his neck standing out to resemble a fan, he was clearly going to blow. His muscles swelled until his shirt tore across his shoulders and back.

"Oh no," Elsa murmured.

She clung to her spear, but the weapon would do little good against an enraged berserker and lycans.

"Not here," Gromuck grunted as she stomped across the floor to the berserker. "You start fight. You go."

Only an orc would feel comfortable storming up to a berserker and grabbing them by the neck. Gromuck plucked the man from the ground and carried him to the front door with his feet dangling over the floor.

Not even a lycan could pull off that move.

The ground quaked from Gromuck's footsteps as the scarogs went crazy outside. The berserker kicked and hit as he spun in Gromuck's hold, but the few blows he succeeded in landing did nothing to deter the orc.

Stopping before the door, Gromuck held the berserker away as Boris rushed to help her with the door.

No. The word froze in Sahira's throat as panic built inside her.

The berserker couldn't stay here—he and the lycans would only tear this place apart and probably kill a few of them if he did—but Gromuck couldn't open that door either.

"Be ready to fight them off," Boris said as he rested his hand on the thick metal bar barricading the door.

Sahira stopped breathing as she shifted her hold on the spear and prepared for battle.

CHAPTER SIXTY-TWO

GROMUCK NODDED TO BORIS, and he lifted the metal bar.

No. No. No!

The word repeated in Sahira's head as the other immortals got to their feet. They weren't armed.

She was sure they had some weapon or another on them, but nothing would help against the scarogs if they got in here. Her heart hammered as, beside her, Elsa edged forward a little.

Their spell wouldn't do any good if they opened the door and let the scarogs in here. It would keep the building safe, but if they provided the opening, there was no stopping the scarogs.

Boris held the metal bar as the warlock swung the door open. When Gromuck tossed the berserker out, the beetles immediately descended, but they also swarmed toward the door.

All Sahira could see were giant black bodies, large mandibles, and beady black eyes as they surged toward Gromuck. Boris smashed one of them with the metal bar, knocking it down as a dwarf lunged forward to slam the door shut.

Before she could get the door to close, more of the beetles

crashed into it. The warlock shouted as one of the scarog's claws crashed down on his arm.

Another one crashed into Gromuck, pushing her back. When more of them swarmed over the doorway and poured inside, Sahira knew they'd lost the battle.

There was no keeping the scarogs out anymore.

The front pincers of the one who entered first clicked, much like a scorpion's, as it skittered up the wall. One of the dwarves threw their battle-ax at it, but the throw wasn't good and bounced off the creature's thick, armored thoracic area.

Its antennae clicked as they circled like windmills searching for something. Its mandibles were at least a foot long outside its gaping mouth—a mouth that would consume them after those claws and mandibles tore them apart.

Exhausted with being tired, threatened, and trapped in this place, Sahira bit back a scream of rage. It echoed in her head but didn't resonate throughout the room as she lunged forward and plunged her spear into the next beetle to shove past the warlock.

Reeling back, the beetle tried to free itself from the spear as she twisted it deeper. Leaning into the weapon, she used her weight to push it farther in before ripping it free with a sucking, slurping sound that turned her stomach.

Elsa and Boris were driving their spears into another creature as the other immortals started shouting for the key to the weapons room. Still trying to close the door, Gromuck yanked the key over her head and threw it across the room.

Before a dark fae could snatch the key, a beetle scurrying across the ceiling fell onto her back. The dark fae shrieked as the beetle's mandibles and pincers tore into her flesh.

The agony in those screams was like needles taken to Sahira's eardrums, except the shrieks didn't rupture her eardrums and bring sweet, noiseless relief like the needles would have. She'd like to say the screams ended fast, but the beetle relished its meal.

Sahira spun and drove her spear into the creature as a dwarf scampered forward to retrieve the key. The beetle reared back.

All its hideous legs opened and closed as it sought to free the spear. With its belly exposed, Elsa lunged forward and plunged her spear into it. The creature screeched as someone else's screams filled the air.

The skittering of more feet and the rustle of wings alerted Sahira to more beetles scampering across the ceiling. The one on the dark fae fell over, revealing the hole it left in the woman's forehead.

The horrifying realization it had eaten her brain, or sucked it out, wasn't slow in coming, as clearly only empty space remained, but her mind shouted denials while her eyes absorbed the gruesome details. She had no idea how the beetle had done it, and she didn't want to know.

Getting the answer meant she had to get too close for comfort.

The dwarf unlocked the weapons room and dashed inside. Weapons started to flow out as more screams pierced the air.

The warlock and a witch had fallen beneath the beetles. A light fae screamed as she ran out of the library, only to have a flying scarog swoop down and catch her.

The light fae screeched as she flew into the air before crashing into the bookcase with a thud that rattled more books free. Pinned to the wall, her screams ratcheted up a level as the beetle started feeding.

Sahira couldn't recall a time she'd been this frightened or unnerved. Even during the war, when they took down the Lord and wendigos were all around them, she hadn't been this scared.

These things shredded their flesh and sucked out their brains. Was there anything worse?

Yes. Dying because of one of them would be worse.

"Must go!" Gromuck bellowed as Boris threw a battle-ax from the weapons room.

Gromuck swung it down on a beetle's head, bashing it into the ground. Yellow pus exploded from the creature to coat the floor. Sahira swallowed the bile surging up her throat as she danced away from the sloppy mess.

Going would be great, but the legs and antennae of more beetles were already wrapping around the doorframe. Gromuck sliced those legs off as she stopped trying to hold the door closed and ripped it open.

They didn't have a choice: try to get to safety or stay and die. Gripping her spear, Sahira followed Gromuck, Elsa, and Boris out the door and into chaos.

CHAPTER SIXTY-THREE

"SOMETHING IS GOING on at the library," a light fae said.

Orin turned his stool to see where the light fae stood with her eye against a small hole in the center of one of the shutters.

"What is it?" a dwarf asked.

"I don't know. I can't see much, but the beetles are swarming it and hovering over the road near it."

A vampire nudged the light fae out of the way and pressed her eye to the hole. "There's dozens of them over there."

"I wonder why," the mermaid murmured.

She'd managed to avoid the beetles before they fully descended, but the lake was far away, and the library was her closest option. Orin had never seen her in the pub before, but she either worked nearby or was in town when The Reaping started.

"Let me see," Belda said as she pushed through the crowd gathering around the shutter.

The tall lycan bent to rest her eye against the hole. She remained there for a minute before rising and frowning at the shutter.

"Gromuck says the books often fall from the shelves when the beetles swarm over the building, and that's why they tend to focus there when they arrive. I've never seen them like that before. Maybe the falling books have really set them off this year."

"Why would they do that now, after all these years?" an imp asked.

"If I had all the answers, we wouldn't be here anymore," Belda retorted.

"What if they turn their attention to us next?"

"Then you better be ready to fight. We've never had any problems before, but we'll pull the booze off the shelves."

She waved at him and Carmella to indicate they should get to work. Orin rose but had no intention of helping Carmella until he saw what was happening.

He brushed past the berserker, still pacing like a restless tiger as he glided toward the closed shutters. Belda watched him as she leaned her shoulder against the wall. Her eyes continued to bore into him when he looked out the hole.

Despite his determination to remain indifferent, an unexpected sinking sensation formed in the pit of his stomach when he spotted the beetles crawling over top of the library and turning the air above the road black. The six-foot-long bugs were enormous killing machines and had found their feast as they dipped and swooped while screams filled the air.

"Shit," he muttered. "I think they left the building."

What is going on over there?

A nervous murmur ran through the crowd as they shifted around him. These things had a twenty-four-hour killing pass. They could devour almost everyone in this town by then if they'd somehow figured out how to breach the library.

"Don't worry," Belda assured the others. "We're safe in here. Something happened over there, but we *won't* let it happen here."

"At least, if they've already eaten, they'll be gone in a day," a vamp said.

Orin shot him a look as he rested his hand against the shutter and bowed his head to think. Cole wouldn't be happy if he returned without Lexi's aunt, nor would the queen of Dragonia.

He preferred to keep his ass firmly intact, something that might not happen if he went out there and tried to save the silly witch, but he couldn't let Lexi and Cole down.

I think they'd understand, a small voice whispered in his head.

And maybe that was true, but would *he* understand? He'd never been a coward, but he'd also never given a rat's ass about most immortals or people and had been perfectly content to watch countless numbers of them fall.

But the idea of leaving Sahira to this horrible fate made him pause. She was a strong, capable woman and a powerful witch; she could care for herself.

He pressed his eye to the hole again. The sky over the library was now so choked with beetles they blocked out the setting sun, turning it night over there.

And they were moving, flowing down the road as those inside sought to evade them.

Why did they leave that building?

But the *why* didn't matter. They were already out and fighting to survive. *Sahira* was fighting to survive.

"Shit," he muttered as he tugged at his hair.

Stepping away from the hole, he rested his hands against the metal shutter as he tried to think past the emotions battering him. Was that *fear* deep down in his belly?

He'd experienced it a time or two before, when he'd watched his brothers fighting for their lives, and when that wendigo gored him and he'd been certain it was over. But never for someone who wasn't blood or himself.

And why was he experiencing it for Sahira? Sure, she was almost family, and he sort of liked the woman, but she wasn't his problem.

It would suck if she died before he fucked her, but he'd been disappointed before and would be disappointed again. Such was life.

But he still couldn't walk away from this shutter and return to his seat to let fate unfold.

Damn witch, always getting herself into trouble.

Pushing away from the shutter, he met Belda's curiosity-filled eyes. "I have to go out there."

Her mouth pursed as her lips twitched toward a smile before compressing again. Orin had no idea what the lycan thought about his words, and he didn't care. He couldn't leave Sahira out there alone.

It might already be too late; Sahira's skin was most likely being shredded, but he couldn't leave her out there when there was a chance he could help her.

"Someone has to close the door behind me," Orin said.

"What do you think you're doing?" the berserker demanded.

"I have family out there, and I'm not leaving her to die. Most of the beetles are focused on the library; I can slip out while they're distracted."

His hand fell to the dagger strapped to his side before he shifted his attention to his room. He had a sword tucked under his mattress, and there were weapons below, but too much time had passed since the scarogs swarmed the library. He couldn't waste any more by going upstairs to retrieve it.

He lifted the bar from the door as some immortals lunged forward to try to stop him. When hands grasped his arm, he spun to destroy those who *dared* to touch him.

Most of them retreated with their hands in the air. There were certain immortals they could screw with and others they couldn't. He was one of the ones they couldn't, and they all knew it.

"Let him go," Belda commanded, and more of them fell back.

She strode over to rest her hand on the metal bar barricading the door. "We might not be able to let you back in."

"That's okay. I'll find somewhere safe until this is over."

Fred fluttered down to hover in front of him. "Good luck."

Before Orin could reply, the pixie darted away, and Belda lifted the bar. Orin threw the locks and pulled the door open.

The creak of the door drew the attention of some scarog beetles. They scuttled down the street toward him as the door closed and the bar settled into place with a click behind him.

Orin enveloped himself in shadows and descended the stairs as the beetles charged toward where he once stood but no longer did. With the shadows tucked securely around him, he headed down the street in pursuit of a witch with an attitude.

CHAPTER SIXTY-FOUR

SAHIRA HELD off one of the scarog beetles with her spear while she kept her back to Elsa, who fought another one off with a sword she'd scooped up from a fallen imp. Her spear had been broken in half shortly after they left the library.

About half of the remaining immortals with them had pulled away and fled down the street. Their screams rebounded off the buildings surrounding them as the scarogs peeled their flesh away and crunched their bones with sickening precision.

She couldn't decide if the screams or the crunching was worse, and her stomach continued to roll as she focused all her energy on surviving this battle. Gromuck, Boris, and the pixies led the way as Gromuck used her battle-ax to hack through the beetles.

Their wings fluttered overhead, and Sahira ducked as one of them dove toward her. When its legs skimmed her neck, a shudder of revulsion ran through her.

She threw up one hand; air circled through her fingers as she weaved them in an intricate pattern until power built between them. "Air beneath my fingers, air beneath my hands, swell and grow and make a stand."

With that, she thrust up her palm. A wall of air rose to shield her, Elsa, and those who remained from the beetles above.

As soon as the spell was in place, a beetle, unaware of its casting, dove down and crashed into the wall of air. The impact caused it to shriek while spiraling away.

Its legs and mandibles flailed before it crashed into another, and they both fell to the ground. They bounced down the road together before jumping up with a screech.

"That's not good," Sahira said as they skittered toward her with mandibles snapping and antennae whipping. If one of those things hit her, they'd crack her back.

Sahira yanked her spear from the scarog she'd been holding back and spun in time to smack one of the charging insects upside the head with the bottom of the shaft. She threw all her weight into the blow, knocking its head down as its momentum carried it forward.

Leaping out of the way, Sahira managed to avoid the thing hitting her, but she also separated herself from Elsa by doing so. A battle-ax crashed onto the back of the second one, severing it in half.

Sahira gave Boris a nod of thanks as he ripped the ax free of the still-squirming creature before chopping off its head. Elsa twisted to look over her shoulder at Sahira and stretched her hand toward her before another scarog cut them off.

The first charging scarog came back at her as more of them swarmed between her and Boris. He was swept away by the crush of beetles pursuing what remained of their group.

She lost sight of Elsa as their distance weakened her spell over the others. It became mostly centered above her. Spinning, she grasped her spear in both hands as she backed down the street.

She'd give anything to be able to teleport right now; it would come in handy for saving her life, but this realm seemed determined to destroy her. She couldn't see them, but Sahira tried to catch up with the others.

She knew where they were going... or at least they hoped to reach the stable. And she hoped to get there too.

Until then, she had to find somewhere safe to shelter, but she didn't think any of these buildings could survive the wrath of these creatures.

When more of them scampered closer, she used her spear to beat them back. She didn't dare plunge it into one of them; the others would charge once it stuck in a beetle.

She didn't have time to cast another spell. The second she had to stop beating them away, they would pounce like a cat on a mouse.

The best she could do was hold them back, and it was working... for now. She glanced at the buildings surrounding her as she tried to decide if she could make it into one.

She glimpsed Boris's tall, blond head about thirty feet away before he turned a corner and vanished. She was completely on her own out here.

The scraping of feet rapidly approaching her back alerted her they were trying to surround her. If that happened, she would be dead.

Twisting, she turned to face the scarogs coming from both directions as she backed toward the steps of a small home with a farmer's porch. Her feet thudded against the wood as she battled the scarog lunging for her.

This one, faster than the others, snatched her spear between one of its claws and snapped it. With her weapon ruined, Sahira threw the broken ends of the spear at it before turning and fleeing the rest of the way up the steps.

She prayed to Hecate that it was unlocked as her hand fell on the doorknob. Hecate must have been listening, as the door flew open, and she half staggered, half ran into the house.

She managed to throw the door shut before the scarog crashed into it. It rattled in its frame, and the windows near it shook, but the door held up against the creature's impressive weight.

That wouldn't last.

CHAPTER SIXTY-FIVE

WITHOUT LOOKING BACK, Sahira sprinted through the house as glass shattered behind her. She was almost out of the living room when a scarog crashed into the couch a few feet away.

Sahira bit back a scream as the furniture exploded into pieces of wood and straw that pelted her as she ran into the kitchen. While she moved, she searched the house for any weapon longer than her dagger but didn't see anything useful before reaching the back door.

She pulled open the door and dashed outside. She didn't bother looking to see what she ran into; it was the same as what hunted her from behind. Slowing down to take in her surroundings would only get her killed.

Trying to stay in one of these houses would also prove useless. After what they'd done to that house, she knew there would be no stopping these things. She had to lose them, then find somewhere to hide.

Considering they were everywhere, it was a pretty shitty option, but it was her only one. And she somehow had to retain the strength to keep moving when her use of powers and so much exertion was only making her hunger worse.

She heard and felt them coming as she raced across the street. The air spell she'd cast to protect her had fallen apart as soon as she was out of the open and inside the house; she didn't have the time to stop and cast another one.

She could only hope one of those things didn't dive down to tear into her like a human with a lobster. She wasn't ready to be some monster's entrée.

Zigzagging across the street in the hopes she could avoid the ones above, she ran faster than ever before as she bolted up the stairs to another home. A scarog crashed into the building beside her as she arrived at the front door.

The wood splintered as its mandibles pierced it. The creature's feet kicked, and its wings flapped while it tried to free itself.

Sahira didn't stick around to see if it was successful before she flung open the door, sprinted inside, and did everything she could to get farther away from them. This time, as she ran, she spotted an iron hook in the corner.

She had no idea what they used it for but snatched it from the wall. Spinning it in her hand, she turned as another beetle barreled toward her. The floor shook beneath its massive weight and its six legs.

Lifting the six-foot-tall hook, she used it like a spear and drove it into the creature's open mandibles. She glimpsed a hideous tongue with strange little bumps covering it before those bumps parted to reveal the dozens of teeth within each one.

These things have teeth on their tongues! Just when she thought they couldn't get any worse or more disgusting, they proved her wrong.

And from the center bump, the biggest one in the middle of its tongue, a snakelike appendage rose and started to unfurl as it stretched across the distance separating them. At least now she knew how it sucked the brains out of the dark fae.

She could have happily lived the rest of her life without learning that answer.

With the hook firmly embedded in the creature, she held it back as the appendage snaked toward her. She tried yanking the hook free, but it remained fixed inside the beast, and that snaky thing was getting too close for comfort.

Releasing the hook, she turned and ran for the back door, but another one crashed into it before she got there. The impact tore the door from its hinges and flung it into the house.

Sahira managed to avoid being leveled by the thing as she skated around the corner and into a bedroom. It was practically useless, but she slammed the door shut behind her.

Her fingers weaved in an intricate pattern as she breathlessly cast a protective barrier over the door. It wouldn't do much to stop those beasts, but it would slow them down.

She grabbed the dresser beside the door and flung it down as an additional barricade. Drawers fell open, and clothes spilled around her feet as she turned and ran for the windows.

Sweat cleaved her clothes to her body as her heart pounded her ribs. During the battle against the Lord, she'd come close to dying a few times, but she never felt the cool hand of death gripping her nape as it did now. It clung to her, refusing to let go while it laughed at her useless attempts to survive.

No matter how fast she sprinted or how many houses she fled into, it wouldn't let go, and she would run out of options and time. Those beetles were coming for her and determined to feast.

She went to unlock the windows before realizing the latches weren't locked. In this realm, and outside of the original, more secure buildings, there was no reason to lock doors and windows.

Everyone here relied on each other to survive and handled their battles in the pit. If they caught someone stealing, they were banished, and the problem was solved.

She was thankful for that, as the lack of locks had given her a bit of a reprieve through these houses, but the fact that *no one* was in either place underscored how unsafe they were against these things.

All the occupants of the homes had fled for the much sturdier and safer build of the original structures. Now, she had to get to one of them again.

The others had gone for the stable because it was closest, but that wasn't true for her anymore. She might be able to make it to the mercantile.

Though that deathly hand continued to caress her nape, she wasn't willing to admit defeat. Being eaten by one of those things was a horrible, painful death; the screams of agony and wails for mercy continued to replay in her head. She'd fight against that fate with every fiber of her being.

A loud bang shook the door behind her. Wood splintered, and when she glanced back, a crack zigzagged down the center of it.

They were coming, but she didn't see any behind the house... yet. Lifting the window, she threw her leg over the sill and dropped to the rocky alley separating this house from the one ten feet away.

Sahira scrambled toward the other house and placed her hands against the glass; planting her feet, she started pushing up. She'd gotten it open enough to climb through when something clamped over her mouth and yanked her back.

CHAPTER SIXTY-SIX

ORIN KEPT his hand plastered over Sahira's mouth as he cinched his other arm around her waist. She squirmed and kicked against him as he called forth the shadows to envelop her too.

"Stop moving," he hissed in her ear. "They won't be able to see you if you *stop moving*."

She went stiff against him before relaxing as her head bowed. Her body remained molded against his as he edged toward the house until his back pressed against the wall.

He kept his hand at her waist as a scarog beetle passed within inches of them. Its legs hooked over the windowsill where Sahira had opened the glass, and it lifted itself off the ground.

Glass shattered and fell in a tinkling wave around their feet as the creature shoved into the house. It landed with a thud on the other side.

His lip curled in disgust. These things were repulsive, and he was out here with them when he should be nestled securely in the pub.

He wanted to blame the witch, but he'd made this stupid choice, and now he had to ensure they survived it. A loud bang sounded from the house she'd fled, and then a strange, inhuman screech filled the air.

Orin waited for something else to break free of the house. Sahira rested her hand over his and tapped his fingers.

He lowered his hand as she turned to him to whisper, "Protection spell."

Orin rose again as another screech followed the first. This time, a few seconds later, one of the revolting beasts erupted from the window and hit the ground. Much like him, they'd broken through the spell, but he hadn't been such a whiny bitch about it.

As the scarog skittered away, Orin rested his head against the wall while surveying the street. Sahira's heart beat so rapidly that he felt her pulse at her waist. Her chest rose and fell with her breaths as her head fell forward.

Despite being out here with these lethal things, he couldn't help admiring how her body fit his in *all* the right places. And damn if he didn't crave touching all those places, even with giant flesh-eating bugs chasing them around.

Or maybe it was because of the bugs chasing them around. What better way to prove they were alive than to fuck?

And he was so hungry. He could blame the witch for that, too, but in his determination to have her, he'd allowed himself to get to this state. It was something he'd remedy as soon as this was over... with or without the witch.

After another one scampered by, he lowered his lips to her ear. "They can't see us, but we have to get to the pub... *soon.*"

With the sun setting, the shadows were dwindling. Depending on the moon's arc, there might not be any shadows. If that happened, they'd be sitting ducks out here, and he wasn't about to be plucked.

They could try for the mercantile, but with the number of beetles rampaging over this place, they might not get in. At least the pub had more than one entrance and a secret little hiding spot that could come in *very* handy right now.

He kept his mouth against her ear and continued. "Stay as close to me as possible."

When she nodded, he shifted his hold on her but kept his arm around her waist. He enjoyed running his hand across her flat belly and rounded hip before hugging her against her side.

He smiled when she glowered daggers at him but didn't stop; if there was one thing he thoroughly enjoyed, it was irritating his little witch. Without speaking, he nudged her forward, and they stepped away from the wall.

The hum of wings beating overhead filled the air as dirt kicked up around them. One of the massive beasts momentarily blocked out the sun as it swept past them.

The beetle swooped out of sight, but not before another skated around the corner and nearly went down. It righted itself and barreled toward them. The thing couldn't see them, but it would feel them if it hit them.

Orin pulled Sahira against another wall, and they flattened themselves against it as the monster lumbered by them and toward the end of the alley. It skittered out of view a second before someone started screaming, and more of them descended from the air.

Sahira lurched like she would rush to help, but he pulled her back and locked her against his side. He expected another disgruntled look from her, but her attention remained on the alley where the scarog disappeared as the woman shrieked for help.

Then, like the intelligent woman she was, Sahira resisted only briefly when he turned her away from the dying immortal. They couldn't do anything to help against so many of those things. Besides, it was already too late.

Orin led her swiftly down another alley to the end, where they stopped. To their left was nothing. Blood splattered the street to their right, and a single skull remained to mark where an immortal lost their life.

So stripped of flesh and blood, the skull looked hundreds of years old instead of an hour or two. Its jaw hung open as its eyeless sockets stared toward the end of the road and the nothingness beyond. A single hole was in the center of the skull.

That they'd left the skull and nothing else intrigued him, but he didn't intend to learn more about these things or get close enough to examine one.

Sahira hesitated when he tried to lead her into the open street. He understood she wasn't as comfortable moving through the shadows as him, but they didn't have time for this.

Refusing to let her balk against it, he kept his arm firmly across her back as he guided her onward. Beetles soared above them while others skittered over the surrounding walls and buildings.

More of them scampered in and out of the homes, through the doors and windows they'd broken. As they approached the library, Sahira's head turned toward it, but she didn't say anything.

From the open doorway, two skulls looked out at them. Each skull had a hole in the center of it where a beetle had sucked out its brain.

A beetle skittered out the door. It ran up the side of the library while another charged across the road, coming within feet of them before taking flight.

The flutter of its wings blew back his hair and clothes. It came so close he saw blood clinging to its legs and bloated belly. He hated these things.

Determined to escape, he guided her into another small alley between some homes. They moved onward through another as they made their way down the roads until they finally emerged across the street from the pub.

It was immediately clear they weren't getting in the way he'd exited, as scarog beetles crawled over the front of the building, scampered across the porch, and felt their way along the metal shutters.

He didn't dare tell Sahira where they were going, as the beetles were thicker through here than they'd been throughout all the alleyways. But then, these monsters probably knew most immortals had run for the original buildings and taken refuge in them.

Orin said nothing as he guided her away from the pub entrance and toward another alley. They passed between the store containing some of the concoctions the witches could make in this place and a tailor.

Scarogs had broken into the witches' shop. He couldn't see inside too well, but glass fell to the ground as they bumped and fumbled through the small space.

When they made it to the end of the alley, he guided Sahira to the back wall of the tailor's building, and they flattened themselves against it as they crept past the scarogs happily devouring what remained of a dwarf.

The back of the pub and the wall that hid the secret room came into view. Scarogs were everywhere as they sought some way into the pub and the feast beyond. The beetles crept up the wall of the pub and littered the back alley.

They had to get inside that room, and as darkness spread across the land, they had to do it soon, or they would be the next ones bloating these bugs' bellies. Orin jerked his head to the right and released Sahira's waist before sliding along the wall.

They scurried around a scarog sniffing the air with its antennae flicking back and forth. When one of the antennae swiveled toward him, Orin resisted the impulse to break it in half.

He'd very much like to kill every one of these things, but

with only a dagger to fight them off, his chances wouldn't be good.

Then the thing's head swiveled toward them, and its antennae locked on him.

CHAPTER SIXTY-SEVEN

ORIN DIDN'T KNOW if a shift in the wind brought their scent to it, if they made a sound only this creature could hear, or if it was because it was getting darker and the shadows were slipping, but he saw the second it registered they were there.

With an inhuman screeching sound, the scarog lunged for them. He pushed Sahira away as one of its mandibles swung toward him. The sharp appendage sliced his shirt open but didn't touch his flesh as it arced across his middle.

Bending his knees, Orin leapt up and landed on the scarog's head. When the creature reared, it drew the attention of its friends as Orin ran down its back and jumped on its ass.

A yellowish pus burst out as he smashed it into the ground. The scarog reeled onto its hind legs as its mandibles and pincers flailed at the air.

While the thing was in the air, Sahira ran past it and toward him as the other scarogs scampered forward in a rush of ticking feet and clacking pincers. The shadows slipped away from him as the sun vanished, and no moon rose to replace its light.

The moon would eventually rise, but not in time to provide them cover again. Orin pulled the dagger at his side free. It was practically useless against these things and would let them get far too close for his liking, but it would cut off a few legs and create some holes.

Pushing Sahira ahead of him, he spun as one of the scarogs charged him. Its large claw aimed to hammer him into the ground as it swung at his head.

He threw himself to the side and rolled away in time to avoid getting bashed into the earth. The creature expected him to try to get away and charged forward, but instead, he rolled toward the monstrosity and beneath its head.

As its head came toward him, he plunged the dagger into the sensitive area beneath its mouth. The scarog wheeled back with a screeching cry as Orin ripped his blade free and rolled out from beneath the beast.

He scrambled to his feet as Sahira made it to the wall with the hidden door. One of the scarogs raced toward her while she searched for the mechanism to unlock their only chance of survival.

The scarog was nearly on her when Orin jumped onto its back. His weight shoved its front into the earth as he lifted the dagger above his head and plunged it into the creature's skull.

The thick plating on the scarog's head resisted the dagger's blow, but he threw his weight into the weapon until it cracked the shell and plunged into its brain... maybe. He was pretty sure this thing's brain was the size of a pea, but the dagger sure pissed it off.

Orin tore the blade free as the scarog wheeled while swinging out its claws. Its spinning antennae sought to whip him off its body as they lashed at him.

"Orin!" Sahira screamed. "It's open! Hurry!"

Orin wanted to tell her that he was a little busy right now, but it took everything he had to hold on to the scarog and not end up beneath it, where it would either trample or eat him. Swinging out, Orin managed to grasp one of the creature's antennae; he snapped it over as he swung himself off the scarog and out over the earth.

The creature screamed again, but this time it had nothing to do with him. He spotted Sahira slicing her blade up through the scarog's belly a second before he hit the ground.

She ripped her blade free and sprinted toward what looked to be a solid wall. Sahira reached it first and, pulling the door farther open, turned to wave him onward.

Like he needed encouragement.

Racing past her, he turned as she shut the door behind him. Absolute darkness descended a second before a beetle crashed into the wall.

CHAPTER SIXTY-EIGHT

"They can't get in here," Sahira whispered.

She didn't know if she was saying it to reassure herself or if it was true as more of them crashed against the door and the side of the building.

"No, they can't," Orin said. "We're safest if we remain in here. Even if they get into the pub, like they did the library, they won't find this room."

Sahira looked around the room, but it was pointless. The darkness was absolute.

"Why were you out there?" she inquired.

He should have been safe inside the pub; it was his day to work. Had he been out there for some other reason, or had he really gone out there for *her*?

"To find you."

A lump formed in her throat, but she squeezed the word out. "Why?"

"It was obvious something went wrong at the library."

Sahira didn't know how to respond or what to make of that. The answer was so out of character with the man she knew.

"What happened there?" Orin asked.

She almost jumped when his voice came from a little closer than before but managed to restrain herself. Did he have to be so quiet?

"A fight. A stupid fight that caused everything to get out of control. Gromuck opened the door to throw out a berserker about to lose it, but the beetles pushed inside before she could close it again."

"Was the fight because of you?"

Sahira recoiled as if he'd slapped her. "*Why* would it be because of me?"

"Were the witches and warlocks starting a problem with you?"

"Oh." Her shoulders slumped a little as she leaned against the wall. "No, I wasn't the problem this time. He accused some lycans of cheating at cards, and it got out of control."

"You've never been the problem. They are."

She had no idea why those words pleased her so much, but they did.

"Fucking berserkers," Orin muttered. "Asshole should have known better."

"I'm pretty sure he's dead."

"Good."

A thud sounded from her left as his feet connected with what she assumed was the bottom step. "Found it," he murmured.

When another resounding bang hammered the wall behind her, Sahira jumped. They couldn't get in here, but the sound of them banging and scrambling over the surface set her teeth on edge.

"Easy," Orin murmured as his hand settled on her waist.

She jumped again. She never heard him move before he stood beside her and touched her again.

Like when he first found her out there, she became acutely aware of him as his fingers caressed her hip. Heat spread up from where he touched, crept through her chest, and sent her heart into overdrive.

She attempted to swallow to get some moisture back into her suddenly parched mouth, but it was pointless. Everything in her became hyper-focused on him as her breasts tingled. She yearned for him to ease this constant *need* his touch evoked in her.

The steady, strong beat of his heart didn't help. Every thump of his pulse reawakened the thirst she'd managed to push aside in her desperation to survive. It was back now with a raging ferocity that left her knees weak.

She should get away from him, but her legs wouldn't move, and she'd planted her feet on the floor.

Move!

No matter how loudly she shouted the word in her head, she didn't retreat when his hand settled against her belly and he pulled her back a step.

This is what he wants! This is all part of his game!

She had to admit that him leaving the pub to come after her couldn't be part of his game. He was determined to win and hell-bent on breaking her, but he wouldn't risk his ass for a game.

She had no idea why he'd done it. It certainly wasn't out of the goodness of his black heart, but he had, and she probably would have died without him.

That didn't mean she owed him anything. He'd chosen to risk his life.

However, her feet remained frozen as he moved closer until her back was firmly against his chest. His body was so unyielding and everything she'd forgotten a man could be.

As prickles of electricity raced up and down her body, she relished their differences. He was hard where she was soft; locked like this and nearly a foot taller than her, he towered over her, but she felt safe and secure instead of intimidated by it—something she'd *never* expected to feel with Orin.

His cinnamon-and-clove scent enveloped her as it dug its

way into the fiber of her being. His hand was tender against her, but his touch spoke of confidence and strength.

Then he turned her toward him, and though her mind still screamed to run, she didn't fight as he brushed back the strands of hair that had fallen free during her flight from the scarogs.

She didn't know how he could tell where her hair was, considering she couldn't see him, but his fingers didn't hesitate as they skimmed her neck and cheek while he brushed her hair aside.

When he leaned closer, her fangs lengthened before she could stop them. *Why does he have to be so close? And why does his touch make me feel so... alive?*

It was more than her starvation making her desire him. It was the man himself.

She loathed him and everything he represented, but couldn't deny she wanted him. Lust was a treacherous bitch that had burrowed under her skin, burrowed through her veins, and taken root like an alien species that would forever corrupt her.

CHAPTER SIXTY-NINE

HE'S A DARK FAE!

But the reminder wasn't the repellent it would have been a few short weeks ago. This realm had stripped so much from them, changed and strengthened them. It had also made them worse.

If she caved to him, he'd never let her forget it. He'd be a constant, thorny, smug asshole afterward.

Thinking about it made her blood boil, but when his thumb found her lips and traced the bottom one before prodding one of her fangs, she forgot all about her pride and his arrogance.

She tried to turn her head away, but it wasn't in time to stop blood from beading on his thumb. Her nostrils flared, and she barely restrained herself from throwing her arms around him as the coppery aroma engulfed her.

"Easy, witch," he murmured as his lips found her cheek. "You've gone too long without feeding."

Those words managed to evoke some of her lost fury at this man. "Whose fault is that?"

"You could have come to me at any time to feed."

Maybe so, but she'd be damned before she asked him for anything. Now, she had no choice as pain twisted in her belly.

She bit back a whimper as her eyes closed and his other hand gripped her nape. With gentle prodding, he brought her mouth toward his throat.

Heart hammering, her dry mouth flooded with saliva as her fangs throbbed in anticipation. Every part of her was on fire with her thirst for blood.

His erection pressing into her belly didn't help, and she rubbed against it. She'd almost died today and so many other times recently, but *today* she'd felt the hand of death on her neck. It had taunted her with its presence and its knowledge of her fate.

A fate it was denied, and largely because of Orin, who cared little about much in life, but he'd left the safety of the pub for *her*. Sahira closed her eyes as she swayed toward him; she couldn't resist anymore and didn't want to.

The flesh of his neck was warm against her mouth. She couldn't stop her tongue from flicking over his skin, just above his enticing pulse. He tasted of salt, sweat, and man in the most delicious ways possible.

He kept one hand on her nape and the other on the wall beside her head while leaning into her. Her nipples hardened when his chest brushed hers. *Every* part of her sought more of a connection to him.

Before she could think about it anymore, and her hunger could tear her to further shreds, she gripped his nape with both hands and locked him into place as she sank her fangs into his throat. As soon as his blood hit her tongue, she reacted as if struck by lightning.

She jerked against him as his blood and power filled her. And there was so much power in Orin that she knew, with absolute certainty, he had far more ciphers than he revealed.

The man was exquisite; she'd feasted on countless others over the years, but no one as powerful as him. And his strength flowed through his blood and into her as it nourished and energized her.

It had been so long since she fed that anyone's blood would have made her half crazed, but his power caused her head to spin. She didn't recall thinking about releasing his neck to grasp his shirt until it shredded in her hands as she tore it from him.

Feeding could awaken an overwhelming lust in vampires. They became aroused by someone else's nearness, the life flowing into them, and the intimacy of it all. Their bloodlust was quenched by sex and feeding; she was only getting one of those things.

A vampire could control their bloodlust, and she'd kept it restrained in the past, but she was nearly mindless with it now. She didn't know if it was because she'd gone so long without feeding, the strength of his blood, or if she simply *wanted* this.

Hecate help her, she really *did* want this, and for far longer than she'd ever admit to anyone… including herself. This man drove her insane; she despised everything about him but still yearned to fuck him.

Call it curiosity or simple, irresistible attraction, but she wanted him. And she *would* have him.

CHAPTER SEVENTY

ORIN HAD KNOWN the little witch would be wild, and she didn't disappoint. He hadn't expected her to be this passionate and ravenous, but he wouldn't complain as she ground against him while he pushed her pants over her hips.

Without breaking her bite on him, she kicked off her boots and wiggled her pants down far enough to kick them off. When his hand settled on her ass, she jumped up to lock her legs around his waist while she bit harder.

Orin stiffened against the pain before it faded and the pleasure that often came from a vampire's bite replaced it. His cock throbbed as her hands jerked at the button on his pants until it tore free.

The button clattered as it bounced into the darkness before resting somewhere. He caressed her silken skin as he savored the feel of her. He'd waited and schemed to get to this point; he should bury himself inside her and feast, too, but he lost himself to the exquisite sensation of her in his arms.

She felt so good he was half convinced she wasn't real. None of the countless women he'd screwed over the years had been as warm, supple, or inviting as her. He didn't want the moment to end, even as hunger shredded his insides.

Orin shoved his pants down and sighed in relief when he freed his erection from its prison. That sigh became a groan of ecstasy when she shifted her hips to tease the head of his shaft with her wet entrance.

Shit!

Had anyone ever been so wet and ready for him? If Orin wasn't careful, he'd come before entering her, something he'd never done before, not even when he was a teen. He'd been faster than he should have been back then but never embarrassed himself by spilling his seed before entering a woman.

Shifting her hips again, the witch drew his head into her. When she drew him deeper, he gritted his teeth against ramming into her until he finally found the release he craved.

But that wouldn't be much fun for him, and he'd sworn he'd hear her scream his name in ecstasy. She cried out as she took him deep into her until he was settled fully inside her warm, inviting body.

Orin's head tipped back as her sheath clenched around him. *Fuck, she's tight!* And felt *amazingly* good.

Resting one hand against the wall, he held her while her hips thrust forward. She slid up until he was nearly out of her before sliding down again. Her calculated movements were a ruthless tease as her fingers bit into his nape and she drank from him.

As their joining created sexual energy in the air, he feasted on the strength of it as his hunger abated. Gradually, her movements became more demanding as she rode him with a savagery he more than matched. She wasn't the only one who was desperate to feed.

Grasping her nape, he held on to her as she planted her hands on the wall behind him. He sensed the increase in her pulse and the small tremors working their way through her before they unfurled into something more.

With a loud cry, she finally broke her bite on him as her back bowed and her body trembled like a plucked bowstring. And he'd most certainly enjoyed plucking her, though he would have preferred some light to watch her come apart.

He'd remedy that soon.

She leaned forward in his arms and rested her hands on his chest. If she thought she would stop this now, she was sadly mistaken.

But she didn't try to push him away. Instead, her fingers raked his flesh as she started moving again, and the energy they created rose between them.

He feasted on it while she leaned forward and bit him again. Her bite didn't last as she released it to move down to bite his shoulder. He released her and her feet hit the ground as she moved down his body.

The pleasure and pain she created mingled until he was on the verge of coming while their bodies worked together to give and take in equal measure.

When her lips found his, he clasped the back of her head and kissed her. She tasted of honey, blood, rapture, and sin; he relished it as their tongues entwined. She cried out his name against his mouth, and he grinned at the sound.

"Say it again," he commanded.

"Orin," she gasped as she came.

This time, he followed her over the edge as he came so hard his teeth clamped shut, his back bowed, and tingles raced up and down his spine. The force of his orgasm left him shaken as she collapsed in his arms.

CHAPTER SEVENTY-ONE

SOMETIME LATER, Sahira came to enough to take in her surroundings. Hours ago, she'd removed her protection spell above so Orin could go upstairs, retrieve the mattress from her bed, and bring it and a candle down.

The things they'd done to each other in the hours since should have made her blush, but it had been centuries since she was a blushing maiden. Still, she'd never done those things or been that uninhibited with any other man.

Maybe it was because he was a dark fae and had some knack for making his partners less reserved, or perhaps it was because she was so far gone in sating her bloodlust, she hadn't stopped to think about what they were doing. And even if she had, it felt too good to stop.

Now, she woke to discover herself nestled against Orin's side. Occasionally, the scarogs would still slam into the side of the building. She didn't know if they were still seeking a way in or were simply crashing into things out there.

Either way, they didn't scare her. They wouldn't get in here, and though it was foolish of her, she felt safe in Orin's arms.

You're an idiot.

It was true, and this little cocoon of theirs would soon end, but for now, she felt secure and more satisfied than ever before.

She'd also come more times than she could count throughout the night, more times than with any other man, and impossibly, she craved *more.*

While she could blame their first time together on having gone without feeding, which intensified her bloodlust until it made her out of control, she couldn't blame their second, third, fourth, or fifth times on that. And she couldn't blame her need for more on it either.

She was more sated on blood than she'd been in years. It hadn't clouded her judgment at all; she'd given herself to him because as much as she didn't want to desire him, she did.

She was a fool, but she was a thoroughly fucked, fed, and happy fool.

When Orin's fingers ran lazily up and down her arm, she was alerted that he was awake again too. When she sensed a change in his heartbeat and touch, her body reacted to it.

She couldn't get enough of him. Despite that, she didn't worry she might become one of the shadow kissed the dark fae sometimes left in their wake. She could never let herself turn into one of those mindless sex slaves.

She now understood how easy it could be for an immortal to lose themselves to the dark fae's touch and give over control of themselves, but that would never be her. No matter how good this felt and how lost she'd been to him, she'd managed to retain part of herself.

After everything they'd shared, she hadn't believed it possible to want him again, but she did. It was as if he'd somehow become a part of her, and his needs were hers too.

Before she could lift her head, he clasped the side of her face and rolled toward her. His mouth found hers in a gentle kiss that reawakened a passion that should have been well-sated but wasn't.

Their tongues entwined as his hands roamed over her with an expertise that brought every part of her to life. She practically begged for more while he kissed his way down her body to between her legs.

Sahira's arms stretched over her head as she savored his tongue against her clit. She loved watching him as the light played over his muscles and emphasized his ciphers while he awakened and teased her until he finally drove her over the edge.

She threaded her fingers through his thick, silken hair and screamed his name, something she'd learned he enjoyed. The shadows embraced him as he lifted himself over her.

Her eyes held his while he kissed her again before claiming her hands and locking them above her head. When he entered her again, he broke the kiss to watch her as he moved leisurely in and out.

Sahira yearned to touch him, but he didn't release her hands, and she couldn't break free of his hold. She couldn't stop looking at him either; she lost herself to those black eyes, the way they devoured her every move while his other hand found every tender spot on her.

And as he watched her, he learned what made her gasp and react as he played with her nipples, stroked her breasts, and lowered his hand to caress her clit. He reclaimed her mouth and plunged deeper into her when she came again.

He shuddered against her as he groaned. Deep within her, she felt the pulse of his cock as he spilled his seed.

After their second time together, she'd regained enough control to inquire about birth control. She hadn't bothered with it yet, but as she'd suspected, he was taking a potion for it.

"I think you're more an enchantress than a witch," he murmured before withdrawing from her and collapsing on the mattress.

Sahira barely had time to catch her breath before he encircled his arms around her again and locked her against his side. This time, she didn't doze off but slipped into a deep sleep as exhaustion claimed her.

CHAPTER SEVENTY-TWO

THE SCAROG BEETLES' occasional thumps against the side of the building came to a halt. The ensuing hush only emphasized Sahira's steady breaths while she slept beside him.

Her warm body was nestled against his. When she rolled toward him a little bit ago, she'd draped her arm over his chest. At the time, her head settled perfectly beneath his chin; it remained there.

He'd finally gotten the chance to see his witch with her hair down, tumbling around her shoulders and down her back, as she rode him with abandon. And she'd rode him to the point where his dick almost couldn't get hard, but recalling her naked and crying out in ecstasy caused his exhausted appendage to stir again.

His trusty friend had never let him down before and wouldn't now. However, it needed a break, and so did she.

Without thinking, he lifted a silken strand of her long hair and slid it through his fingers before letting it fall to her shoulder. Its warm mahogany hue shone in the candlelight flickering over them.

He couldn't help admiring its color or how every part of her was supple, warm, yielding, and beautiful. She also fit perfectly against his side; it was as if she was made for him, but that wasn't possible. He wasn't a lycan seeking a mate or a vampire's consort; he was a dark fae, which meant he had no mate, and that was how he liked it.

Still, she felt incredibly good against his side. Too good. He didn't want to get up and leave when it was past time for him to do so.

Judging by the silence, the scarogs had spent their twenty-four hours here and retreated. It was time to see the damage and move on to a new bedmate.

This had been a fun game, but it was over. He'd won.

He'd conquered his stubborn witch, and while she was *fantastic*, he was now free to move on to other women. There was always an endless supply of them. Life was grand that way.

But he didn't get up. He told himself it was because he'd been awake for over a day, things had been a bit stressful during The Reaping, and his little witch had about fucked him dry, so he was too tired to move.

It had *nothing* to do with how good her breasts felt against his chest, how much he enjoyed her soft breaths against his skin, or how she now smelled of him. Still, as he stared at the closed-off floor above, he relished his scent all over her.

She wasn't the first woman he'd lain next to in bed. Of course she wasn't, but she was the first where he *enjoyed* being there. He hadn't once contemplated chewing off his arm to escape.

With those women, if he didn't fall asleep when he finished with them, he'd just laid there and endured it. He never stayed because he wanted to. It was always because there weren't other options for another bed, he'd passed out, or they'd been good enough to stay for another round after some rest.

That's why he was still here, he decided. The witch was a

great lay, and while he'd already taken her six times, he'd gladly give her another spin.

He wasn't still lying here because she'd somehow managed to get under his skin. She hadn't. That could *never* happen to him... not with a woman.

No one got under the skin of a dark fae... except Lexi had stolen Cole's heart. *But he's part lycan, and emotion rules those beasts.*

It was true, but as he smiled over that confirmation, a dark truth niggled at his brain. *Father fell in love with Cole's mother.*

He recoiled at the idea of love. That was an *insane* possibility and as far from what this was as it could get.

Yes, somehow Cole's mother, a lycan, had managed to make the king of the dark fae, a man renowned for his black heart, fall in love with her. That heart only warmed for his wife, Caitrin, and his sons.

His father was a fair ruler but also a renowned, brutal bastard. None of his fury ever touched his sons. They'd remained immune to his wrath, even when they royally pissed him off as Orin had *many* times, but the man never stopped loving him.

It would have been so easy, and maybe expected of his father, to have favored Cole—the only child who came of the king's love for his wife—but he didn't.

Orin grew up knowing Cole's mother was the only woman his father ever loved, the only one he would ever marry, but he'd never felt any less loved than his older brother. And he was sure the rest of his siblings felt the same way.

Yes, his father had fallen for a woman and married, and so had other dark fae, including his mother, but not him. *Never* him.

The witch intrigued him, and she'd been a delight as well as a great source for him to feast on, but he didn't have feelings for her. He prided himself on his black soul and cold heart, a heart that, much like his father's, only warmed for his siblings.

It was not, and never would be, affected by a woman.

Then why are you still here?

Much to his mounting frustration, he couldn't answer that. It didn't matter how good she fucked, smelled, and felt; he shouldn't be here anymore.

But he didn't move as he savored her warmth while also enjoying not being hungry or horny for the first time in weeks.

He was... *content.*

The word caused his lip to curl as he sneered at the ceiling. He hated every second of this... except he didn't.

It was peaceful here, warm and safe. She brought a sense of calm and rightness he'd never experienced with a woman before. He'd never believed it possible for him to feel this way, but here it was, and as much as he *loathed* it, he also *liked* it.

What is wrong with me?

He had no idea, but this wasn't him, and he hated that his emotions were in a tailspin. This was *not* who he was. He didn't *cuddle* or lie in bed and breathe in the scent of a woman.

Whatever this was, he couldn't allow it to continue. He had no room in his life for any changes and didn't want them.

He was perfectly content with his life, enjoyed it a lot, and wouldn't let it change. He didn't care how good a woman smelled.

Determined not to let anyone or anything interfere in his life, he carefully removed his arm from under Sahira and rolled away. As soon as they separated, a pang of loss tugged at his heart, but he shoved it aside as he gathered his ruined clothes and left the sleeping witch behind.

CHAPTER SEVENTY-THREE

SAHIRA HAD no idea what time it was when she woke, but she knew, without having to search for him, that Orin was gone. The coldness of the spot beside her told her he'd been gone for at least an hour.

Sitting up, she tried not to think about what his disappearance meant while she searched the small hidden space. She *knew* what it meant. From the moment they entered this room and she bit into him, she knew this was how it would end.

So why did a pit of uncertainty and sadness fester inside her like an infected wound?

She'd messed up by having sex with him; there was no denying that. It was a mistake. He'd never let her forget it, but it wasn't like she loved him. She could barely tolerate the man, but... damn it... what *was* that between them last night?

Over the years, she'd had a *lot* of sex but never experienced anything like that. It was *amazing*.

But he was a dark fae; she'd never been with one of *them* before, and they knew what they were doing. He'd most certainly had *lots* of practice. Maybe this was how everyone felt after a night with a dark fae, but she doubted it.

His blood and the way he felt inside and against her had all been so *right*. How could something so right also be so bad for her?

And it was *so* bad. He was the worst possible thing for her, a man who gave few shits about anything. She would never be one of the things he cared about either.

Lowering her head, she clutched it in both hands as she fought against the sudden panic threatening to overwhelm her. *Get it together. Get up and move!*

Taking a tremulous breath, Sahira dropped her hands and studied the sputtering flame of the nearly burned-out candle before planting her palms on the mattress and pushing herself up. With jerky movements, she gathered her clothes.

She was acutely aware Orin's were already gone. He hadn't bothered to wake her before leaving, but she hadn't expected anything else.

So then why did it hurt?

She had no answer. None of it made any sense to her—*none of it.*

When she finished tugging on the remnants of her clothes, she hauled her mattress and the candle upstairs. Once she had everything above, she slid the stairway cover back into place, set a protection spell over it, and cautiously approached the shutters.

Resting her hand against the metal, she leaned forward to place her eye on the small hole in the center. She didn't hear the beetles bouncing off the walls anymore, and the light outside indicated it had been about twenty-four hours since The Reaping started, but she still held her breath.

When she spotted immortals walking the street, she lifted the bar. She swung open the shutters, rested her hands on the sill, and leaned out to examine the town.

Immortals hurried back and forth, carrying supplies and debris. A fire burned in the pit; it grew bigger with every piece of broken lumber and furniture tossed onto the pile.

The immortals also carried and threw the remains of the dead beetles onto the fire. Their shells cracked and popped as the flames devoured them, and sparks flew.

She shivered at the reminder of what those things could do and stepped away from the window. She went to close the shutters again but stopped; they had at least a couple of weeks before the new year started, and a possible return of the beetles, so it was safe to leave them open. This room needed some fresh air, and so did she.

Sahira had no idea where Orin was and wouldn't look for him. Gathering some fresh clothes, she headed for the door.

A shower, where she could scrub Orin's scent from her, would help her feel a lot better. The idea of removing the evidence of what passed between them caused inexplicable sadness to creep through her, but it had to happen.

No, she would *not* do this. She would shower and get to work. There was plenty to do out there; the library would be a mess, and she had to earn extra supplies to get out of here.

It was time she got as far from this town as possible.

CHAPTER SEVENTY-FOUR

THE STARS HAD STARTED to pierce through the thick velvet night when Sahira left the library with Elsa. They'd spent the entire day in there with Gromuck and Elsa as they pieced the place back together.

The beetles had unleashed a ton of devastation on the books and building. Not to mention, they'd left behind a bloodbath no amount of water and scrubbing could remove from the wood and pages.

It would take weeks for them to get everything fixed and cleaned, but they'd made a good start today. They'd done what they could to salvage the books the beetles destroyed.

She and Elsa had worked to repair the broken spines, torn pages, and trampled covers. They still had a giant pile to go through, but they'd saved all those they worked on today.

Sahira was glad to see Elsa had survived the beetles' attack, and the witch had hugged her when she walked through the door. "I thought we'd lost you."

Astonished by the woman's warmth, it took Sahira a second to respond, but then she'd hugged her back. Elsa had no way of knowing how much Sahira needed that hug.

Many of those from the library didn't reach the stable, but Gromuck, Elsa, the pixies, and a few others got there. When they arrived, Zeth let them in.

She was also glad to learn the demon had survived. He'd come by the library earlier to check on her, and she'd assured him she was great, even if she wasn't.

But she'd survived when many others hadn't; their skulls, littering the town, were a stark reminder of that. And each of them had a hole in the center.

She'd come so close to being one of those skulls. Apparently, they were the only things a scarog beetle didn't eat. They were all buried during the day, but the memory of walking through town this morning and seeing all those picked-clean skulls made her skin crawl.

That could have been her if Orin hadn't helped her. She tried not to think about him, but the annoying man had a way of creeping back into her thoughts.

She was alive, fed, and should have been ecstatic, even if she'd had an incredibly *bad* moment of weakness last night. The more time passed, the more she kicked herself in the ass for giving in to Orin, but Zeth didn't have to know that.

And once he left, she had only her memories and work to keep her occupied. Her thoughts were determined to drive her insane as they kept returning to Orin and what passed between them. She couldn't stop recalling how his body moved, how his arms felt around her, and the false sense of security she'd experienced while with him.

Yes, he was strong and had saved her, but in many ways, he was as treacherous as the scarog beetles. And just as dangerous to her.

She'd known that and still chose to have sex with him. She couldn't blame it on out-of-control bloodlust either; she'd experienced it before—granted, not with the same intensity as last night—but she'd never given in to it.

She'd given in to Orin because it was what she wanted, even though she'd known it would come back to bite her in the ass.

But it hadn't felt wrong. Not then and not now as the reality of her choice weighed her down. And the truth was, she'd *really* enjoyed herself and wanted more from a dark fae who had probably already moved on to someone else.

She closed her eyes against that reminder. Everything about last night had felt so right that it made the reality of today and waking up alone worse.

And now, as she approached the pub with an armload of books tucked against her chest and Elsa at her side, she was dismayed to realize the place was in full swing. Shouts of revelry poured out from within, singing punctuated the night, women and men danced on the front balconies, and the place was so packed, immortals overflowed onto the porch.

Her steps slowed as they neared the raucous place. She should have expected all these immortals to celebrate, even after working to clean the wreckage left by the scarogs.

"I guess everyone's celebrating their survival," Elsa said.

"Yeah," Sahira muttered.

She wasn't sure how she would get through the door as the immortals crammed around it focused on the inside while downing their drinks. More of them filtered onto the porch but didn't leave.

"You can stay at my place tonight," Elsa offered. "I have an extra bedroom."

Sahira's eyes widened; they'd become friendly since she started working at the library, but she hadn't expected that. "I don't think the other witches and warlocks would like that."

They'd both chosen to work in the library and, therefore, had to see each other every day, but Elsa didn't have to offer Sahira a room in her home. It wouldn't go over well with the others if Sahira went there tonight.

Elsa shrugged. "I don't care. I've always been more of a lone witch, and I like it that way. Besides, I don't dislike someone because of *what* they are. I'll hate them because of *who* they are, though."

Sahira chuckled while studying the pub and the chaos that had taken over. She was very tempted to say yes.

Not having to fight her way through the crowd was a good reason to avoid Orin. She could even talk herself into believing the crowd was her only reason to take Elsa up on her offer.

However, Zeth and Elsa were the only two sort-of friends she had here. She didn't consider Orin one; no matter what passed between them, she couldn't trust him enough to be his friend, and she doubted he wanted that from her.

Sahira couldn't cause any problems for Zeth or Elsa. And no matter what Elsa said, the other witches and warlocks could make her life a living hell for helping Sahira. She wouldn't allow that.

"I really appreciate the offer, but I should return to my room," Sahira said.

"You won't bring any trouble down on me."

"We both know that's probably not true. We have to work together, but I don't have to go to your house. They'll see that as a betrayal on your part."

"I'm not loyal to them. They've done nothing to earn it."

The bitterness in her voice piqued Sahira's curiosity, but she didn't question Elsa. She understood not having anything to do with witches and warlocks; she had her reasons, and apparently Elsa did too.

Elsa scowled at the pub as a drunken berserker staggered down the stairs with his arm draped around a dark fae's shoulders. "I hope you have a silencing spell."

"I use it every night."

"Good. I'll see you in the morning."

"See you then."

CHAPTER SEVENTY-FIVE

SAHIRA STARTED toward the pub but stopped when she spotted two lycans screwing against the wall. Trying to act casual, Sahira watched Elsa stroll toward the end of the street. There, she made a right and jogged up the steps of a small log cabin.

Most witches and crones stayed in the tepee-like lodgings on the other side of town near the lake. The warlocks preferred more elegant accommodations; their larger homes had been built near the witches'.

Warlocks and witches didn't always get along. Some warlocks didn't hate vampires—that was the witches' fight—but in this realm, they'd grouped together and exerted strength in numbers.

Yippee for me.

Elsa had used her home, a whole town away from the other witches, to further distinguish herself from them. Sahira wondered if the other witches gave Elsa any trouble over this and why she'd separated herself when it would have been safer to align with them, but those were questions for another day.

Now, all she wanted was to get past all the commotion at the door, a hot shower, and sleep. She absolutely did *not* want Orin to somehow fit into the lovely picture she'd painted in her head.

When the memory of his mouth against hers and having him inside her tried to intrude, she shoved it away. She had no expectation of him coming to her room tonight... or ever again.

He'd won, and now he would move on.

And she would be left to pine for him. Her body, which he'd awakened in ways she hadn't known possible last night, still craved his touch when it should have been beyond satisfied.

She'd almost worry he'd shadow kissed her, but even in her moment of *great* weakness, she hadn't allowed that to happen. Yes, the sex was amazing, but she'd never lost herself enough to become shadow kissed. And she never would.

Which meant this misery was all *her* doing. She had no idea why he affected her as badly as he did, but she had to get it together, or her life would turn into a never-ending nightmare.

When the lycans finally finished having sex and returned to drinking with their pants around their ankles, Sahira took a deep breath and slogged up the steps. She elbowed her way past the vampires, lycans, and dwarves gathered around the doorway.

They finally parted enough to grant her entrance to the mobbed pub. She came up against a wall of backs as she tried to weave through the crowd.

She slid sideways around one immortal, ducked under the elbow of another, and almost got on her hands and knees to scoot past two dwarves with their arms locked as they waved their battle-axes and belted out a battle song.

The pub always smelled of alcohol, sex, and immortals, but now the stench was overwhelming as liquor spilled across the bar top, tables, and sloshed from the glasses immortals raised while shouting cheers. Some held their glasses over their heads as they sang, and more than a few drops rained onto her.

Sahira brushed away the trail of alcohol running down the

side of her face. At any other time, she might have joined the celebration, too, but she was too exhausted to party.

She'd made it about ten feet into the pub and was contemplating backing out and heading for Elsa's house when she spotted Orin sitting at the bar. He lifted a glass into the air and clinked it against others as a raucous cheer ran through the crowd.

A big smile lit his face, but then he had every reason to be happy, as he had alcohol and a pretty nymph sitting on his lap. Her pink hair spilled over his hands, and what little clothes she wore left nothing to the imagination.

Something twisted inside Sahira as she swallowed the sudden lump in her throat. She couldn't decide if she was hurt, angry, or jealous as an unexpected tidal wave of emotions bombarded her.

She'd told herself this was going to happen, told herself not to expect *anything* from this man. After all, he was a dark fae, and *this* was what they did and who they were.

Despite mentally preparing herself for this, seeing him sitting there was still a kick in the chest. He had his hand on the thigh of a woman who happily wiggled her ass all over his crotch.

Move!

Somehow her brain slammed back into action while her body remained a useless, immobile lump. She couldn't stand there, trapped like a deer in the headlights, and *stare.*

Would there be anything more humiliating in her life than to have him look up and catch her? No, there wouldn't.

She had to go and couldn't retreat, as the immortals had created a wall behind her. It was like they knew she was experiencing the most mortifying moment of her life and were determined to make her face it.

And she would face it. She would use the memory of the nymph now pouring beer down her chest to drown out all the memories of what passed between them last night. When Orin bent his head to lick the alcohol away, Sahira focused on getting through the crowd.

She dodged a berserker and almost swatted away Fred when he flew into her face before bouncing off, burping, and darting away. "Toots," he slurred before crashing into an imp.

A trail of red dust clogged the air behind him; she waved it from her face. When the air cleared, she wished it hadn't, as her new position gave her a great view of *Orin*... who was now staring at her with an amused gleam in his crow-black eyes.

CHAPTER SEVENTY-SIX

SOMEHOW, and she had *no* idea how, she managed to keep her face impassive as the nymph draped her arms around his neck. Orin's cocky grin set her teeth on edge, and when he wiggled his fingers at her in a little wave, she wished she was close enough to cut off those appendages. She doubted he'd still smile with his fingers all over the bar.

Juggling the books in her arms, Sahira smiled as she waved back. Then she turned her attention to getting through the rest of the crowd.

She had to get out of this place, get some fresh air, and *breathe,* but that wasn't an option. She could only keep going.

Sahira refused to look his way again as she weaved through the crowd until she *finally* made it to the stairs. Her eyes kept trying to return to Orin and the bar as she climbed, but she refused to let them.

She could be as casual about all this as him. No, she wouldn't jump into someone else's bed tonight, like him, but she could pretend none of this bothered her.

Maybe she could make it true if she kept faking it.

When she finally reached her room, she closed and locked the door behind her. She set the books on her bureau, cast her silencing spell, and inhaled a shaky breath as the noise from downstairs dissipated.

Bending, she rested her hands on her knees and closed her eyes. The image of that nymph on his lap popped up to haunt her.

"What am I going to do? *Why* does he have this effect on me?"

He was an asshole—a womanizing jerk who followed his dark fae instincts without caring about what he left in his wake.

But then, he didn't have to care. Every immortal, in all the realms, knew what the dark fae were. *None* of them expected anything more than a good time from them.

And she hadn't either. She'd known it would never be more than a onetime thing, so why did she still crave his touch, and *why* couldn't she get him out of her head?

Tears burned her eyes, but she had no idea what to make of the emotions battering her. And since she couldn't begin to sort them out, she decided ignoring them was her best option.

It didn't matter what, or *who*, Orin did. She was leaving this place and him behind as soon as she could. She'd been steadily saving supplies to make her move, and it was almost time to go.

She'd been dreading it but suddenly couldn't wait to make a trip into the Barren Lands. The unknown monsters awaiting her were far preferable to this place.

~

ORIN'S TEETH scraped together when Sahira closed her door. He wasn't sure how he expected the enchantress to react to seeing him with another, but it was more than what she gave him.

He'd been thinking about her all day. At one time, he almost made the humiliating decision to go to the library to ensure she was okay.

Thankfully, when he realized what he was considering, he decided against it, but it never should have been a thought. He didn't check on women; he didn't *want* to see them once he finished with them.

That was *not* his way.

And once he realized this woman was getting to him, he'd become determined to prove it wasn't true. Sure, he wanted and would have her again, but he'd have plenty of others in between too.

He was *not* about to tie himself to one woman for any length of time, not even for two days in a row. Sahira would know that, and so would he.

Now, he'd made his point to himself and her. No woman got under his skin. Sahira would see she wasn't anything special.

A niggle of doubt tickled the back of his mind. *Was I wrong to do this?*

His being wrong about anything was an extremely rare occurrence, but it happened from time to time. Something strange had passed between them, and something *was* different about her.

He couldn't explain what it was or put a finger on it, but there was a reason why she wasn't far from his mind today. He couldn't deny he liked the witch as more than a way to get off. She was smart, stubborn, and stronger than almost everyone he'd ever met before.

She could have easily sat and whined about her bloodline and the unfairness of the way the witches treated her. She could have let fear rule her, stayed hidden in her room after Radagast's attack, or refused to go anywhere alone.

Many would have cowered and broken from far less, but she kept going with a determination he admired. Yes, she was different, and it was driving him nuts.

He nudged the nymph off his lap, ignoring her little moan of protest as she jiggled her very lovely breasts in his face.

There was a time when his dick would have jumped in appreciation and he would have fucked her on the stool; she'd made it clear she was more than up for it. But apparently, that time was not tonight.

It's only because my dick hasn't recovered from last night yet. But he'd done it before without any problems, and if Sahira was squirming all over his lap, he was sure he could do it again. Which only pissed him off.

The nymph was sexy and one of the few women he hadn't been with in this realm; he should have been all over her. Instead, he wasn't in the mood.

Besides, he had work to do. Something Belda made clear as she glowered at him from the end of the bar while pouring bourbon across the glasses set up before her.

Orin strolled behind the bar to start helping again. As he set up more glasses, his eyes returned to Sahira's room.

He didn't expect to see her again tonight but wondered what she was doing. Maybe he'd go to her room after work.

After the thing with the nymph, it would probably take a little coaxing, but he was sure he could get her pretty thighs to open for him again. After all, he knew how much of a good time she had last night. If she was pissed at him, that could make tonight better.

Where the nymph hadn't caused his shaft to stir much, the possibility of fucking an irate Sahira did. What fun it would be.

He shut his thoughts down when he realized he was obsessing over the witch again. He didn't care how good Sahira was or how much he liked her. No one would interfere in his life or have any sway over how he lived it.

He wouldn't go to Sahira's room tonight or any other night. She'd come to him; she would need to feed, and when she did, he'd be more than happy to accommodate her in every way.

Until then, he'd find someone else to screw.

Maybe not today or tomorrow, but plenty of other women in this realm could keep him occupied. The enchantress was only one of many.

CHAPTER SEVENTY-SEVEN

"ARE YOU PLANNING TO LEAVE TOWN?"

Sahira shifted her attention from the weeds she was pulling in the gardens to the demon whose shadow had fallen over her when he stopped a few feet away. She and Elsa had been the only ones in the gardens until Zeth entered through the small gate on the other side of the space, easily the size of a football field.

Unfortunately, the scarogs had damaged a fair amount of the plants, but they'd removed them and seeded new ones. Beside Zeth's right foot sat the bucket of water she'd brought from the lake for the new seeds she and Elsa were planting.

The other garden workers had already gone home when their shifts ended an hour ago. Her shift at the library ended then, too, but she had to work extra to earn more supplies.

Elsa often worked in the gardens after the library, although Sahira never asked why. She suspected Elsa was a little lonely in her log home, but she didn't visit the witches, and she only went to the pub to eat on occasion or to talk to Belda.

Sahira understood how she felt; loneliness permeated every

inch of this place. Even when surrounded by others, as she often was at the pub, she felt completely alone without her loved ones and Shade.

And she'd never felt more alone than when smiling while walking by Orin these past few days. She pretended his smile and douchey little wave didn't irritate her, but it was a daily dagger to her battered heart.

Despite the anguish it caused, and her infuriating inability to shake him from her system, she always smiled and waved back at him. The whole time, she did so through gritted teeth while hoping his next fling bit off his cock.

"Are you planning to leave town?" Zeth asked again.

Sahira leaned back and draped her arm over her knee as she looked up at the demon. Beside her, Elsa stopped working to study her.

"Yes," Sahira said.

"To go *where*?" Elsa demanded.

Sahira's gaze shifted toward the pit and the land beyond. She couldn't see them from the gardens' location near the lake, but she could picture them perfectly.

"Into the Barren Lands," she said.

"Why?"

"Because staying here to rot or be killed by witches isn't an option," Sahira said more defensively than she anticipated. Then, taking a deep breath, she continued. "I need answers. I have to know what is out there. Maybe it's nothing, maybe I'll come back here or die, but I *have* to know."

"They say there's nothing but monsters out there," Elsa said.

"There isn't," Zeth agreed, "or at least not that I saw."

"I have to see what's out there, and I'm going to keep going until I have answers."

"Do you plan on trying to come back if you can't make it?" Zeth inquired.

Sahira yanked a stubborn weed from the ground. "I don't know."

They exchanged looks before focusing on her again. Sahira tossed the weed aside as she tapped her shovel against the ground.

"I haven't discussed my plan with anyone but Belda. I had to tell her because I needed to work more to get more supplies; she wasn't giving those up without reason. I've been gathering a stash that will hopefully help me get through the Barren Lands. I have to know what, if anything, is beyond this town... even if it kills me."

"So you're willing to die for that answer instead of staying here where it's safer?" Elsa asked.

"Is it safer for *me*?"

Elsa plunged her shovel into the ground. "The witches and warlocks have been leaving you alone."

"For how long? And is it only because The Reaping distracted them for a bit, and soon they'll return their attention to me? Or is it for good? Do you really think they'll let Radagast's death go?"

"You didn't kill him, and he deserved it."

Sahira stupidly beamed over Elsa's words. She was never quite sure what to make of the witch or why she had tried to create a friendship between them, but it was good to have someone on her side, even if she didn't completely trust Elsa and might never be able to do so.

"The witches don't blame Orin for his death, and if they did, he still wouldn't be the one they went after," Sahira said.

"That's because they're a bunch of cowards."

Elsa's muttered words caused Sahira's eyebrows to rise. Looking at Zeth, she saw the same surprise mirrored on his face.

"Maybe so, but they won't let what happened with Radagast go. They'll come for me eventually, and I can't spend the rest of my life looking over my shoulder, waiting for them to strike. I have to try to find a way out of here."

Elsa sat back on her heels and rested her dirty hands on her knees. "I'm coming with you."

CHAPTER SEVENTY-EIGHT

SAHIRA BLINKED at her and started to shake her head, but Elsa continued speaking. "I've been here for decades, just hoping something would change, but nothing has, and I haven't done anything to create that change besides read more books than I'd ever considered possible. And not *one* of those books has given me any answers or hope. I'm ready to try something new. I'm going too."

Sahira liked Elsa, and other than being a witch, the woman had never given Sahira a reason to doubt her motives. But the witch thing was a pretty *big* reason.

She didn't think Elsa was trying to set her up to kill her, but she couldn't be certain either. And out there, in those Barren Lands, she'd have to put a lot of trust in anyone who went with her.

But going out there alone was a lot more dangerous than with an ally. Could Elsa be that ally?

"I'm coming too," Zeth said. "She's right; I've been here for too long. I've tried going out there and failed, but I was alone. I'll prepare better this time, and we'll have a better chance of success as a team. We can do this *together*."

He was right, and Sahira wanted to believe they could do it, but she also couldn't be the reason one, or both, of them ended up dead. "Belda said there are things out there that make the scarogs look like fun. You have no idea what we could run into."

"I encountered some things when I explored it before. I'm still here to tell the tale, and so is Belda. I didn't find any answers or some miraculous way out, but we'll go farther this time," Zeth said. "Even if we don't survive, at least we tried."

"And at least we're not just sitting here, rotting," Elsa said.

"If you leave with me, the witches and warlocks will paint a bull's-eye on your back," Sahira told her.

"In case you haven't noticed, I'm not one of them. I don't live *with* them, I don't live *like* them, and I've had *nothing* to do with them since arriving."

"Why not?"

Elsa's problem with the witches and warlocks wasn't her business, but if the witch intended to make this journey with her, then Sahira deserved answers. It could also help build her trust in Elsa.

Elsa glanced toward the cluster of witches' tepees on the other side of the lake at the edge of town. Beyond them were the fancier homes of the warlocks.

A group of them had gathered near the lake and were bathing nude while others lay on the shore. Their numbers had taken a hit during The Reaping but not enough to make a real dent in their strength.

"Witches and warlocks killed my parents," Elsa stated.

Sahira's eyebrows shot up, and she exchanged a glance with Zeth. She wasn't sure what to say; she was tempted to press for more details, but she couldn't ask Elsa to relive those memories.

"I'm sorry," she said.

"So am I," Zeth said.

"Don't be. You didn't kill them. It was those judgmental assholes who did it, and all because my parents committed the cardinal sin of saving a child attacked by a wendigo," Elsa explained.

"How was that a sin?" Zeth demanded.

"The child was a vampire. The wendigo had already killed its parents."

Zeth and Sahira both sucked in a breath.

"Oh," Sahira murmured.

"My father was a warlock, and my mother a witch, but they were always outsiders to their kind. They didn't reside with the witches and warlocks; they'd found their own little realm and settled onto it.

"They preferred to be away from the drama and fighting that often came with being a part of those worlds. I know it sounds unusual, considering most witches and warlocks grow up in that life and it's all they know, but they found each other when they were children.

"They loved each other from when they were nine years old and simply wanted to start a family together. It shouldn't have been too much to ask for, but apparently it was, as the two groups refused to let them go.

"My mother's sister would often drop by without any warning. My mother believed she reported back about them, and she was right.

"They had just found and brought the child home to help him heal when that bitch arrived. My mother kept her out of the house, but she must have seen something. That night, with my aunt in the lead, the witches and warlocks came for them. The two sides had grouped together to destroy what they deemed to be the traitors amongst them."

"Warlocks don't usually hate vampires like the witches," Sahira said.

"I know, but they *never* liked that my father preferred to live a simple, happy life with his wife and child. His family always tried to get him to return and were pissed that he wouldn't fall in line.

"The child gave them the excuse they needed to make him pay for what they deemed as his disloyalty. They preferred to see him dead rather than happily living with my mother and me; how awful is that?"

"It's pretty awful," Zeth said while Sahira nodded her agreement.

"They killed the child and my parents. Then they took me away. At first, they forced me to stay with my aunt, the woman who helped kill my parents and tore my perfectly happy life apart. I was twelve when it happened, and as soon as I could start opening portals, I left and never looked back.

"I'm seventy-five now, and until I entered this realm, I had succeeded in staying far away from witches and warlocks for over fifty years. For the past decade, I've had to interact with them in this realm. None of them know who I am or the so-called atrocity my parents committed, but I worry about the day when someone who knows me arrives. Then, like you, they'll turn on me too. I can't be here when it happens."

"You're risking them turning on you by spending as much time with me as you do," Sahira reminded her.

Elsa ran a hand through her chocolate-colored hair as her chestnut eyes surveyed the gathering on the other side of the lake. "I don't like judgmental assholes, and that's all they know how to be. Do I want them to turn on me? No. But I won't live in fear because I'm spending time with someone they don't approve of. Who are they to approve or disapprove of anyone?"

"A bunch of pricks," Zeth said.

Sahira agreed. "What reason did you give them for choosing to live separately from them?"

"I didn't give them one. I don't owe them any explanation about my choices, but when I arrived here, the previous resident of my cabin was just killed in The Reaping. I hated living in the pub, so I moved in there. Some might have found it morbid, but I like morbid."

The grin she flashed showed off all her white teeth and beautiful smile. At seventy-five, she was young for an immortal, yet she seemed so much older, probably because of what she'd endured with her family. Her devilish smile made her appear more youthful, and Sahira grinned back at her.

"I got rid of most of the previous owner's things and made their home my own. When the witches asked why I hadn't joined them, I told them I was a solitary practitioner. It's the truth, but they don't trust me as much because of it. I'm okay with that."

Solitary practitioners were rare, but they did exist. Sahira had considered herself more of one before meeting Kaylia, but any existing coven would have shunned her.

Even with Kaylia, she didn't consider herself part of a coven; she had a friend to create potions and spells with, and the other witches didn't spurn her as much. She was happy being mostly alone or with Kaylia. She enjoyed her privacy and the freedom that came from not being tied to a coven.

"I don't know what they'll do if they discover my history. When I was a child, they didn't hold me responsible for my parents' actions, but who knows what they decided after I ran away from them?" Elsa continued.

"Who knows, indeed?" Zeth murmured before shifting his attention to Sahira. "When I saw you were working in the gardens *and* the library, I suspected something was up. I'm coming with you too. Over the years, I've stashed extra supplies away in case it all went to hell here. I never considered returning to the Barren Lands, but maybe I always knew I would."

"I've managed to save some things too—not a lot, but some. If you can wait another week, I'll also put in extra hours and earn more from Belda," Elsa said. "With all of us going out there and with more supplies, it should be safer, and we'll make it farther than ever before."

"Plus, if we go with you, you'll have a blood supply," Zeth said. "Without us, you'll have to rely on catching some of those things out there, and believe me, they're not mouthwatering morsels."

Sahira inwardly recoiled at the idea of drinking anyone else's blood after experiencing the ambrosia of Orin's, but it had to happen. She suspected that bastard was smugly biding his time until she returned to him to feed.

She was sure he anticipated her jumping his bones again when she did, but that wouldn't happen. After his parade of women these past few days, there was no way she was screwing him again.

The idea made her skin crawl while a part of her yearned for his touch. She *loathed* that part but would have to get used to disappointment.

She didn't hate herself after her one mistake—or more like *six* of them—but she would if it happened again.

Everyone made poor choices sometimes; life would be a *lot* less interesting if they didn't. But if she continued to make the same poor choices, she would be an idiot, and she'd never considered herself one of those before.

She could blame one bad choice on her hunger, lack of sex for decades, and the fact that even if Orin was the biggest douchebag she'd ever met, he was handsome and charming. Plus, he'd helped save her life; of course she made a bad choice after having death nipping at her heels.

Those reasons wouldn't exist next time, or she hoped they wouldn't.

Besides, once she was out of this town and away from him, the temptation would be gone, and everything would be a *lot* better.

"Okay," she said. "We'll leave in a week."

They smiled at her.

CHAPTER SEVENTY-NINE

THE NIGHT before they were supposed to leave, Sahira packed all her supplies in a blanket she'd cut and stitched into a bag to hold everything. Small and sturdy, she could sling it over her shoulders like a backpack.

She had everything she needed and was ready to go... except for one thing. With a sigh, she pulled on a cloak and buttoned it at her throat.

Winter had settled into many of the realms, but this place remained relatively warm. Still, she wanted the cloak and hood to keep others from seeing her.

Sahira kept telling herself she wasn't doing anything wrong, but it felt like it as she pulled the hood over her head. The trapdoor and secret entry would keep her from being seen by anyone, but she couldn't risk opening the door and discovering someone standing on the other side.

There were rarely any immortals in the alley behind this swath of buildings, but it wasn't a risk she was willing to take. Even if this was her last night here, she didn't want someone else sneaking into her room. Besides, they could return to this town, so she wasn't about to let that secret out of the bag.

She strode across the room and to the window. Below, immortals hurried about, so jumping out and coming back in through the window wasn't an option either.

That meant she would have to go through the pub, where Orin was. At least it had calmed down a lot over the last week, but that meant she would be *more* likely to see him.

Stop being a coward and go.

She had no other options, and it was the last time she'd have to see Orin, so that was a bonus. Sahira bowed her head, opened her door, and took in the calmer pub below.

A few immortals sat around the gaming tables, and a couple sat at the bar where Orin was filling their orders. He looked damn good, with his black hair shining and his eyes twinkling beneath the glow of the chandelier.

It only reinforced her hatred of him, and she didn't look at him again while she descended the stairs and swept out the door.

None of the other immortals paid her any attention as she made her way to Zeth's home, but the streets were starting to clear out. Night had descended, but the moon hadn't risen yet, and no stars decorated the sky.

With every step she took, her heart thundered, and it wasn't just because of the thirst clawing at her belly again. It was because of what she would do, what she was here to ask for, and how much she *craved* and *loathed* it simultaneously.

Gliding up the stairs, she took a deep breath as she lifted her hand and held it before Zeth's door. *Do it!*

Without allowing herself to think about it anymore—she'd done too much of that over the past week—she rapped on the door. Stepping back, she clasped her hands in front of her while she waited for Zeth to open it.

Approaching footsteps preceded the opening of the door. A little lantern light filtered out around him and spilled across the porch to her booted toes.

Zeth frowned as he held the screen door open and stepped aside to let her enter. "What's wrong?"

Sahira slipped past him and, once inside, pushed back the hood on her cloak. The last time she spoke with him and Elsa, only a couple of hours ago, they were set to leave tomorrow.

As soon as the sun spread its red tentacles across the sky, they would gather their things and meet at the pit. They'd all agreed to head toward the possibly missing symbol. They had no other leads to follow.

"Nothing's wrong," Sahira assured him. "We're still set for tomorrow."

Zeth shut the door behind her and walked over to sit on a couch made of rocks and twigs. Straw padded the top, and a plush blanket covered it.

"You have to feed," he stated.

Sahira closed her eyes and nodded. She'd considered going to Elsa, but though the witch had said she would provide blood to Sahira while in the Barren Lands, Sahira wasn't ready to test their friendship by asking for this.

Maybe one day she'd be ready, but not yet.

"You're not feeding from the dark fae?" Zeth asked.

"Not in a…." Sahira gulped back the unexpected lump in her throat. *Get it together!* "Not in a while. He was the one assigned to me, but since you and Elsa both said you'd be willing to let me feed from you while we're out there, I was thinking… I was *hoping* maybe it could happen before we left."

"I see," Zeth murmured.

And Sahira knew he did see what had transpired between her and Orin. Feeling completely exposed, she shifted her eyes to the far wall with its strange red symbolic paintings covering it.

No matter how often she told herself it wouldn't happen again, if her lips touched Orin's neck and his blood hit her tongue, it would be over for her. And then she *would* hate herself, and Zeth saw this.

Zeth held his hands before him as the lantern's radiance played over his red horns and yellow eyes. "It would be better if you fed before we left and safer for all of us. If it's been a while, you're hungry and weakened because of it."

Unable to speak, she kept her attention focused on the wall. She'd never seen symbols like them before but didn't ask what they were. They were obviously demon symbols, and he had a right to keep their meanings to himself.

When she felt his eyes on her, she finally met his gaze again, but he was the one who spoke. "The dark fae uses his blood as a weapon against you."

"*Everything* is a weapon to Orin."

"Such is the way of the dark fae." He patted the spot beside him. "Come and sit down."

CHAPTER EIGHTY

TAKING A DEEP BREATH, Sahira straightened her shoulders and strode toward him. After all, this was what she'd come here for, but the idea of feeding from him had her stomach in knots, and those knots weren't because she was hungry.

She lost control the last time she did this; she couldn't let that happen with Zeth. Being with someone other than Orin made her nauseous, and she wasn't ready to jump into someone else's bed.

Still, she had to feed and couldn't go to Orin to ease her thirst without risking her sense of self. And she couldn't leave this town weakened when they had no idea what they would face out there.

She'd put them all at risk if she did. She could handle making things more dangerous for herself but not for Zeth and Elsa.

When she perched awkwardly on the couch beside him, she discovered it was far more comfortable than it looked. That did little to ease her nerves.

They'd gotten to know each other over the past month, but this was such an intimate thing. Not to mention, after what happened with Orin, she was half afraid she'd lose control and maul the demon.

While she wasn't against a good lay, she felt no attraction to Zeth. There was no room for that when Orin kept haunting her waking and sleeping moments.

She wanted his smell, feel, and taste out of her head, but he was worse than a poltergeist as he continued to haunt her. *Damn him!*

She pushed the dark fae out of her mind and focused on why she was there. She edged closer as she tried to figure out how to do this. The bony hooks on Zeth's shoulders would be difficult to navigate, but she could do it.

With a smile, Zeth took pity on her and held out his wrist. "I think this would be easier, and my wife would appreciate it more."

"You have a *wife*?" she blurted.

"And a son waiting for me at home... I hope. I've missed a lot of his life but intend to be there for the rest of it."

It now made more sense why Zeth went to the pub, drank, and played his games but never interacted sexually with any women or men. She'd assumed he brought them home to entertain them here, but it was because his heart belonged to another.

"Why didn't you mention them when you were talking about your family?" she asked.

His gaze darted away, and his eyes closed as anguish crossed his face. "Some things are too difficult to talk about."

She almost reached out to comfort him but sensed that he wouldn't welcome a woman's touch. "I'll go. I can ask Elsa or wait. I'm not *that* hungry."

"I told you I would do this and meant it."

"I don't want to do anything that makes you uncomfortable or would upset your wife. I don't need a demon on my ass.... is she a demon?"

"She is." His eyes took on a far-off, dreamy look. "And she's so beautiful."

His sorrow tugged at her heart, and she fisted her fingers against touching him.

"I know what can happen to a vampire when they feed, and if it becomes an issue, we'll stop, but I *will* be able to stop it," Zeth said.

Sahira knew that meant he would do whatever it took to stop it, which was fine with her.

"My wife is my life. We were almost always together and would have been the day I got stuck here if I hadn't been running an errand for my uncle while she was busy with our son," he continued.

"What kind of an errand?"

"I was searching for the demon who turned on us and killed my father."

"I'm sorry."

"It was many years ago, but I found him here and took him to the pit. He no longer graces this realm."

The one time he found himself in the pit, she realized. "Good."

"My thoughts exactly." He lifted his wrist toward her again. "Go on now."

Sahira stared at the thin blue lines beneath his dark skin before grasping it. His heart beat out a steady rhythm that called to her, but unlike Orin's pulse, his didn't push her to the brink of madness.

It did, however, prick her appetite for more as her fangs lengthened, but she wasn't out of control. She also hadn't bitten him yet, so that might change.

Sahira closed her eyes and braced herself before sinking her fangs into his wrist. Zeth jerked a little but didn't try to pull away.

When his blood filled her mouth, power flowed through the

sweet, intoxicating liquid, but it didn't unleash the same wild abandon in her that Orin's did. She didn't lose control or suddenly want to jump on him.

Instead, tears burned her eyes. She squeezed them closed so no tears spilled free, but a sob caught in her throat and reverberated around her chest.

She had no idea what was wrong with her or why Orin had gotten under her skin and taken such a strong hold over her, but no matter what it took, she would break that hold. Until then, she would have to get used to feeding in misery.

CHAPTER EIGHTY-ONE

ORIN SAT in the dark with his feet propped on a chair and his hands clasped on his stomach while he rocked back in his chair. The clock ticked away the seconds as night crept toward dawn, but though he was tired, he wasn't going anywhere.

For the past week, he'd suspected the enchantress and her two friends were plotting something. They were all working more hours, barely around, and constantly had their heads together when they walked down the road or during the one night they ate dinner here.

After the three of them left that night, he had a conversation with Belda and confirmed his suspicions. His sneaky little witch planned to leave, and she wasn't going to tell him about it.

He suspected, after she snuck out of here with her cloak last night, she would leave soon... most likely today.

He'd pushed Sahira too far. It sometimes happened in games, but he wasn't ready to stop playing. And he sure as shit wasn't going to let her walk out of here, and possibly this realm, without *him*.

Instead, without his little witch's knowledge, he'd also started hoarding supplies and working to earn extra from Belda.

He'd expected Sahira to come to him to feed before she left, but she hadn't done so.

She wasn't stupid enough to go into the Barren Lands without being at full strength, especially not after what happened with the scarogs, but she hadn't come to him. And he was beginning to suspect she wouldn't.

When a door above creaked open, his suspicions were confirmed. He didn't move while Sahira descended the stairs. Her step was as light as a feather drifting to earth, and not a single step creaked beneath her weight.

On her back, she carried a blanket she'd sewn into a backpack and filled with supplies. She'd pulled the hood of her cloak over her head. A scarf hung around her neck, but she hadn't placed it over her mouth.

As he watched her walk, his sense of betrayal rose. She really planned to leave here without discussing it with him.

He'd considered them allies in their attempt to leave this place and was certain she'd return to him to feed and fuck. He'd let her have this space because, even though he hated admitting it, he'd required it too.

She'd rattled him, and he'd been waiting for *her* to return to *him* so he could enjoy her again. And the enchantress had other plans.

No one fucked him over. *No one.* Not even a beautiful witch with a body built for pleasure and the untamed passion of a wildcat. He'd considered them allies, and now, they would be enemies.

She was only a few feet from the door when he spoke. "Going somewhere without me?"

A small squeak escaped before she suppressed it and spun toward him. Orin's eyes narrowed on her flushed face. Her eyes twinkled with a vitality that wasn't there yesterday.

When she'd shuffled into the pub yesterday afternoon, she'd been pale and drawn, with shadows under her eyes as she plodded up the steps. Watching her, he'd been certain she'd soon break and come to him within the next week or two for sustenance and sex.

His shaft had readied itself in anticipation. He'd seen her slip out again later, but when she returned, her hood hid her face. It didn't hide her now, and as he studied her, the truth sank in.

She fed.

The realization was an unexpected dagger to his heart as the first two legs of his chair hit the ground with a thud that rebounded through the hush enshrouding the building. Rising, he prowled toward her while scenting the air.

Her honey scent was crisp and too damn tantalizing. Her golden skin glowed as he stopped only a few inches away from her.

"Where are you going, witch?" he growled.

"That's none of your business."

"You're wrong." When he stalked closer, she backed away. "You came here for me; you'll leave here *with me*."

"Plans change."

Her casual, dismissive attitude grated on his already-fraying nerves. During her slow retreat from him, her foot caught a chair leg, and it spun toward her as it squeaked across the wood floor.

When she staggered a little, he clasped her elbow to steady her. She yanked it away as her fangs flashed in the dim light of dawn.

"Don't touch me!" she spat.

He smiled, but it was more a baring of his teeth than a real smile. He was too pissed to smile, and his anger had nothing to do with her planning to leave without him.

The more he considered it, the more he realized her trying to sneak away was all part of their game. They enjoyed turning the screws into each other, and she'd upped the ante with this one, but since she wasn't as good as him, he'd caught her.

No, her little bit of deviousness here wasn't what upset him at all. It was the realization she'd pulled a move he *hadn't* anticipated.

She fed!

"If you found your way out of this realm, did you plan to tell my brother you never found me?" Orin murmured as he tried to control his rising temper.

"I wouldn't lie to Cole."

"So, you plan to tell them you abandoned me here?"

"I have a feeling he'd understand."

He slapped his hands over his heart, but although he would have found her words humorous before, he wasn't amused. In fact, he was growing more pissed off by the second.

"You wound me, witch," he growled.

"You'd need a heart for that. Nothing can hurt that deadened black thing in your chest."

A flicker of something ran through him as her words upset him more than he ever would have believed possible. He shoved away the possibility it could *actually* be hurt as he resumed prowling toward her while she backed away.

When her heel connected with the wall, ending her retreat, she lifted her chin and scowled at him. Orin stopped before her, and resting his hand on the wall beside her head, he lowered himself until they were at eye level.

"You fed." The words were more accusatory than he intended.

Her dainty one-shoulder shrug caused his nostrils to flare as his teeth ground together. He'd been waiting for her to return to *him*, waiting to take her and feast like he had the last time. Waiting to lose himself to the exquisite pleasure she gave, and she'd gone to *someone else*.

She'd changed the game; she wasn't playing by *his* rules. He'd been waiting, and she'd turned to another.

"Was it the demon?" he demanded.

Again with that *fucking* shrug. Before he could think about

how he was losing control of his emotions—something a dark
fae rarely did, and he *never* did—his other hand slammed into
the wall beside her head.

Wood cracked and indented beneath his palm. She jumped as
her eyes widened a little.

"Did you fuck him?" Orin snarled.

She didn't speak as her eyes remained on his. Curiosity
shone in those amber depths, as did wariness and uncertainty.
She'd never looked at him like that, and he'd never expected to
see it from her.

Something inside him was unraveling, something dark and
primitive that sought to tear this town apart. At this point, he'd
gladly give in to his urge to do so, even if it meant he'd be more
like the lycans he'd always disdained for their lack of control
over their emotions.

He wasn't one of those beasts. He was a dark fae with all the
control and emotional distance dark fae possessed. Women
didn't get under his skin and rile him.

He'd never cared who those he'd bedded screwed before or
after him. He never had, and he wasn't about to start now... but
as much as he hated to admit it, a part of him cared about her.

And he loathed himself and *her* because of it.

CHAPTER EIGHTY-TWO

SAHIRA DIDN'T KNOW what to say or how to respond. She'd never seen Orin this enraged before; she'd never considered it possible for him to be like this, given his usual indifference, disdain, and flat-out coldhearted demeanor most of the time.

His crow-black eyes glimmered with fury as they ran over her while his lip curved into a sneer. His body vibrated with barely leashed violence as his gaze returned to hers.

Despite the murder he radiated, she wasn't afraid of him. He was a vicious, brutal killer who never let anything stand in his way, and he was staring at her like she was the enemy, but her pulse didn't spike with trepidation.

It did pump a little faster when his scent filled her nostrils and she recalled having those arms around her in a passionate embrace. Being attracted to this man was the bane of her existence; being attracted to him *now*, when he looked ready to destroy her, was insanity.

And maybe she was a little insane. Maybe this realm, or *he*, had completely broken her, but she couldn't deny her attraction to him remained as strong as before she'd watched him bounce from one woman to another for the past ten days.

She didn't know how to respond or what to do, but she wasn't about to back down or give in, even if her body begged for him.

~

ORIN HAD no idea what he was doing or what was wrong with him, but the idea of that demon feeling her bite, and the wildness it unleashed while she screwed him, made his blood boil.

What did he care if she screwed the demon?

He had no idea what the answer was, but her actions mattered despite his every intention to deny it. He wasn't done playing with her, and she wouldn't be with anyone else until he finished.

It wasn't the first time he'd been a completely selfish prick, and it wouldn't be the last. But it was what he wanted, and because he always got his way, he would have it, even if it meant ripping the demon's head from his shoulders and shoving his horns up his ass.

That was how he took care of competition, and when it came to the witch, he wouldn't allow any competitors to stand in his way.

And then an unsettling possibility occurred to him. *Is this jealousy?*

Was that what this ridiculous emotion battering him was? He'd heard of it but never experienced it before, and he'd certainly never felt it churning within *him*.

But that wasn't possible. He didn't get jealous. He'd never even been jealous of Cole, the one everyone had deemed to be the bigger, better brother.

Cole was welcome to have his over-glorified, boring role in the world while they were growing up. He got to be the brother with much more freedom and fun than King Tove's firstborn.

No, he didn't get jealous, but this little witch had done something to him. Maybe she really was an enchantress who'd cast a spell over him while they were having sex.

He would have noticed that. He'd never seen her fingers working their magic on anything other than his cock, and if she'd tried to cast a spell and he somehow missed it, he would have felt a shift and the rise of her power in the air.

So then *why* was he like this? He couldn't think of any logical explanation.

He liked her, he admired her strength and courage, but that still didn't explain this unfamiliar intensity of emotion he was experiencing. And he couldn't let it go either. He had to know.

"Did. You. Fuck. Him?"

At least this time his words were more controlled as he bit them out, but anger still seethed in his tone.

The little witch lifted her chin. "I don't inquire about your abundant sexual partners and sex life; don't inquire about mine."

"Do you want to know?" he murmured as he leaned closer.

He was pleased when her breath kicked up a little and she flattened herself against the wall. She was trying to get away, but the slight parting of her lips and the way her eyes fell to his mouth before returning to his told him all he needed to know. The enchantress still wanted him too.

With the back of his knuckles, he caressed her cheek. "Would you like to know who I've fucked since you?"

She slapped his hand away. "You're disgusting."

Orin chuckled as he found himself back on familiar ground. It was better when she was the riled one while he was calm and pulling the strings. It was better that she believed he'd been blowing through all those women when, in truth...

He hadn't believed it possible, but he became angrier because the truth was he'd been waiting for her. He'd enjoyed twisting the screws into her while biding his time for when she returned.

She'd been a feast the likes of which he'd never experienced before; he was still mostly sated from their time together, though hunger was starting to creep in again. Still, he hadn't needed to bed anyone else, so he hadn't.

Was that entirely unusual for him? Yep, but he'd been okay with it.

Now, he was infuriated at himself for being so sure of what would happen, while she was playing by a different set of rules and screwing someone else. He had a new game to play with the little witch: fuck her, break her, and make her pay for this.

"I'll tell you a secret." He leaned so close his lips brushed her cheek and ear while he spoke. "None of them were as good as you."

She planted her hands on his chest and shoved him back. "Get away from me!"

Orin relented a little as he leaned away again but kept his hands on the wall beside her head. "And picturing you helped me get off with all of them."

"I hate you."

He stroked her cheek again. "Maybe that's what makes it so good between us. We'll find out again soon."

"I'm *never* having sex with you again."

"And at one point, you said you'd die before fucking me, but you're still alive, so never say never, little witch. Your body belongs to *me*."

He skimmed his hand down to her waist and smiled when she squirmed away from him. He saw the punch flying toward him a second before he caught her hand only centimeters from his cheek.

He chuckled as he lowered her hand. "That fire is what makes you such a good fuck."

Keeping a firm hold on her fisted hand, he held it while studying her. Now that he was in control again, he could think better, and they had bigger things than sex to deal with.

"Where are you going?" he asked, releasing her hand and stepping away.

"That's none of your business."

"But it is, because I'm coming with you."

"You're not going anywhere! We've been planning for this and gathering supplies to keep us alive out there. You're not ready, and I wouldn't want you with us even if you were."

Orin strolled over to the chair where he'd been sitting. Bending, he lifted the bundle he'd wrapped in a canvas sheet. He'd cut and stitched it to sling over his shoulder and across his chest. He lifted his sword from the table and swung it onto his back.

"Did you really think I'd missed your plotting?" he asked. "I've been preparing, too, witch. You're not leaving this town, or this *realm*, without me."

A flash of red ran through her eyes. Aside from her bite, it was the most vampiric thing he'd ever seen from her. He liked it.

Yes, he definitely enjoyed pissing off his little witch and igniting her fire. Soon, he'd also enjoy making her pay for turning to the demon by fucking any memory of that creature from her. And then he would go out and screw every woman he encountered; he might even make her watch.

That would be great fun.

He sauntered over to her and held out his arm; she ignored it as she shoved past him. "We don't want you with us."

"That doesn't matter, Sahira. We're in this together, whether you like it or not."

When she stalked over to the door and threw it open, he followed her onto the porch and down the steps. He fingered the dagger at his side and the crossbow under his cloak while strolling beside her as she stomped toward the pit.

"Go back," she said. "If we find a way out, I'll send someone for you."

"I'm not stupid enough to believe that."

"I wouldn't leave everyone else here to spite you."

He did believe that, but he wasn't about to let her wander the Barren Lands with only a demon and a witch. She needed more protection than that.

When they rounded some of the buildings and the pit came into view, a sneer curved his upper lip when he spotted the demon waiting with the other witch. The two of them exchanged uneasy looks as he and Sahira approached.

"He's coming with us?" Elsa inquired.

"Believe me, it wasn't part of my plan," Sahira said. "He was waiting for me when I came downstairs this morning. Apparently, he managed to figure out we were planning to leave."

"I'm not stupid, witch," Orin sneered.

"I disagree," Sahira muttered.

Zeth laughed loudly as Elsa grinned. Orin glowered at the demon, who smiled back at him. Orin contemplated killing him now, but Sahira would probably refuse to leave if he did, and getting out of this town was their only chance of escaping this realm.

"I told him we didn't want him with us," Sahira said, "but Orin doesn't give a shit about what anyone other than Orin wants."

He draped an arm casually around her shoulders as he leaned closer. "That's not true. I also care about my family."

She shrugged out from under his arm and focused on the others. "I'm sorry about this. I should have been more discreet, but I didn't think he was paying attention."

Orin wasn't about to tell her that he'd paid a whole lot of attention to her over the past ten days. He'd never give her that kind of information to use as a weapon against him.

"It's fine." Zeth handed her one of the two spears he held. "He adds another layer of protection. Plus, he's got supplies and can help."

Yep, Orin was going to love killing that asshole.

"He's going to make things more miserable," Sahira stated.

Elsa rested her hand on Sahira's arm but didn't say anything as they turned to face the Barren Lands. Once they went out there, they wouldn't turn back.

Belda had warned him about what awaited them in all that sand. Now it was time to find out for himself.

Without looking back at the town, Orin flanked Sahira's side as they started into the Barren Lands. He was sure it wouldn't take long to encounter the horrors that lay beyond.

Let the games begin... again, he decided with a smile.

∼

Read on for an excerpt from *Sinful Curses* Book 8 in the series, or download now and continue reading: brendakdavies.com/SCwb

Stay in touch on updates, sales, and new releases by joining to the mailing list: brendakdavies.com/ESBKDNews

Visit the Erica Stevens/Brenda K. Davies Book Club on Facebook for exclusive giveaways and all things book related. Come join the fun: brendakdavies.com/ESBKDBookClub

SNEAK PEEK

SINFUL CURSES, THE SHADOW REALMS
BOOK 8

"Look out!" Elsa cried as something erupted from the sand.

Sahira threw her hands over her head and ducked as whatever it was took flight. Impossible, frightening *flight* as sand rained down on them.

Blinking against the grainy bits clinging to her face and lashes, she tried to clear her vision as she craned her head back to take it in while lifting her spear. The beast's arms, wings, or whatever, were spread wide like a phoenix rising into the sky, but this monstrosity was no beautiful phoenix.

Instead, the thing appeared to be made entirely of sand as pieces of it continued to speckle them before it plunged back into the loose, red earth beneath their feet. She jumped to the side as the sand plowed up like a giant earthworm was racing toward her.

When she kept moving, it turned in the sand and rushed toward her. Sahira lifted her spear as she prepared for battle.

They'd survived three days in the Barren Lands; she wouldn't die now at the hands of this *thing* or... not hands, but sandy bits all grouped to become some killing machine. And Sahira was sure this creature was lethal, even if it was dirt.

As the thing burst free of the sand, she thrust her spear up to stab it in what should have been its belly, but it was impossible to tell as the sand monster erupted into millions of tiny particles. Her skin turned red and bruised as the sand pelted her flesh.

Skin stinging and welts already forming on her forearms, Sahira slowly lowered her spear to wipe away the sand coating her eyelashes and face. She wanted to speak, to ask what that was, but so much sand coated her lips that she didn't dare open her mouth.

Over the past three days, she'd probably inhaled and eaten a gallon's worth of sand; she didn't need any more in her system. Refusing to let go, it clung to *every* part of her.

"Are you okay?" Zeth inquired.

Sahira could only nod as Orin walked over to study the ground around her. When he lifted his black eyes to hers, they shone with hard, steely light, but she didn't think it was because the thing had attacked her. It was most likely because he was still infuriated with her.

Ever since he'd accused her —wrongly— of sleeping with Zeth, he'd been distant toward her. After they had sex, he happily returned to his womanizing ways with who knew how many more sexual partners without any care, but because he believed she had sex with Zeth, he was pissed at her for it.

The hypocrisy of his attitude wasn't lost on her… or appreciated. She could *never* deny her intense attraction to the dark fae, which lingered even as her dislike of him grew. She never would have believed it possible to hate him more than she used to, but Orin, and his shitty attitude, had proven she could.

"What was that?" Elsa whispered.

Sahira's eyes flicked toward the pretty witch whose chestnut brown eyes were wide as her gaze ran over Sahira. She'd pulled her chocolate brown hair into a braid wrapped like a crown around her head. The red sand sticking to it had turned her hair a different shade, but pieces of its pretty color peeked through.

"I have no idea," Zeth answered. "I've never encountered anything like it during my travels into the Barren Lands, but I rarely encountered the same creature twice, and it always felt like the place was changing around me."

Wonderful, one more thing to worry about in this endless hell of sand and sun.

~

WITH A SIGH, Sahira tried wiping away more of the sand, but it also clung to her fingers; she was just spreading it around. It had gotten into crevices where it should never be and refused to come free. It covered *every* part of her.

It hurt to walk as it rubbed against her, making her legs and ass raw. She never could have imagined that *sand* could make life so miserable, but it had.

She'd always loved the beach and ocean but hoped never to see sand again after this. Waving her fingers in front of her face, she whispered, "Air in front of me, mote it be, mote it be. Air protect me, mote it be, mote it be."

Though she couldn't see it, a small wall appeared before her eyes to keep the sand from blowing into them. From experience, she knew this reprieve wouldn't last; eventually, the sand found its way in again, but it would give her a little break at least.

"Anyone else?" she asked as she waved her fingers.

"No, mine's still working from the spell you cast earlier," Zeth said.

Elsa shook her head. "I have my own."

As much she hated doing anything nice for Orin, and knowing he would probably refuse, as he had the other times she offered, she shifted her gaze to him. He was almost always a complete asshole, but she wasn't that type of immortal and wouldn't be, not even when it came to him.

However, he wasn't paying attention to her, and she wouldn't go out of her way to offer her help. Orin surveyed the sand where the thing had disappeared before turning to examine the area where it first emerged.

"What is it?" Elsa inquired.

When he shook his head, sand flew from his black hair. When his disheveled hair settled back into place, the tips of his pointed ears poked through the top. He brushed a few strands away from his forehead.

With his narrow face, high cheekbones, slightly pointed chin, and hawkish nose, he radiated an air of menace. Unfortunately, his handsomeness also hid his cruel, soulless heart.

The only things Orin cared about were Orin and his family. Technically, once Lexi and Cole wed, they'd be related by marriage, but she was *not* on the list of things he cared about.

And she was fine with that. Sure, she could admit that his rejection of her after they had sex, which was still one of the best nights of her life, had hurt, but she'd moved on since then.

Or at least that's what she told herself while his smell of cinnamon and clove caused her to yearn for him. And she would have to get used to being disappointed because, while she'd made the mistake of falling into his bed before, she wouldn't repeat it.

"What is it?" Elsa asked again.

Orin turned away from the horizon and focused on the witch. Wearing his cloak, a long-sleeved shirt, and pants, she couldn't see the ciphers running across his upper chest and arms before ending at his wrists, but they were there.

During her night with him, she'd traced each of those marks until she knew their ebb and flow. Those ciphers indicated how much power a dark fae possessed, and while his older brother Cole had more than him, she hadn't seen any other dark fae with as many markings as Orin.

And those were only the ones he'd allowed her to see. Though he kept them hidden, she was certain far more marks covered him. Each of those ciphers was like fire and water as they flowed like a river but possessed the sharp points of flames. She couldn't see them, but she knew them well.

"Nothing," Orin finally said. "We should keep moving."

Sahira didn't want to encounter another one of those things, but at least, even if it had been a weird, frightening creature, it wasn't much of a threat.

That wouldn't last long in those bleak, Barren Lands.

～

Download *Sinful Curses* and continue reading now: brendakdavies.com/SCwb

～

Stay in touch on updates, sales, and new releases by joining to the mailing list: brendakdavies.com/ESBKDNews

Visit the Erica Stevens/Brenda K. Davies Book Club on Facebook for exclusive giveaways and all things book related. Come join the fun: brendakdavies.com/ESBKDBookClub

FIND THE AUTHOR

Brenda K. Davies Mailing List:
brendakdavies.com/News

Facebook: brendakdavies.com/BKDfb

Brenda K. Davies Book Club:
brendakdavies.com/BKDBooks

Instagram: brendakdavies.com/BKDInsta
Twitter: brendakdavies.com/BKDTweet
Website: www.brendakdavies.com

ALSO FROM THE AUTHOR

Books written under the pen name
Brenda K. Davies

The Vampire Awakenings Series
Awakened (Book 1)

Destined (Book 2)

Untamed (Book 3)

Enraptured (Book 4)

Undone (Book 5)

Fractured (Book 6)

Ravaged (Book 7)

Consumed (Book 8)

Unforeseen (Book 9)

Forsaken (Book 10)

Relentless (Book 11)

Legacy (Book 12)

The Alliance Series
Eternally Bound (Book 1)

Bound by Vengeance (Book 2)

Bound by Darkness (Book 3)

Bound by Passion (Book 4)

Bound by Torment (Book 5)

Bound by Danger (Book 6)

Bound by Deception (Book 7)

Bound by Fate (Book 8)

Bound by Blood (Book 9)

Bound by Love (Book 10)

The Road to Hell Series

Good Intentions (Book 1)

Carved (Book 2)

The Road (Book 3)

Into Hell (Book 4)

Hell on Earth (Book 5)

Into the Abyss (Book 6)

Kiss of Death (Book 7)

Edge of the Darkness (Book 8)

The Shadow Realms

Shadows of Fire (Book 1)

Shadows of Discovery (Book 2)

Shadows of Betrayal (Book 3)

Shadows of Fury (Book 4)

Shadows of Destiny (Book 5)

Shadows of Light (Book 6)

Wicked Curses (Book 7)

Sinful Curses (Book 8)

Gilded Curses (Book 9)

Whispers of Ruin (Book 10)

Secrets of Ruin (Book 11)

Tempest of Shadows

A Tempest of Shadows (Book 1)

A Tempest of Thieves (Book 2)

A Tempest of Revelations (Book 3)

A Tempest of Intrigue (Book 4)

A Tempest of Chaos (Book 5)

Historical Romance

A Stolen Heart

Books written under the pen name

Erica Stevens

The Coven Series

Nightmares (Book 1)

The Maze (Book 2)

Dream Walker (Book 3)

The Captive Series

Captured (Book 1)

Renegade (Book 2)

Refugee (Book 3)

Salvation (Book 4)

Redemption (Book 5)

Vengeance (Book 6)

Unbound (Book 7)

Broken (Book 8 - Prequel)

The Kindred Series

Kindred (Book 1)

Ashes (Book 2)

Kindled (Book 3)

Inferno (Book 4)

Phoenix Rising (Book 5)

The Fire & Ice Series

Frost Burn (Book 1)

Arctic Fire (Book 2)

Scorched Ice (Book 3)

The Ravening Series

The Ravening (Book 1)

Taken Over (Book 2)

Reclamation (Book 3)

The Survivor Chronicles

The Upheaval (Book 1)

The Divide (Book 2)

The Forsaken (Book 3)

The Risen (Book 4)

ABOUT THE AUTHOR

Brenda K. Davies is the USA Today Bestselling author of the Vampire Awakening Series, Alliance Series, Road to Hell Series, Hell on Earth Series, The Shadow Realms Series, A Tempest of Shadows Series, and historical romantic fiction. She also writes under the pen name, Erica Stevens. When not out with friends and family, she can be found at home with her husband, son, and pets.

Printed in Dunstable, United Kingdom